Prai...

Scent to ...

the first Bath and Body Mystery

"An appealing, credible heroine."   —*Publishers Weekly*

"Clever, often humorous, and definitely complex . . . The start of what smells to be a winning series."
          —*Midwest Book Review*

"Lots of good and relaxing beauty tips thrown in."
          —*I Love a Mystery*

"A great start to what will surely be a successful new mystery series."   —*The Romance Reader's Connection*

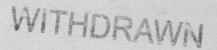

Bath and Body Mysteries by India Ink

SCENT TO HER GRAVE
BLUSH WITH DEATH
GLOSSED AND FOUND

GLOSSED
and
FOUND

A BATH AND BODY MYSTERY

India Ink

BERKLEY PRIME CRIME, NEW YORK

THE BERKLEY PUBLISHING GROUP
Published by the Penguin Group
Penguin Group (USA) Inc.
375 Hudson Street, New York, New York 10014, USA
Penguin Group (Canada), 90 Eglinton Avenue East, Suite 700, Toronto, Ontario M4P 2Y3, Canada
(a division of Pearson Penguin Canada Inc.)
Penguin Books Ltd., 80 Strand, London WC2R 0RL, England
Penguin Group Ireland, 25 St. Stephen's Green, Dublin 2, Ireland (a division of Penguin Books Ltd.)
Penguin Group (Australia), 250 Camberwell Road, Camberwell, Victoria 3124, Australia
(a division of Pearson Australia Group Pty. Ltd.)
Penguin Books India Pvt. Ltd., 11 Community Centre, Panchsheel Park, New Delhi—110 017, India
Penguin Group (NZ), Cnr. Airborne and Rosedale Roads, Albany, Auckland 1310, New Zealand
(a division of Pearson New Zealand Ltd.)
Penguin Books (South Africa) (Pty.) Ltd., 24 Sturdee Avenue, Rosebank, Johannesburg 2196,
South Africa

Penguin Books Ltd., Registered Offices: 80 Strand, London WC2R 0RL, England

GLOSSED AND FOUND

A Berkley Prime Crime Book / published by arrangement with the author

PRINTING HISTORY
Berkley Prime Crime mass-market edition / January 2007

ISBN: 978-0-425-21294-3

BERKLEY® PRIME CRIME
Berkley Prime Crime Books are published by The Berkley Publishing Group,
a division of Penguin Group (USA) Inc.,
375 Hudson Street, New York, New York 10014.
The name BERKLEY PRIME CRIME and the BERKLEY PRIME CRIME design are trademarks belonging to Penguin Group (USA) Inc.

PRINTED IN THE UNITED STATES OF AMERICA

10 9 8 7 6 5 4 3 2 1

To my fellow Witchy Chicks:
Lisa, Linda, Candy, Terey, and Maddy.
Long may we blog.

Acknowledgments

Always, thank you to Samwise, my beloved, and my gurlz, who purr me to sleep, meow me awake, and generally make life livable.

Thank-yous go out to my agent, Meredith Bernstein; my editor, Christine Zika; and so many of my dear friends. To all the makeup mavens and cosmetics junkies like me, who revel in the passionate search for just the right shade of lipstick. And for this series, a nod and thank-you to Aphrodite and Venus, goddesses of both inner and outer beauty. As always, to Mielikki, Tapio, Rauni, and Ukko.

To my readers: As always, thank you for buying my books, and I hope you enjoy this one. Even though I write this series under a nom de plume, India Ink is just an alter ego of mine. You can reach me via my Web site, www.galenorn.com, or via snail mail. Join our Reader Forum boards on our site to discuss the books, if you like. And if you write to me snail mail, please send a stamped, self-addressed envelope for reply. Signed bookplates and bookmarks are available. See site for further information.

The Painted Panther
Yasmine Galenorn aka India Ink

Foreword

The recipes in this book are my own concoctions. I've spent many years blending magical oils, and here I give you perhaps not magical recipes but ones to heighten your senses, to bring new experiences into your lives.

Essential oils can be expensive, so yes, you may use synthetics if you can't afford the pure ones, but bear in mind that the fragrance may end up differing slightly. However, this should not be a significant problem. Also, some oils may irritate the skin, so if I make a note to the effect of: "Do not get on your skin," I mean it. Cinnamon can irritate the skin. Black pepper and other oils can burn delicate tissue.

The oil and other bath recipes are obviously not for consumption, but I am stating it here to clear up any potential miscommunications: *Don't eat them or drink them.* They're meant to be used as fragrances, for dreaming pillows, sachets, potpourris, and the like.

*She's the kind of girl who climbed the ladder
of success . . . wrong by wrong.*
Mae West, 1893–1980

Chapter One

Life was good, I thought as I brought my legs up to form a perfect *V*. My hands were behind me, pressed against the rubber exercise ball as I balanced on my butt, breathing slowly. *Inhale. Exhale. Inhale. Exhale.* I focused on one of my favorite photographs that I'd framed and hung on the wall: a picture of a group of Shaolin monks from their U.S. tour during 2003. When tickets went on sale in Seattle, I'd been first in line and had soaked up every moment of the performance.

Someday I promised myself that I'd travel to China, to the foot of Songshan Mountain, where I'd visit the ancient Shaolin Temple. Of course, there were hundreds of tourists there, but I didn't care. Ancient ruins begat ancient energy, and the whispers of the monks would still be engraved on the walls, in the statues, on the passing breeze.

I sucked in another deep breath, gently bringing my focus back to the photograph. I'd built up to holding this pose for almost five minutes, and today I planned on taking it a step further. I cautiously lifted one hand from the ball, and then—inch by inch—raised the other hand, holding my arms straight out so that my butt was the focal point, the only part of me touching the ball as I balanced without support.

As I exhaled, willing myself to remain still, a loud pop startled me, and the next thing I knew, I hit the floor squarely on my tailbone, a thin yoga mat the only thing separating my ass from the hardwood. The thud shook the room. Blinking, I sat there wondering what the hell had happened. Then footsteps sounded from the stairway, and I heard Auntie calling me.

"Persia, Persia? Are you okay?"

"I'm in here," I said, finding my voice. "I'm in my workout room."

I stared at the floor a moment, debating on whether I should stand up. Was I hurt? Maybe; I didn't think so, but it was hard to tell from where I was sitting. No sharp aches or pains, no feeling that something was broken. Just a general sense that all was not right with the world.

I was used to thumps and jolts from my martial arts classes and the self-defense classes I taught, along with numerous other activities—such as fighting off the occasional bad guy (or woman, as the case may be). But this . . . this was something else.

I'd never had an exercise ball break on me before. I usually replaced them once a year, not trusting them to withstand all the punishment I put them through for any longer than that. But I'd only had this ball . . . When did I buy it? Five . . . six months ago? It shouldn't have burst, and even if it had sustained a small puncture, the damned thing should have deflated slowly.

"God almighty, girl! What happened?" Auntie bustled into the room.

I accepted her hand, gingerly pushing myself off the floor to tower over her. My Aunt Florence might be the most intimidating woman on Port Samanish Island, but she was still a good seven inches shorter than me, though she had me beat in the weight department.

"I have no idea. One moment I was on my ball, and the next thing I knew, I was viewing life from a distinctly different perspective." As I examined the exercise ball I noticed it had ripped, not on the seams but across the ribs. "I think it was defective. Look at the way it tore open."

"Never mind that. Are you okay?" Auntie asked, leaning down to pick up the bright blue rubber that ripped even further as she touched it.

"I'm in a little bit of shock, actually," I said, unable to focus. I closed my eyes. My back felt stiff—I'd landed hard. My butt was sore, and my neck was beginning to ache. "I think I'm okay, but to tell you the truth, I don't really know. I'm a little shaky." I winced as I slowly bent over to touch my toes.

"You'd better make an appointment with Cynthia," Auntie said. "Can you make it downstairs to breakfast? We need to be at Venus Envy early today." She gave me a pat on the back and a nasty twinge in my glutes made me think that maybe I'd managed to injure myself after all.

An hour on the massage table would do me good. "I'll call her, then take a hot shower. I'll be down to breakfast after that." As I cautiously crossed the hall to my study, a glance at the clock told me it was ten minutes after eight. I picked up the phone and dialed our masseuse.

Cynthia answered on the second ring. "Radiant Massage Therapy, Cynthia speaking. May I help you?"

I smiled. *Radiant* was a good word to describe her. Cynthia glowed, and she had a way of making every client feel special. "Persia Vanderbilt here. I just had a nasty little tumble off my exercise ball, and I think I should come in. Can you squeeze me in tonight at five?" I flipped open my Day-Timer and glanced through my appointments. The morning was taken up with clients looking for custom fragrances for the coming holiday season. I was cleaning up by making one-of-a-kind Christmas presents.

During the afternoon, I planned on drafting out my column for *Pout Magazine*. After I'd given them an interview about the ins and outs of being an up-and-coming young entrepreneur, the editor asked me if I'd be interested in writing a monthly beauty hints column, and I'd agreed. I could always use an extra five hundred a month, and the column would bring more attention both to Venus Envy and to my custom-blended oils.

Things had snowballed after that, with the column leading to a half-hour special segment on *Northwest Island Living*, a cable-access television show local to Gull Harbor and Port Samanish Island, where I answered callers' questions about beauty, fragrance, and fitness. The show's producers were trying to talk me into a regular spot hosting an early morning exercise and beauty show, which I was seriously considering. All I had to lose was a little extra sleep. And perhaps my dignity, if the show went the route my workout had gone this morning.

Cynthia confirmed me for a five o'clock appointment, and I penciled it in, then headed for the shower. I slid out of my leotard and turned on the water as hot as I could stand it, then took a shaky step into the glass-enclosed shower. What I really wanted was to fill the freestanding claw-foot tub up to the brim and just soak, but Auntie and I needed to be at the shop early, so bubbles were a luxury that would have to wait until later.

As the spray beat down on my back, I was aware of a growing ache in my tailbone. Damn, this was the last thing I needed. While the self-defense class that I taught was over until the end of January, I was signed up for a workshop on intensive bodywork for women that was supposed to start in two weeks—three days of grueling, push-it-to-the-max exercise and body detox work. The last thing I needed was a backache, neck ache, or any other type of ache threatening to bench me. I leaned over, back to the shower head, as the streaming water tapped out a staccato drumbeat on my coccyx.

After my shower, I slipped into a gray tweed walking skirt and a royal blue V-neck sweater that shimmered with sparkling white beads. The sleeves ended two inches below my elbow and my bluebell faerie tattoo wound around my left arm like an old friend tagging along for the ride. I changed my belly button ring for one with a delicate polished garnet in it—my birthstone. In a month and a half, I'd turn thirty-two years old. A pair of mile-high Chanel round-toed pumps completed the ensemble. Sweeping my waist-length hair into a thick chignon, I fastened it in place with a pair of black lacquered chopsticks and then headed down to breakfast, wincing a little as my lower back complained about the two flights of stairs.

Auntie had made a huge omelet with bacon bits, bell peppers, onions, cheddar, and diced zucchini. As I set the table, she fed apples, carrots, and pears through the juicer. I'd picked up the contraption a few weeks earlier, and we were on a juicing craze. I'd tried just about every combination of fruits and vegetables that I could think of—a few of which immediately ended up down the drain. Never again would I attempt to juice a kohlrabi.

As I settled down at the table, the muscles around my tailbone spasmed again, and I winced. "Damn, I think I threw something out. I'll call Will and schedule an appointment before I head over to see Cynthia." Will Cohalis was our chiropractor.

Auntie handed me a small plastic cup full of vitamins and supplements and the plate of toast. I buttered two slices of toast, swallowed the pills in three gulps with my juice, and dug into the omelet. "Yum, this is really good. I'm hungrier than I thought."

"With the workload we've got coming up today, I figured we'd want something more substantial than cereal. We're heading into the busiest season of the year, and there's a nasty bug going around. I don't want anybody out sick during the holidays."

Auntie had gone on a modified health kick herself, hence the handful of supplements and antioxidants we were now taking with our morning meals. She told me that she might be as wide as she was tall, but she wasn't about to let herself go. Her blood pressure was good, her cholesterol was spot-on, and she spent three nights a week at an aqua-aerobics class for older women down at the Gull Harbor Aquatic Center, known as the GAC for short.

When I was four years old, Auntie had taken me in after my mother died and my father abandoned me, and now—twenty-seven years later—I owed her for everything I had and everything I'd become. She'd been my inspiration and my comfort, and now that she'd bestowed upon me half interest in Venus Envy, her bath and beauty shop and day spa, she was also my business partner. Last year, I'd returned home to the eccentric, artsy, high-tech town of Gull Harbor after a tiring stint in Seattle during which I'd gotten involved with an embezzler. Now, it was as if I'd never left Port Samanish Island.

"What are you doing tonight, Imp?" she asked, clearing away our plates.

Imp was her nickname for me—short for *impetuous*—and it fit. I patted my lips with my napkin and pulled out my lipstick and compact. "I'm meeting Lisa at six thirty at the GAC for a half hour for another swimming lesson. Then Barb and I'll connect at the Delacorte Plaza. Neither one of us has anything worth wearing to the Gala, and we've decided to play it up glam." Done with breakfast, I carefully lined my lips with a burgundy liner and then stained them with Merlot Vision, the newest lipstick from Urban Gurlz.

Auntie slipped the dishes into the dishwasher. "How's Lisa doing on her lessons? She seems like such a strong girl, to be so afraid of the water."

We'd recently hired both a hair stylist and a makeup

artist for Venus Envy, expanding our day spa offerings by double. Seth Jones was a master with the scissors, and Lisa Tremont was a whiz with makeup and manicures. Lisa and I'd become friends in short order. Although she was closer to our cashier Tawny's age, Lisa was more mature. She'd been through the wringer, and it showed in both her attitude and her eyes. And yet she was terrified of the water and asked me if I'd help her overcome her fear. We'd been working together for the past month at the pool, one step at a time, trying to acclimate her with the more pleasant aspects of swimming.

"Childhood trauma. She almost drowned when she was five. She was swept out toward the ocean during a riptide, and her father didn't notice at first. He finally saw her struggling in the surf and managed to swim out and save her before she went under, but by then, she'd freaked. She's never been back in the water since. At least, never in anything bigger than a bathtub." I eased out of my chair and slid into the new black leather jacket Killian—my boyfriend—had given me. It was tailored and fit me like a glove. So did he, for that matter.

Auntie wiped her hands on the dish towel. She was dressed in her usual mu'umu'u; today it was fuchsia, the color of her straw hat with the beloved and very-late Squeaky, who'd met his death via electrical cord. The bird was affixed to the hat with a glue that held stronger than steel. She shrugged into the long wool cape that I'd bought her for her birthday and plunked the hat on her head.

"Ready to go?"

I nodded. "Meet you there. And Auntie, *please* call the garage and have them stifle that beast of yours before Kyle finally gives in and slaps you with a ticket. He's not going to look the other way forever, you know." Baby, Auntie's convertible, was louder than a jet engine and desperately needed muffling.

Auntie shrugged. "One of these days, my dear. One of these days."

❧

Our shop, Venus Envy, was on Island Drive, the main drag of Gull Harbor, Washington, the town that sprawled across a good share of Port Samanish Island in Puget Sound. We attracted the renegade techies and artists, the summer millionaires, and those fleeing the frenetic pace of Seattle's java jive mentality. Oh, that's not to say that caffeine didn't still rule the community and that we weren't still in the loop, but the islanders had managed to pull in the best of both worlds. Seattle was only a half hour away by ferry, and yet the island was removed, a world away from the grime and the haze and the concrete. We did get the rain— in fact, more than the city proper by a measurable amount—but we were tweeners—between urban and rural.

I pulled into my parking spot and dashed across the street, shielding myself from the rain with my handbag. The clouds were thick and looming ominous, the streets wet from the night's downpour. Lucky for me, morning rush hour was over, and the matrons of the town hadn't come out to shop yet, so parking was easy and the slick pavement clear.

Venus Envy was nestled between the Baklava or Bust Bakery on one side—owned by my best friend Barbara Konstantinos and her husband Dorian—and Starbucks on the other. Barb lived for Starbucks, while I thrived on black tea and lemon. On the corner was our favorite hangout, the BookWich, a café-slash-bookstore where you could read and eat. Downtown Gull Harbor had all the charm of an old-fashioned town, with all the boutiques of a thriving metropolis. It was the perfect blend of tradition and cutting edge.

I dashed through the door. Tawny was already at work, and I saw that Seth had come in early, too. I waved at them as I headed back to the office. A few months back we'd been facing ruin, thanks to a ruthless competitor. After I'd managed to expose her dirty game, our customer base rebounded higher than ever, including a few clients who sheepishly returned after deserting us for Bebe Wilcox and her low-cost, low-quality wares.

But I had to admit, thanks to the crap that Bebe had pulled, we were smarter. We now kept all valuables locked in the office, our computer was secure, our files were backed up, and I'd created copies of my oil recipe journal, both on the computer and hard copy. Difficult lessons all, but vital.

I checked for messages as I slid out of my leather jacket and hung it up behind the door. The tranquil mauve and sea-green color scheme always calmed me down, even when I was in a rush, and now I exhaled slowly as I listened to the string of callbacks waiting for us. Most were for Auntie, one was for Tawny, and one was a client who had to cancel her fragrance consultation.

As I turned off the machine, I realized that my butt still hurt. Hopefully, Cynthia would be able to take care of it, but I put in a call to Will Cohalis and scheduled an adjustment for four fifteen, just to make sure. Finished with the morning administration, I left my purse in the bottom drawer of Auntie's desk and headed back to my station.

My first two appointments were business as usual, but when I glanced at the schedule, the third name stood out in bold screaming letters to me. I glared at the writing and hurried over to Tawny.

"What the hell is this?" I shoved the book under her nose. "You know better than to schedule an appointment with the Albatross!"

Don't get me wrong. I liked Tawny, she was a good worker, but she had a few specific orders that were sacrosanct. And refusing service to my ex-boyfriend Elliot was at the top of the commandments. I'd been compiling a long list of his stunts in the hopes of getting a restraining order, but he always stopped right before crossing the line. A few times I'd managed to chase him off by threatening to beat him to a pulp if he didn't get the hell out of Dodge. He knew I could do it, too, and he knew that I would, if pushed.

Tawny paled. "Oh Persia, I'm sorry! Let me see that." She took the book from me and squinted. "That's not my handwriting. I'll bet Seth took down the appointment when I was on break, and I just never noticed."

"Oh Lord, I'm sorry, Tawny." I let out a long sigh. Had I warned Seth about Elliot? Lisa knew, but when I tried to remember if I'd told Seth, I came up with a blank. "Forgive me? The sight of his name was just a shock."

Tawny winked. "I'd have done the same thing. Maybe you'd better let Seth know, though, so it doesn't happen again." She glanced at the clock. "Do you think I have time to call and cancel his appointment before—"

The shop chimes sounded, and I grimaced. Even though I hadn't turned around, I knew who it was. I knew as sure as I could smell the pathetic knockoff version of Calvin Klein's Obsession. I whirled around, jaw set. Elliot stood there, a smile of triumph on his face.

What had I ever seen in this man? There must have been something that attracted me at one time, but over the past eighteen months, I'd totally forgotten what it was. I'd dated Elliot Parker, former accountant-turned-embezzler, for several years before moving in with him, never having a clue as to his criminal alter ego. Five years later, the Feds caught up with him.

I cut my losses and ran, leaving Seattle to return home to Auntie's house. Elliot managed to finagle a deal and got off on a plea bargain, and he followed me to Gull Harbor, where he rented a dive, took odd jobs to keep himself alive, and pestered me at every turn.

"What the fuck do you want, Elliot? I told you to never darken the doors of this shop, and if Auntie finds out you were in here, she'll hunt you down like the dog you are."

Hands on my hips, I glared. In my heels, I was well over six feet and towered over him.

He stared up at me, his eyes glittering with thoughts that were hard to read, probably a good thing for both our sakes. "I'm a paying customer—"

I looked around. By now most of our customers knew about my volatile connection with the jerk, but I still didn't like causing scenes in the shop if I could avoid it. However, there were only three customers in the shop, and they all gave me knowing smiles as I glanced at them.

"What you *are* is an asshole! Now get out before I help you find the door." I took a step forward and glared.

He swallowed, the nervous tic in his face starting up. He hadn't had that until he moved to Gull Harbor and took up drinking as a sport. "Persia, when are you going to admit you still want me—"

"That's it!" I took hold of his elbow and within seconds had twisted him around as I propelled him to the door. He tried to break free, but I held fast until we reached the rainy sidewalk. As I let go, I whispered, "You come back, and I'll have to get rough. Got it through that alcohol-sodden skull of yours?"

He coughed, backing away as I cracked my knuckles, and then without a word, turned and stumbled off down the street. Just as I thought, he was already on his way to being soused. As I dusted my hands on my skirt and headed back into the shop, I wondered what else was going to go wrong today.

⁊

By lunchtime, I was ready for a bowl of chicken soup and a sandwich. I'd created five custom blends for my regular clients, sorted out an inventory mistake that left Tawny bewildered and almost in tears, and tried to console an angry Lisa who had gotten yet another letter from the creditors who were hounding her and her sister.

"We'll talk about it at the pool tonight. Maybe there's

something I can think of to help," I said, staring at the demand for payment.

Lisa and Amy were trying to pull together the remains of their father's estate after he'd died of a long and arduous ordeal with cancer. They were up to their necks in fending off the sharks who wanted their money from an estate that had fallen far short of everyone's expectations.

She sighed. "It's just been so hard, Persia. We're trying to save the family house, but I'm not sure if we have time to save it." An odd look crossed her face, and she shrugged. "I do have one idea, but I'm not sure if it's going to work. I'll know more soon, though." I handed her a tissue, and she wiped her eyes and blew her nose. Luckily, Lisa wore waterproof mascara, or she'd be a runny mess by now.

I patted her on the arm. "Don't cry. We'll figure out something." A glance at the clock told me I was running late. "I'm meeting Barb for lunch now, but we'll talk this afternoon at the pool. I promise." As Lisa nodded, I grabbed my wallet from Auntie's office and waved as I headed out the door.

Barb was waiting by the door of the bakery, and as she swung out to meet me in stride, I could smell the delicious scents of fresh bread and pastries. She looked wiped.

"Busy?" I asked.

"The week before Thanksgiving?" She snorted. "Persia, we're going down for the third time. Not only are people ordering breads and rolls and pies for their dinners, but we're catering the pastries for the Gull Harbor Thanksgiving Gala tomorrow night."

The Gala was an annual dance sponsored by the Chamber of Commerce and various Gull Harbor small businesses. All proceeds went to the Helping Hands Center and the Port Samanish Island Food Bank. Tickets were one hundred dollars per person, and Auntie and I had decided to spring for Trevor, Tawny, Seth, and Lisa. They'd all be attending, dates included. It was the one posh affair of the year that was open to the public, and everybody who was anybody would be there.

"So not only are we run ragged," she said, playing with her straw, "but guess who decided to show up just to make my life miserable?"

"At least it wasn't Elliot. He dropped into Venus Envy this morning." I shook my head, wondering just who'd gotten on Barb's bad side. We'd been so busy lately we hadn't had a chance to really sit and dish for several weeks. "Who's the thorn in your side? Maybe we can take him—or her—and Elliot at the same time. Tie them to cement blocks, and toss them in the ocean or something."

"Don't I wish, but that's not going to happen. Mama Konstantinos showed up a few days ago for a visit." The look on her face said it all. Barbara and her mother-in-law were in a constant struggle over who had the most claim on Dorian. The battle was usually on hold, since Mama Konstantinos lived in Greece, but since she'd actually made a trip to the States, it was guaranteed that the war would rage with a renewed fury.

"You pick a place to stash the body yet?" I grinned at Barb, and she let go of the pinched look that was threatening to add a few wrinkles to the faint laugh lines that crept around her eyes. A decade older than me, at forty-two she still looked closer to thirty.

"I wish," she muttered as we swung into the BookWich and waited at the hostess's stand. Within minutes, Tilda was there to lead us back to a booth that afforded a little more privacy.

"Haven't seen you girls in a while," the older waitress said. Tilda was a good soul, and she treated us like we were her nieces. I always overtipped. Considering her age and how strenuous the job was, she deserved it.

"Busy, Tilda, so damned busy," Barb said, sliding into the booth with one of those sighs that says it all. She leaned her head back against the seat, and I could see the strain tightening her neck and shoulders.

I slipped into the opposite seat and took a long drink of water. Tilda handed us menus and asked, "The usual drinks, girls?" We nodded, and she took off for the kitchen.

"Actually, what I want is a good stiff screwdriver right now. More vodka than OJ." Barb inhaled deeply, then slumped. "I tell you, Persia, that woman is the root of all evil. I hate her—I really hate her. And Dorian adores her."

"Doesn't he see how she treats you?" I asked, playing with my glass. Just one more reason I never planned to walk down the aisle. As much as I liked Killian, I'd seen too many bad marriages. I'd rather have commitment than a license any day. In my book, the two didn't always go together.

"You know Dorian, he never wants to make waves. And he never thinks she acts as badly as she really does. I can't tell him what she says to me when he's not around—he wouldn't believe it. I just hope that having her on my turf makes a difference. She hasn't been to the U.S. in six years, you know." Barb shook her head in disgust. "So, what's up with you? How's Killian?"

"Well, other than almost breaking my butt this morning, I'm fine." I gave her a slow smile. "Killian's good, in more ways than one." And that was no lie. Killian and I had been together since August, and the sex was so good that I almost thanked Bebe Wilcox for the trouble she'd caused us. Her machinations afforded me the opportunity to get to know Killian Reed, former owner of Donna Prima, a cosmetics company that Wilcox had managed to put out of business. Killian and I meshed in so many ways it was spooky; and like me, he wasn't looking to formalize our relationship any time soon. We'd agreed to remain exclusive—the energy we raised between us was too intense for anything else—but that was enough for now.

"The Gala should be fun, at least," Barb mumbled, her mouth full of a breadstick. She perked up a little. Barbara loved parties and playing socialite, and she did it well, without snobbishness but with a pizzazz few could mimic.

"I haven't the faintest idea of what I want to wear. Something sparkly. The gloom's really getting to me this autumn. I miss the sun." I was a sun bunny at heart. I loved being outdoors, hiking, swimming, taking long walks on the beach. I still hiked and camped during the autumn and winter, but it was a hell of a lot harder when rain ruled the skies and fog rolled in to cloud the islands of Puget Sound.

Barb broke into a grin. "I know exactly where we're going to shop tonight. A new store moved into the plaza last month. Sarina's. Gorgeous dresses, designer wear. A real upscale boutique."

I nodded as Tilda came to take our orders. An evening of shopping with my best friend may just be what the doctor ordered. Now, if I could figure out a way to boost Lisa's mood, everything would be just peachy.

Chapter Two

Lisa was waiting for me when I arrived at the aquatic center. My chiropractor and masseuse had both taken great pains to keep me from *having* great pains, and they both agreed that a nice stint in a warm pool afterward would be just the ticket. As I sat on the bench in the locker room and changed into my suit, Lisa huddled in her cover-up. She had a great body, but her fear of the water made putting on a bathing suit torturous.

I slid out of my skirt, sweater, and underwear, hanging them in the locker. Auntie and I rented our lockers by the year since we were both here so often. As Lisa watched, a faint smile on her face, I stepped into the sleek one-piece twist bandeau suit that had become my current favorite. With diamond cutouts on the sides and sturdy underwire support, the crimson wonder—as I'd dubbed it—both showed off my figure and supported me for serious swimming.

"You ready?" I asked her, braiding my hair and pinning it up to keep it out of the way.

Lisa blanched and stared nervously at the door. "No, I'd rather be anywhere but here, but I guess that's part of the reason I *am* here, isn't it? I wish I wasn't so afraid, but I can't seem to forget." She twisted the belt of her terry cover-up, nervously wringing it with her hands. "The waves were so huge, and I was so little. And then I couldn't breathe, and everything was a roar of water. Then my daddy caught me up, and the look on his face terrified me. I knew then that he'd almost lost me. That he almost didn't save me."

I'd heard the story over and over, but the past few times I noticed it had gotten shorter, as if she no longer needed to go over each and every detail quite so compulsively. I let her ramble on but gently steered her toward the shower. Taking a deep breath, she slid out of the cover-up, and we rinsed off, then headed for the pool.

As we entered the main room, the scent of chlorine overwhelmed me and almost sent me reeling. I hated the stuff. It made me queasy, and every public pool in the area seemed to overuse it. But if I wanted to swim indoors, there was nothing I could do until I could convince Auntie to build an add-on with our own swimming pool, so I bit the bullet and made sure to shower thoroughly afterward.

There were actually three pools: one for the little waders, one for lap swimming and general splashing around, and a therapy pool. Since Lisa was so afraid, we always went to the therapy pool, because at its deepest the water was barely four feet. Deep enough to get her acclimated but not so deep that she'd be in over her head. But getting her to the four-foot end was going to take some doing; she was still afraid, even when the water only came to her knees.

I'd managed to steer her down the ramp, which was used by a number of physical therapy patients, and into the water three times by holding tightly to her hand and slowly easing her in. Pressuring Lisa would backfire; I knew that from the start. With each session, I encouraged her down the ramp step-by-step.

Now, I spoke softly to Lisa as we edged our way into the pool until the water covered our feet. I glanced at her. She was breathing heavily, and her shoulders were hunched, but her eyes were determined.

"You're doing great. Just a little farther. We're almost there, and then we can sit and chat for a bit." The therapy pool had a built-in bench in the shallow end where patients could sit and soak in the warm water. That's what we'd done last time, when I finally managed to coax her off the ramp. The first two times, we'd stopped at the bottom, where she started to panic. Today, however, I had hope that we'd make it over to sit down.

Lisa paused, sucked in a deep breath, and let me lead her to the bench. Her eyes were closed, and she was trembling, but we made it the last two yards.

"You can sit down now," I said.

She opened her eyes and looked down at the water that was rippling around her knees. "I feel dizzy," she said.

"Come on, have a seat. The bench is raised, so the water won't be any deeper than your lower back. Can you manage that? Think of it like a really big bathtub. I'm right here, so you're safe." Still holding on to her hand, I sat down on the bench, and after another moment she joined me, still shaking. Once she was seated, she took another deep breath and let it out in a long sigh.

"I hate this. I hate being so afraid, Persia. I can't believe I'm sitting here, but I look at the people in the main pool who are swimming and diving, and I feel like I've got a thousand miles to go. Why can't I do that? Why can't I just go over there, jump in, and have fun like they are?"

"Fear is a powerful force. Don't sell yourself short. Within just a few tries, you've made tremendous strides. Eventually, you'll be walking on the beach by yourself and coming here to soak and swim. But give it time. Working through any fear takes both time and determination. Don't beat yourself up over it." I leaned back, relaxing as the soothing warmth cushioned my tailbone. I was still sore from the fall this morning, but the water helped, and I gently shrugged my shoulders, trying to release some of the tension.

Lisa gingerly settled back against the rim of the pool, bracing herself as if she expected a tidal wave to sweep through the building. "I guess this does feel good, kind of like a Jacuzzi. Thanks, Persia, for helping me out."

"No problem, I don't like to see fear overshadow someone's life, and any excuse to get in the water's a good one to me. So tell me more about the collections letter you received. What have you and your sister done so far about your father's estate? Maybe Auntie's lawyer can consult with you on a pro bono basis." If anybody could figure out a plan, Winthrop Winchester could, but it wouldn't be cheap. I had no idea where he stood on freebies, but we could find out. "I can't promise anything, but we can try."

But instead of launching back into the horror story surrounding her father's estate, Lisa surprised me. "I don't think there will be a problem much longer. As I said, I have a plan. I have to check out something first, but I'm pretty sure I know who took the money and how to get it back."

"Who took it? You think somebody stole it?"

She shrugged. "It makes sense, with what I've found out."

At last something was going right for the Tremont sisters. "Do you want to talk about it? I'm a good sounding board," I said.

She shook her head. "Not yet. I want to be certain I'm right before I say anything. I don't dare accuse anybody without proof. I haven't even mentioned this to Amy yet, so keep it under your hat, if you would. I don't want to get her hopes up. But if I play my cards right, we'll be back on our feet in a few weeks."

Wondering what rabbit she'd managed to pull out of

the hat, I kept my silence. Lisa would talk when she was ready. Or not. It wasn't my place to pry. I knew what everybody else knew: the two sisters had returned to Gull Harbor to be with their father during the last months of his dying and once here, discovered the family fortune had vanished. According to what little they could find out, it sounded as though their father had gambled the money away on the Internet, but Lisa refused to believe it.

Amy was older than Lisa and had several years' teaching experience, but the only position open was that of substitute teacher at Pilsner Middle School, so she took temp jobs to make ends meet. Lisa had a background in cosmetology but had been scraping by as a waitress at the Davenport Diner, a dive in the seedy part of town, until we hired her at the shop. Together, they barely managed to keep the family home afloat, but they were facing the threat of having to sell it in order to meet their father's debts and medical bills if a miracle didn't show up on their doorstep pretty soon.

After awhile, I glanced at the clock. We'd been in the water fifteen minutes, and Lisa was starting to fidget. "Okay, then. How are you feeling now?"

She swallowed. "Scared, still."

"Do you think you can go in a little deeper tonight?" I stood up. "It's up to you. Whatever you feel you can handle."

She glanced at the water farther along in the pool. A wistful look crossed her face, but I could see the shadows of fear there, too. With a shake of the head, she said, "I can't go another step tonight. This was almost too much. Maybe next time?"

I held out my hand. "Not a problem. I'm so proud of you for coming this far. Next time, we tackle a few more steps into the water. Okay?" As she nodded, I added, "Come on then, let's take our walk around the pool and then shower."

Our first few visits had consisted solely of walking

around the pool. Lisa was as afraid of walking by the water's edge as she was of being in it, so we began with that. Now she could circle the pool if I was by her side, but she was still skittish, especially when we passed by the deeper end.

After we'd made our circuit, I led her back to the door leading into the shower room. She began to breathe easier the minute we stepped out of sight of the water. With an apologetic grin, she stripped off her suit.

"Did you want to take a few laps, or would you like to get coffee?" she asked, slipping under one of the showers.

The clock told me I had half an hour until I was supposed to meet Barb. "A rain check on both, I'm afraid. I'm going shopping with Barb at the Delacorte Plaza in thirty minutes. Lisa, you did a good job in there. You actually sat in the water again. That's progress in my book." I wrung out my suit over the drain, then scrubbed down with a cucumber-ginseng body wash and lathered shampoo in my hair.

"Tomorrow's going to be insane at the shop," I warned her. "The appointment book is jammed with makeovers and haircuts. We'll need you there on time. By the way, who are you going to the Gala with?"

I rinsed the conditioner out of my hair and stepped out of the shower, aware of the eyes watching me in the locker room. I was comfortable in my body, and I knew that shook up other women more than my height, my boobs, *or* my muscles. Wrapping a towel around me, I padded over to the bench by my locker. Lisa joined me.

"I told Mitch Willis I'd go with him. You know who Amy's going with?" She leaned forward, at ease again now that the pool was out of sight.

I grinned. "Who?" Lisa loved to gossip, and while it wasn't usually in my nature except with Auntie or Barb, we'd fallen into an easy way of chatting that felt comfortable, if a bit chummy.

"Chief Laughlin. I was in the kitchen the other night

when he came over to visit. They've been talking a lot, ever since Amy volunteered to head a committee to keep guns away from kids. He dropped off some information, and I heard him hemming and hawing until he finally got up the courage to ask her out. I think they really like each other." She giggled, rolling her eyes. "He's nice, but a cop? I dunno."

I blinked. Kyle? Dating? A brief flush ran up my face, and I examined the feeling behind it, wondering if there'd be any fleeting feelings of jealousy. After all, he'd pursued me since I returned to Gull Harbor. But when I listened to my heart, all I could feel was a quiet sense of satisfaction.

"Amy and Kyle seem to match well in temperament," I said. And Amy was a lot like his late wife, if what Barb had told me was true. Quiet, firm-willed, but not outspoken. Happy with the simple things in life, Amy Tremont might just be the ticket to heal Kyle's loss; something I knew I could never do.

"Well, they both listen to country music, so that's a start. Okay, I'm dressed and out of here." Lisa snuggled her threadbare coat around her shoulders and swung the waterproof bag holding her suit and towel over her shoulder. "See you tomorrow!"

"Mañana," I said, waving as she dashed out of the room. I didn't have time to dry my hair so braided it to keep it from tangling, then quickly dressed and slid on my leather jacket. I packed my suit into a plastic tote bag and, snagging up my purse and keys, headed out to my car. Time to meet Barb and do some serious shopping.

◆

The Delacorte Plaza was across the street from one of the seediest apartment buildings in town. Unfortunately, I'd lived there for a few days earlier in the summer, and I cringed every time I drove past it. But the plaza itself was a plethora of shops and boutiques, including a four-thousand-square-foot interactive aquarium that I liked to meander through, looking at the jellies and eels and all the other creatures that I found mesmerizing. Who needed aliens when you had a box jelly floating around in a tank?

I parked my Sebring and once again thought I should look into getting a new car. It wasn't like I didn't have the money to afford the payments, and I was getting antsy for something a little smaller that gave better gas mileage.

As I dashed through the drizzle to the plaza, I saw Barb waiting just inside the doors. She was standing in line at Jumbo Juice, a new juice bar that I'd introduced her to. Once you got past the wheatgrass and algae glop, most of their combos were pretty good. I slid in behind Barb and tapped her on the shoulder. She jumped and turned around.

"Jesus, you scared me, Persia! I see you didn't have time to dry your hair," she said, staring up at me. Barb was as petite as I was tall, as tiny as I was muscled, and she sported a coppery spiked do that made her look chic without giving any Euro trash vibes. Impeccably dressed, she never looked flustered, even when she was wearing an apron and was covered with flour.

"Hey, I made it on time, didn't I? Besides, I was helping Lisa at the pool. That woman has one hell of an entrenched phobia."

"Hydrophobia . . . not an easy one to overcome. You want some juice?"

I glanced at the menu. "Yeah, I'll take an apple-carrot-ginger juice."

Barb stepped up to the counter and put in my order and the one she wanted, a blend they called Sunshine Joy. With orange, pineapple, lemon, and kiwi, it sounded bright enough to light up the sky.

We sipped our drinks as we meandered through the mall. I, of course, wanted to go to the aquarium, but Barb slapped a moratorium on that thought. "Not until we find our dresses and shoes," she said.

I laughed. "Whatever you say. So, how goes it with

Mama K? You figured out a good antidote to her venom yet?"

Barb flashed me a grateful smile. She couldn't talk openly about how she felt about her mother-in-law to anybody else. Dorian would freak, and Auntie would nod, but there seemed to be a link older women who were in the mama category shared—one that brooded silently over the younger women in the families. As much as Auntie was my friend, she was first and foremost my aunt and substitute mother.

"Tonight, I told her I was going shopping with you so Dorian would be cooking dinner. Lordy, Persia, I thought she was going to have a fit. That man is a god in her eyes, and she thinks I should be his servant. Well, you know just how I feel about *that* mind-set. When I ignored her dire looks, she set into nitpicking about the house. Why do I have a maid? Why can't I just do the housework in the evenings after a long day at the bakery while Dorian rests? Because, of course, that's what *she* would be doing." She let out a sigh. "It's never going to end until that old bat dies. Or until I do, whichever comes first. Honestly, Persia, this is what I hate most about being married. She doesn't want Dorian to grow up."

I refrained from stating the obvious. Or at least, what seemed obvious to me. If Dorian wanted to act grown-up he could tell his mother to back off. Sure, he'd put his balls on the line standing up to his mother, but sometimes personal integrity demanded taking a stand.

I finished off my juice and pointed to a small boutique nestled between a guitar shop and a video arcade. "That the place?"

Barb broke into a giddy smile. Shopping was her solace, and she could outlast the best of the mall rats. "That's it! Let's go get beautiful."

Sarina's was the type of boutique that should have charged a fee just for entering the store. I could tell at a glance that the designs were all about this year; no has-beens allowed. Quality materials, name designers, glitter and glitz all the way. Women drifted through the racks, lingering over the selections as they mulled over a lace sleeve or boned bodice. Coming from the upper-crust set of Gull Harbor, the wives of the software designers, the matrons of old money, the newbies of nouveau riche, their expressions ranged from mildly bored to wistful.

A saleswoman, clad in a suit designed to look professional and yet set her off as an employee rather than a customer, bustled over to us. "May I show you something? Shopping for the Gala?" Her smile was infectious, and both Barb and I beamed at her.

Barb nodded. "I'm looking for something in a size two, petite, that plays up my hair—short, above knee-length. Maybe something in royal blue or forest green. Persia, what are you looking for?"

I blinked as I surveyed the options. "I want to shine. Sparkly but no sequins. Form-fitting with a flare at the bottom, if possible. Long, with low-cut cleavage. I take between a six and an eight, depending on the piece."

The girl nodded, taking everything we said in so seriously that I wanted to pat her on the shoulder and reassure her that we wouldn't keel over and die if we couldn't find anything. She led us through the racks, stopping by one to sort through the hangers. Within minutes, she held out a dress to Barb. It was a simple chiffon sheath made from mousseline de soie, trimmed with a satin belt. The color was so blue that it almost hurt my eyes, and the belt had a rhinestone buckle on it that sparkled against the royal hue.

"Oh Barb, that would be so gorgeous with the color of your hair," I said, staring at the way the blue popped against her skin.

Barb held the dress up to her and smiled. "I have to try this on," she said, and the girl directed her back to a fitting room, then returned to me.

"I think I have the perfect dress for you, too," she said, leading me around to a different section of the store. She poked through two racks before coming up with a triumphant gleam in her eye. "Yes! We still have it. What do you think?"

The dress she held out to me was brilliant. Metallic gold without sequins, the long halter dress caught the light and reflected it with a shimmering ease. It was form-fitting until it hit just above the knees, at which point it flared out into a flurry of pleats. The front hem was shorter than the back and would frame my legs in a sparkle of color. A plunging neckline brought the center almost down to meet the navel, but a pale mesh insert provided a secret underwire support system for the breasts. The back was even lower, draping in a curve right above the butt.

"My God. That doesn't leave much to the imagination, but yet . . . everything important is covered." I gazed at the dress. It fit my style perfectly. Now, if it only fit my body. "Let me try it on."

"Not every woman could pull this off," she said, leading me back to the room next to Barb's. "But I think you have the panache."

Thank God the skirt of the dress had a hidden fastener in the back. I sucked in my breath and zipped it up. The mesh around my bra band was almost invisible with only a faint gold sheen to indicate its presence, but it was molded strong enough to support my breasts. The thin band of mesh hooked in back, where it barely showed against my bra line. When my hair was down, it would be entirely invisible. It looked like gravity had taken leave, and my boobs were floating in the air with just the right amount of perk.

Once zipped, the skirt of the dress molded itself to my hips and thighs, the material stretching across my legs. I cautiously sat in one of the chairs, pleased to see there was just enough give in the fabric so that I wouldn't have to stand up all evening. Pleats gathered just above my knees, framing the front of my legs as they swept down to the floor in back, much like tails on a tuxedo. I shook out my hair, and it cascaded down in a frenzy of damp black curls. Finally, I took a long look in the mirror.

"Oh good Lord." My reflection stood somewhere between runway and red carpet. With the right stilettos, I'd be jammin'. I peeked out of the dressing room to find Barbara, who was looking for me. She looked positively gorgeous in the sheath dress, and her hair shimmered like fire next to the royal blue.

"You're stunning," I said, stepping out of my room.

Barb stared at me, her mouth agape. "Uh . . . you, too. Oh my, I think that beats just about anything I've ever seen you in. Very Marilyn Monroe meets King Midas." She slowly circled me, squinting. "Persia, that's hot. It's almost . . . slutty, but not enough to give people reason to whisper."

I grinned. "That's what I want, then. It works. I feel like one of the old-fashioned glamour girls. But I need new shoes to go with it, don't you think?"

"I think you'd better get spikes, because you can use them to beat the men off. Seriously, that dress is a jaw-dropper. I guess part of it's your height. You tower over every other woman in the room as it is. In that getup, and with stilettos, you'll be impossible to ignore."

I asked her to come into the fitting room so she could unzip me. "That doesn't bother me. I just want to look good. So, who's in charge of the whole shebang? Auntie gave me a quick rundown, but to be honest I wasn't really listening. All I know is that we've been run ragged this week. That's good, though, with the profits from the makeovers and haircuts going to charity."

As I slipped out of the dress and back into my clothes, Barb hung it on the hanger for me.

"Annabel Mason, the grande dame of Gull Harbor. You've met her—she's the president of the Chamber of Commerce, and the Thanksgiving Gala was her brainchild. This is the fifteenth year. It started, if I remember, when the Helping Hands Center was about to close for lack of funding. They made enough to tide it over until they could drum up enough sponsors to help out. Each year, the Gala's gotten bigger, and Annabel plays hostess every year, regardless of how she's feeling. Lovely older woman, about your aunt's age . . . maybe a few years older."

I thought for a moment, then an image came to mind, and I matched the name with the face. "I know who you're talking about. I went to last month's meeting with Auntie and met her there. She seems a little frail, doesn't she?"

Barb nodded. "Yes, she is. Sadly, she inherited her father's heart condition, and she also has rheumatoid arthritis, but she does more than most of the women I know who are half her age." She glanced at the price tag on the dress and let out a low whistle. "Man, I hope you have more places to wear this than just the Gala. For these prices, we should be attending balls every month!"

"Go change, if you've decided on that one, and let's find some shoes to match these gowns." I pushed her toward the door, and she laughingly headed back to her dressing room. I took another look at the price. Barb was right; the dress was outrageously expensive, but even though the thought crossed my mind that I could wear it to Killian's Christmas party in Seattle, I decided against rationalizing. There was no rationale for a dress that cost that much except that I loved it, I could afford it, and I wanted it.

We scoured the shoe stores and came up with glitzy sandals, then spent a quick ten minutes drifting through the aquarium. I tapped lightly on the glass of the octopus tank, watching as the cephalopod swam over to my summons, its tentacles rippling in the water.

"Hey there," I said, whispering to it. "How are you doing? Like it in there, or do you wish you were out in the open water?" Every time I came to the aquarium, I'd stop and spend some time with Ivan, as I'd taken to calling him. He fascinated me, appearing pensive as he watched from his watery world. I'd studied a bit about octopuses and their brethren, and knew just how intelligent they had tested out, and I'd finally admitted that I wanted one for myself. I was researching just what upkeep it would require.

I hadn't sprung that bit of news on Aunt Florence yet, but considering that we already had eight cats, three dogs, and Hoffman, our rooster, who took up residence in the utility room and often joined us for an evening of *Forensics Files*, I didn't see why she would object.

Barb returned after a stint watching the jellyfish. She had a personal grudge against the creatures, and every time I dragged her to the aquarium, she held a staring match with them while I meandered around and said hi to the various tank dwellers.

She sighed. "I guess I'd better get home and face Mama K's wrath. Damn it. I've never been good enough, and never will. If she's not harping on the fact that we actually *chose* to remain child-free, then she's bitching about Dorian's decision to stay in the United States. It's going to be a long visit, Persia. I may need a few sanity breaks."

I put my arm around her shoulders and squeezed. "Honey, any time you need to catch your breath, just give me a call, and we'll take off and go get coffee or lunch or even just a walk down by the lighthouse."

With a resigned wave, she headed to her car. I watched until she made it, then pulled out my keys and jogged the distance to mine. Thank God I didn't have the in-law problems Barb did, because my temper wasn't all that under control, and I wouldn't put up with crap from anybody. If Mama Konstantinos was *my* mother-in-law, I'd be locked up in no time.

By the time I pulled in the driveway to Moss Rose Cottage, it was full-on dark. Auntie would be waiting dinner for me; we ate late most days, usually around seven thirty or eight. I noticed two other cars in the driveway and smiled. Killian and Kane were here. My boyfriend and Auntie's beau. It had seemed odd at first to see Auntie cavorting with a man, but within a few weeks I'd fallen for the Hawaiian who had brought a spark of romantic joy to my aunt's heart. Long ago, his twin brother and Auntie had been engaged, but tragedy intervened. Now, time had come full circle, and Kane was wooing my aunt.

Moss Rose Cottage was a huge old three-story Victorian that had been built well over one hundred years ago by a Captain Bentley, a Navy officer who retired with his family to Port Samanish Island before the turn of the twentieth century. His spirit still walked the halls. Auntie and I had both felt and heard him around since we first moved in when I was ten years old. Occasionally a doorknob would turn, or footsteps would sound in the attic, but we were never afraid; in fact, we always had the feeling that the Cap'n, as we called him, was watching over us.

Set on thirty acres of gardens and orchards, the house was situated across the road from the inlet. We could open the curtains that covered the floor-to-ceiling windows stretching along one entire wall of the living room and watch the ocean crashing as the waves swept the currents in and out of the bay, ebbing with the tides that ruled the shoreline. This was the only home I'd really ever known.

When I was four, my father brought me back from Iran after Mother died and dropped me on Auntie's doorstep in Seattle. He then absconded after giving her full guardianship over me. I grew up traveling the world. At five, I stood at the foot of the pyramids in Giza, and then flew to the UK to gaze silently at the standing stones that encircled Stonehenge. At six, I learned to eat croissants for breakfast at the outdoor sidewalk cafés in Paris. Then Auntie took me to Rome, where I grappled with the beauty of Michelangelo's work at Saint Peter's Basilica. Old women wrapped in black shawls would chuck my chin and hand me yeasty rolls as we wandered through the markets for breakfast and lunch.

Over the next three years, I navigated the throngs of Tokyo where my height—even as a child—made me stand out as a gaijin. I gazed upon the fabled Taj Mahal and memorized the royal love story that inspired the building of it. Frightened by the noise and the beggars, I pressed close to Auntie's side in the crowded streets of Calcutta. With Eva, my nanny and tutor, along for the ride, we criss-crossed the world. She cracked the whip over my studies, and I learned geography via experience far better than most adults did through books.

But on the day I turned ten, Aunt Florence decided it was time to settle me in one place, so she bought Moss Rose Cottage, and we moved in. She continued to travel for awhile, leaving me with Eva during her trips, but the moment we first walked through the door, I knew I was home.

I hoisted my shopping bags and swimsuit tote and headed for the porch. Illuminated by soft lights to guide friends and family to our door through the rain-soaked nights, Moss Rose Cottage beckoned me in, and I knew in the depths of my heart that, no matter where I journeyed, this house would always be the one place I would call home.

From the Pages of Persia's Journal

Intoxication Oil #3

Ronnie Jenks wanted something that would make her smell delicious. Since she can handle rich, creamy scents, I came up with a wintertime version of my original Intoxication Oil. Simple and yet elegant, the scent is yummy enough to make any woman smell like dessert— and to pass muster at any holiday gala.

We talked about other ways in which she could make herself stand out, since she's in the boyfriend-hunting club. I mentioned that while she's a lovely woman, she often carries herself as though she's embarrassed of something. Ronnie's never had a lot of self-esteem, and it shows. So I gave her a few pointers.

- Walk with your head held high. Not *nose in the air*, but proud of your accomplishments, of your strengths. Don't stare at the ground, don't roll your shoulders forward to hide your figure. Be happy to be the woman you are, rather than wishing you were the woman you aren't. Everyone has something special and wonderful they can call their own; find what your unique strengths are and emphasize them.

- When you greet someone, don't be a wilting violet. Take their hand firmly in yours. Smile and say hello in a clear voice. Don't mumble, don't focus on what they might be thinking of you. Most often, people are more concerned about their own lives rather than noticing whether you're a few pounds heavier than you were last year or that you aren't wearing a trendy outfit. The best way to invite criticism is to start ridiculing yourself.

~ Remember, people will treat you like you treat yourself. Respect yourself, and they'll take their cues from you.

~ Be a good listener. People like to feel as though they matter. Nothing invites conversation more quickly than asking about somebody else's life.

~ If you're not sure of party etiquette, buy an up-to-date book about good manners and study it. These books aren't bibles, but they can help you steer clear of making a major faux pas.

Blend and store this oil (as with all oils) in a small, dark bottle. You will need a bottle and stopper or lid, an eyedropper, and the following:

> *¼ oz. almond or apricot kernel oil (a good unscented base)*
> *25 drops peach oil*
> *25 drops musk oil*
> *10 drops vanilla oil*
> *3 drops clove oil*

OPTIONAL:

> *2 dried cloves*
> *A small piece of garnet (you can use chips off a gemstone chip necklace)*

Using an eyedropper, add each fragrance oil to the almond oil, gently swirling after each addition to blend the scent. After adding all the oils, cap and shake gently. At this time, add the cloves and garnets to the bottle for added energy, if so desired.

Garnets promote self-confidence and personal power.

The cloves will intensify the scent and add a decorative touch. Keep oil in a cool, dark place; if left in the sun it will lose potency. As always, remind customers to avoid eating or drinking this oil, and to keep it out of reach of children and animals.

Chapter Three

Killian jumped up the moment I swept through the door and took my bags from me, setting them down on the bench in the foyer. Tall and lean, with short red spiky hair, he was perpetually dressed in black jeans and a turtleneck. He pulled me into his arms, his lips lingering on mine, and I melted into the kiss as he wrapped his arms around my waist. The scent of his cologne left me reeling. Spicy, reminiscent of dark woods on a fiery autumn night, it inundated my senses, and I wanted to drag him to the sofa, to curl up in front of the roaring fire and make passionate love on the rug in front of the flames.

He must have caught my mood. "Good to see you, too," he said, his eyes dancing, twin orbs of laughing blue. "Did you find a dress?"

I held up the bag. "Yes, I found a dress. And it's gorgeous. You'd better wear a tuxedo to match." As I carried my bags into the living room, the aroma of turkey soup and baking powder biscuits drifted in from the kitchen. My stomach rumbled, and I followed my nose to the stove, where Auntie stood, stirring the pot of bubbling broth.

Kane, a stout man of Hawaiian and Portuguese descent, sat in a chair at the table, looking out over the storm-ridden night. His hair was sleeked back into a salt-and-pepper ponytail, and he had a peaceful look on his face, as if he were exactly where he wanted to be.

Beauty and Beast, two of our dogs, curled at his feet. Old Pete was asleep in the dog bed, and I could hear Hoffman clucking away in the utility room. Delilah, Auntie's seventeen-year-old white Persian who was well on her way to a cranky, happy senility, had taken up residence on the counter. She watched Aunt Florence, her ears twitching with every word Auntie said.

I slipped up behind Auntie and wrapped my arms around her. "Hey you, dinner smells wonderful, and I'm starved."

"How did Lisa's lesson go?" Auntie asked.

"Not bad, she actually made it over to the bench again and sat down in the water for awhile. Mmm, can I have a bite?" I picked up the soup spoon and dipped it in the pot, tasting the warm trickle of broth as it ran down my throat.

Auntie slapped my hand. "Stop it, child. Dinner's almost ready. Kane and Killian already set the table, so go wash your hands, and we'll eat."

I retreated to the downstairs bath and washed my hands and face. Home felt comfortable, and with Killian and Kane here, lively. By the time I returned to the dining room, Auntie had poured the soup into the tureen and the biscuits sat in a cloth-lined basket, golden brown and fluffy. The sweet-cream butter was just the right texture, and as Kane poured our wine—a Sauvignon Blanc—I settled myself next to Killian and unfolded my napkin with a flourish, covering my lap with the linen towel.

The floor-to-ceiling windows that graced both dining room and living room gave us a perfect view into the dark night. In the backyard, a long row of low-voltage walkway lighting illuminated the path leading to our gardens, while down the hill and across the road from our house I could barely make out the faint swell of waves as they rolled onto the beach that stretched along the eastern coastline of the island.

Auntie dished up the soup. I took a biscuit and tore it in half, the yeasty scent of fresh-baked bread rising along with the saliva. God help me, if I didn't get something in my mouth soon I'd be drooling like old Pete when he heard the dog food bag open.

"How'd your phone call go today?" I glanced at Killian, hoping for good news. Even though Bebe had tanked his company in the late summer, he was already busy drumming up funding to start a new venture. This time Killian wanted to focus solely on skin care products.

He winked at me. "Great. In fact, they want to see me Monday morning at eight AM. Which means I'll take the ferry over to Seattle tomorrow and stay with Michael." Michael was his stepbrother who worked for Microsoft. He lived in a high-end condo on the Eastside, along with his fiancée. Michael was a good sort, if nerdy.

"Just make sure you come back," I murmured, biting into my biscuit. I closed my eyes, reveling in the flood of butter and bread.

"Persia, did you remind Lisa that she needs to be at the shop on time tomorrow? We won't have a minute to spare right up until closing time." Auntie made sure everybody had plenty of soup and then allowed herself to sit and eat.

I nodded, swallowing before I answered. "I did. She'll be there. We're closing at four, right?"

"Yes, that should give everybody enough time to go home and get ready for the Gala. This year I believe Annabel set the starting time for the dance at eight. That should give us enough time, don't you think?" Auntie frowned, and I knew she was fretting.

"That's plenty, at least for me. I doubt that Tawny will need more than a couple of hours, and Trevor's a shower-

and-shave type of guy. If we lock the door at four PM promptly, we should all do just fine." I noticed that Kane had brought his slack key guitar with him. I pointed at it. "Does that mean you're going to treat us to a concert tonight?"

He winked at Auntie. "If Florence here gives me the word, I might at that."

Comfortably full and looking forward to an evening's relaxation, I let out a long sigh. Just one day to get through, and the Gala would be over, but coming right on its heels would be the Christmas season. We'd already decorated the shop, thank heavens. Evenings like this one were a priceless treat amid the holiday madness.

❧

A glance out the window told me that the day was shaping up to be stormy. Not unusual weather for around here, but I'd been hoping that we'd manage a dry day for the dance. I opened the sash, letting the chill air flow into the room. It was almost cold enough to snow, I thought, and the rain-soaked breeze carried with it the scent of moss and detritus from the gardens and ravines surrounding our home, as well as the briny scent of the inlet.

I decided to forgo any stressful workout. My butt still hurt a little, and a day or two of rest would do me fine. I swung through a soothing yoga routine, then spent twenty minutes on the treadmill before slipping into a calf-length black rayon skirt and a short-sleeved V-neck in hunter green. I braided my hair back and slipped on a pair of knee-high suede boots that I'd owned so long that I'd had them resoled twice. They were still in good condition and so comfortable that I dreaded the idea of ever giving them up.

Auntie had already fixed breakfast by the time I clattered down the stairs. She'd made fruit salad, whole-grain toast, scrambled eggs, and venison patties. Trevor had gone on a hunting trip early in the month and brought down a deer. He gave us some of the meat, and in return, Auntie let him have the nuts off one of the hazelnut trees.

Neither Kane nor Killian had stayed over, so we were just two at the breakfast table, not counting the cats milling around the table and the dogs watching our every move. We usually enjoyed our leisurely alone-time meals, but this morning was different. We had work to do, more than we wanted to even think about.

"Are you stopping off anywhere after work, Imp?" Auntie asked.

I shook my head. "No, I want to come right home and rest for an hour or so before getting ready."

"Then I'll ride with you today. No sense taking both cars since we'll both be at the shop all day and we're coming directly home." She patted her lips with her napkin and delicately burped. "Whenever you're ready, child."

I polished off the last bite of my toast and grabbed my keys and purse. It was unlike Auntie to ever accept a ride with anybody. She loved her Baby more than she loved most of the people in her life. The two were inseparable.

"What happened to your car? I mean, I'll be glad to give you a ride, but you always drive. Is something wrong?"

She let out a loud sigh, a sheepish look on her face. "I didn't say anything last night in front of Kane, but did you know that Kyle had the nerve to give me a ticket? *Me?* I read him the riot act and told him I'd speak to his mother about him if he ever brought up Baby's needing a muffler again. He agreed to tear up the ticket if I'd take Baby into the shop today, and I finally said yes, just to keep the peace. Someone's coming out to take her in later this morning."

I repressed a grin. Kyle had finally won the battle. Good for him, and good for the peace and quiet of the neighborhood. But one glance at Auntie's smoldering look told me it would be wisest to keep my thoughts on the subject to myself, so I made appropriately sympathetic noises and locked the door behind us as we hurried out to my car. The rain shower had turned into a downpour, and the wind was picking up, whipping through the tops of the tall firs. I grimaced as a sudden gust pelted me with a sideways shock of watery bullets.

"I hope the power doesn't go out. That would just frost things for the Gala tonight," Auntie said. As she scrambled into the passenger seat, I raced around to the driver's side and slipped under cover just in time to avoid a flurry of hail that pelted the ground. The ice balls were the size of kitty kibble, small enough to avoid pitting the cars, large enough to smart if they hit bare skin.

"Did you by any chance listen to the weather report to see what they're predicting?" I started the car and cautiously inched down the driveway. We needed a new batch of gravel; the ruts were becoming a little too deep, and last week I'd almost gotten stuck. Auntie had ordered it, but until it was actually in place, I decided to play it safe.

"I barely had time to make breakfast this morning. Buttercup kept waking me up through the night. I think there's a mouse in the walls of my bedroom, because she kept racing around the room, thunking her head when she forgot to slow down." She adjusted her seat belt and cleared her throat. "I've been meaning to tell you that I'm thinking about taking a vacation next month. Kane and I might go to Hawai'i."

I gripped the steering wheel. I hadn't expected to hear that. Auntie hadn't been back to the islands since her fiancé was murdered. "Really? Auntie, is there something I should know? Are you planning on marrying Kane?"

Her laughter filled the car. "Child, I'll go to my grave a single woman. I adore Kane, and he's a wonderful addition to my life, but I have no need or desire to marry. I'm too capricious and set in my ways. I couldn't take living with a man, even though it's nice to have one in my bed again."

Curious now, I stepped into the gray area where I'd always hesitated to pry. "Have you had a boyfriend since your fiancé died?"

Auntie's snort was louder than her laugh. "I've had my share, child, and the last one was . . . oh . . . about two years ago. We broke up a few months before you came back to live with me. Remember Clyde Wilkerson?" Clyde was a friend of Winthrop Winchester, Auntie's lawyer. He was a CPA who owned a thriving business preparing taxes for the Gull Harbor elite.

"*Clyde Wilkerson?* But he's married!" I almost swerved onto the shoulder of the road. I quickly adjusted the wheel.

"He wasn't married a few years back."

"But he's *seventy* if he's a day!" I just couldn't imagine Auntie with someone who looked ready for the country club's smoking room. Clyde always wore a suit, and while he was a stately gentleman, carrying a silver-handled cane with him everywhere he went, he seemed to have as much in common with Auntie as a bull did with a zebra.

"Imp, never judge a book by its cover," she said. "Clyde may look the conservative financier, but trust me, he's got a wild streak, and he doesn't appreciate women who sit around gossiping about the neighbors or whining about how they need a new fur coat. The man has a mind like a fox, and . . ." She paused, then plunged ahead. "And Clyde Wilkerson was one of the best lovers I ever had."

I swallowed, trying not to look shocked. Auntie and I were frank about a lot of things, but this side of her life had always seemed sacrosanct. In fact, I'd seldom connected the term *love life* with thoughts of Aunt Florence.

"Why did you split up, then?" I asked.

"Because, at my age there's more to life than sex, and while we had lovely times together, the man wanted to marry me. He wanted a wife, and I had no intention of walking down the aisle with him. So he married Ruth Gorsky instead, and I sincerely hope they're happy."

When I thought about Ruth Wilkerson, I doubted that

Clyde was all too happy. Ruth might have been an on-the-button lady at one point, but her main focuses now seemed to be shopping, lunching with the ladies, and finding a wife for her son, whom I'd met once. He was the type of man who went out of his way to insult people. I shuddered, thinking Auntie had definitely gotten the better part of the deal.

As we wound through the slick streets leading to downtown Gull Harbor, I began to run through my tasks for the day. I completely missed the turn onto Island Drive and would probably have kept right on going if Auntie hadn't cleared her throat and pointed out that we had overshot the mark. Feeling sheepish, I rounded the block and pulled into a parking spot across the street from the store. We hopped out of the car and waved to Marianne, of Marianne's Closet, and bustled across the street, holding our purses over our heads to stave off the driving rain.

The shop was jumping. Tawny already looked frazzled, and Seth was a flurry of scissors, combs, hair spray, and mousse. I had no more than shrugged out of my leather jacket when my first appointment appeared, and we were off for the day.

Ronnie Jenks wanted something lovely, something that would match her peach-colored gown for the Thanksgiving Gala. As I blended together the musk and vanilla oils, adding a few drops of clove as a top note, I tried to shut out the drone of noise that filtered through the shop. The buzz was incredible, and I began to realize that not only had we rebuilt our customer base after Bebe's sabotage, we'd increased it threefold.

Ronnie loved the oil, and I wrote out an invoice and checked her off in my appointment book. Julia Wheeler was due in about fifteen minutes. I had time to run back to talk to Auntie for a moment. She was between facials, and I caught her washing her hands at the sink in the back of the spa area.

"Auntie, we need to get some help in here. Tawny's run

ragged out there, and if I were her, I'd demand an assistant or I'd quit." I glanced back at the register where there was a line of at least seven people. "We need two registers going during the Christmas rush."

Auntie blinked. She peered around the corner, then blithely smiled. "Good catch, Persia. Why don't you take a moment and run back to the office. Call Trevor and see if he knows anybody who needs a temporary job. We'll pay ten dollars an hour, full-time through Christmas. We might want to consider keeping them on if business continues to pick up like it has been." Her next appointment showed up as I jogged down the hall to the office.

A quick call to Trevor turned up zilch, but then an inspiration hit me, and I punched in Killian's number. He answered almost immediately.

"Listen," I said in a rush. "We need extra help down here on the register. What's the name of that girl who was the receptionist for you at Donna Prima? Do you know if she's still looking for work?"

"Betsy Sue, and yes, she's still looking for work. Both she and her boyfriend Julius will be coming back to work for me if I can get this new undertaking started in the next few months. Want her number?"

"Yeah," I said, readying a pen and Post-it note. Betsy Sue and Julius made one of the most unlikely couples I'd met. She was a perky cheerleader type, and he was the geeky young scientist, but they loved each other deeply.

"It's 555-7700. She can use the work, I'll tell you that. They're expecting."

"A baby?" I sat down, staring at the number. "How far along is she?"

"Only a few months. They wanted to get married right after she found out, but she can't get AFDC if they are married, and right now with being out of work and on what little unemployment she gets . . . it's just not feasible without the state stepping in to help."

"Thanks," I murmured. "I'll call her right away." I put

in a quick call to Betsy Sue, who almost started crying when I offered her the job. "This is temporary, Betsy, but who knows . . . we may be able to work it into something more, though I can't make any promises. At the least, it should tide you over until Killian gets his business up and going again. Can you start Monday?"

She eagerly accepted, and when I returned to the main store, I felt like I'd just bailed her out of a sinking ship. I informed Tawny and Auntie to expect another hand come Monday, for which Tawny flashed me a brilliant smile, and then I dove into the next fragrance appointment, wondering just how busy we were going to get during the coming season.

⋅❧

Around two PM, Tawny frantically motioned to me. As I approached the counter, she asked the next customer in line if she'd mind waiting "just one second," then nodded me away from where the line of shoppers could hear us. As I followed her, I wondered what the hell was up.

"What is it?" I asked, glancing back at my station. "I've got one last appointment—who's waiting on me—and then I'll give you a hand until we shut the doors at four."

"Thanks, but Persia, we have a bigger problem than that. Lisa's vanished. She left a note that I didn't find until I escorted her next appointment back to get a makeover." Tawny handed me a piece of stationery.

I stared at it for a moment before taking it and unfolding the paper. As I read it, a headache a mile wide stabbed me between the eyes. Seven simple lines, but it meant at least three dissatisfied customers and one very irate store owner: me. Two, when Auntie found out.

Persia, I had to take off for the rest of the afternoon. I'm sorry I didn't tell you myself, but I knew you'd be upset. Please believe me, this is very important and relates to what we were talking about at the pool yester-

*day. Don't be mad, please. I wouldn't put you on the
spot if I didn't have a really good reason. See you
tonight, and I hope to have good news to tell you then!*
     Lisa T.

"Damn it, what the hell was she thinking? How many
appointments does she have left for the afternoon?" I
crumpled the note in my hand, furious.

Tawny paled. "Four. One at two, one at two thirty, one
at three, and one at three thirty. What should I tell her two
o'clock?"

Frazzled, I ran my hand across my forehead. "Shit, I
don't know. Ask her if she'd mind waiting for a moment.
Get her some tea and a cookie, and tell her we'll be about
fifteen minutes late."

We didn't have time to call in anybody else. I was
going to have to wing this mess myself. "I used to give
makeovers when I worked the counter at Sashay in
Seattle. It's been awhile, but hell, I'm good with makeup.
I should be able to cover for her. I'll finish up with my appointment as soon as possible and then start taking Lisa's
clients. You be sure to leave a note that I took care of those
clients. I feel very sorry for Lisa and her situation, but nobody puts us in a tight spot like this."

I started to return to my fragrance appointment, then
paused. "Listen, since we're running late, inform each
makeover that there will be a fifteen- to twenty-minute
delay. Make sure the coffee, tea, and cookies are good
to go."

Looking relieved, Tawny whirled around and hurried
back to the counter to implement my orders. I leaned
against the wall, feeling overwhelmed. We'd been unpre-
pared for the crisis. Auntie and I were going to have to discuss backups and the work schedule. I didn't want
anything like this happening again. It made for unhappy
customers and an even more unhappy Persia.

Chapter Four

Auntie called me into her room to help her with her dress, and I couldn't believe my eyes when I opened the door. No mu'umu'us, no floppy pink straw hat. In fact, I barely recognized her, and it took me a good five minutes to close the door behind me.

"Auntie, I've never seen you look so beautiful," I whispered. "Where on earth did you get that dress?"

As she turned around, I found myself sliding onto the bench that sat at the foot of her bed. My aunt was stout—well—more than stout. And short. And usually she looked like an escapee from some tropical island. But tonight she was stunning.

Auntie was dressed in a flowing teal skirt set in chiffon that sparkled with shimmering beads. The hem of her skirt flowed out in an A-line, grazing the bottom of her knees. I was amazed to see how good her legs looked. She was wearing kitten heels—black pumps—and a diamond pendant set in gold rested against the blouson top that she had belted with a simple patent leather black belt. Her hair, normally worn in a braid that trailed down her back, had been coiled in an elegant chignon and was set off with a festive comb decorated with glittery autumn leaves and red berries.

"Auntie," I said, unable to tear my gaze away. "You . . . I've never seen you like this." I knew she dressed up for the Chamber of Commerce meetings she went to, but nothing like this. No, since I'd been a child it had been a steady barrage of mu'umu'us and straw hats.

She smiled, her lips a rusty bronze that mirrored the colors of her barrette. "Well, it is the *Gala*. You weren't here for last year's event, so you didn't see me then, either. I was the belle of the ball." With a twinkle in her eyes, she added, "Well, maybe not, but I knocked 'em dead."

I nodded dumbly, still too shocked to speak. After a moment, I cleared my throat and said, "You're beautiful, Auntie. Always . . . but tonight . . ."

"Maybe you'd be a dear and zip me up in back? I can't quite reach the zipper," she said. I stepped around behind her and drew the fastener closed, thinking that if Auntie wanted to, she could give any of the town matrons a run for their money. Not only did she have brains and heart, but she could put on a damned good show when she wanted to.

"I'd better finish dressing," I said, wanting to stay and chat. She shooed me out of the room though, and I dashed up to my suite. I'd already taken my shower, so I slid into the skintight gold dress and finally managed to get the mesh bustline settled in the right place. I usually wore my hair up, but tonight I decided to leave it down in a tumble of curls. As I added a simple gold chain and a pair of amethyst chandelier earrings, I thought again about Auntie.

If she wanted to, she could probably be married within the month to any man she set her sights on, but she chose to remain single and enjoy life on her own terms. I only hoped to remain as firm in my own resolve, to never settle, never compromise away what I wanted. Auntie wasn't afraid to face the future on her own terms, and I wouldn't be either.

I added a velvet cloak to my outfit and cautiously descended the stairs. My heels were thin—delicately so—and I didn't want to take a tumble that would land me in the hospital instead of on the dance floor. Auntie was waiting below, wrapped in a sable coat. Killian and Kane were both in the living room, Kane in a black suit that looked a few years out of date but still dapper, and Killian was dressed in full tux and tails, including top hat. I tucked the strap of my evening bag over my shoulder and looped my arm through Killian's.

"Ready?" I asked. He nodded. Kane took Auntie's arm, and we left for the Gala, Auntie and Kane in his car, and Killian and me in Killian's Jag.

❧

Oh, the joys of small town island life. Everybody who had enough money to spare for tickets had come out in full force, and the social circles had already formed by the time we walked through the door.

The Gala was held at the Gull Harbor Club Noir, a large multicultural center that hosted dances, plays, art exhibits, and other such events. The lights were shimmering out of the two-story building, which had been built with a Bavarian facade. Snowflake cutouts of dark wood framed the lower level, and row after row of dark beams rested against tan walls, forming a crosshatch design that made your eyes go wonky if you looked at it too long.

The entire roof had been strung with icicle lights that cascaded in long, draping chains. Atop the roof, a brilliant star of twinkling lights emblazoned the sky. The brilliance continued with a large blue spruce that graced the rounded driveway where the valet parking awaited. Alight in a blinding array of multicolored bulbs, the tree was surrounded by illuminated candy canes that cordoned off the grass, guiding guests along the path to the door of the club. There, two men dressed in red tuxedos waited to open the doors for the dancers.

Music echoed from within, and for once there were no requisite retro disco numbers playing. As we swept past the doormen, I found my foot tapping and realized that I was actually looking forward to the evening. Killian had proven to be as good on the dance floor as he was in bed, and my body longed for movement. His hand on my lower back, propelling me forward, only made my desire stronger. Before the night was out, I had the feeling my urge to dance would be turning into a different—though related—urge.

The interior of Club Noir had been transformed from its usual urban grunge décor to a vision in gold. Soft lighting shed a decidedly bronzed cast over the guests, and the dance floor was spotlighted in a shimmer of red, bronze, and orange. My dress would be absolutely stunning, I thought, feeling a little wiggle of joy. A DJ was set up on one side of the dance floor, and I recognized him as one of Killian's friends. We gave him a little wave, and he winked at us.

At the far end of the room there was a long buffet table, and with my heightened sense of smell, I caught a whiff of roast turkey and prime rib. My stomach rumbled, but I told it to wait. No way could I eat a good meal in this dress and then hope to dance. I'd opt for a plate later on.

A lounge and dining area offered dancers a place to rest their tired feet and eat. Over the whole Gala, bouncing against the top of the twenty-foot ceiling, loomed giant balloons of turkeys, pilgrims, and Indians, watching over the party, surreal sentinels that I would only expect to find in a town like Gull Harbor.

And speaking of . . . Gull Harbor's elite had gathered near the lounge—old money, draped in paste copies of their very-real jewels that resided within dark vaults in the bowels of the banks. Then came our circle—the business folk, respected members of the Chamber of Commerce who weren't upper-crust enough to join the elite, yet not considered beneath an air-kissed hello. The techies and their wives—mostly moneyed—formed their own little clique, and they mingled with the artists— moneyed or not.

Then there were the other citizens of Gull Harbor who had forked out the steep fee to attend. Some of them just wanted a little sparkle in their lives; others wanted to contribute to charity, but they also wanted to get something out of their contribution other than a tax write-off. And still others were here because it sounded like fun. They seemed the ones most at ease and likely to enjoy themselves.

The music was decidedly oriented toward the techno-artistic crowd, most of whom were in my generation, and as Don the DJ slapped on a track off of the Gorillaz' *Demon Days*, Killian nodded toward the dance floor. Auntie offered to take my wrap for me, and so we spun out, keeping perfect rhythm to the techno hip-hop that I loved so much.

As the track switched over to the bluesy, sexy-as-hell "Every Planet We Reach Is Dead," Killian pulled me into his arms. I matched my movements to his, hip to hip, barely a finger's width between our bodies. His eyes danced with fire as he gazed at me, and I caught my breath in a swirl of hunger. All he had to do was look at me, and I wanted him. The corners of his lips twisted in a wicked grin, and he spun me out then in again for a dip so low my back almost touched the ground. Then up again and round and round, circling the other dancers so lightly our feet barely skimmed the floor.

Three songs later, I caught sight of Barbara dancing with Dorian and gave her a little wave. She pointed to the buffet table, and I nodded. As the four of us walked off the dance floor, I could feel eyes on me. *Hell yeah*, this dress was good for my ego.

When we approached the table, I saw one table was still free, and we sent the men to hold it for us while we attacked the table. Barb looked gorgeous, but behind the sparkling eye shadow and flawless foundation, deep circles were hiding below her eyes and a glint that told me she was about ready to break.

"Oh God, Persia. So help me, I'm going to break that old bat's neck. Dorian turns a blind eye to every insult she gives me. When she's around, he's her little boy again, and he loves playing the part. He left his boxers on the bathroom floor, and he hasn't done that for years. And this morning he actually yelled at me for not making breakfast for everybody, even though I had to be at the bakery an hour earlier than he did." She was blinking furiously, and I had the impression she was trying not to cry.

I glanced over at the table where Dorian and Killian were talking. Killian had a mild look of distaste on his face, and I wondered just what was going down. Dorian, on the other hand, looked a little too self-satisfied for my taste. I'd always liked Dorian, but he could be a little overbearing, and when he grabbed on to an idea, he wouldn't let go. And it seemed that Mama Konstantinos was filling his head with ideas. And yet, and yet . . . would he listen if he didn't secretly agree with her? Shaking my head, I turned back to Barbara.

"How long does she have left on her visit?"

"God knows . . . she's supposed to leave in about a week. I know she has to be back in Greece by December thirteenth because her sister Angelina is arriving from Brussels." She halfheartedly stabbed an olive with her fork as we returned to the table.

I slid in between Dorian and Killian. "Okay, you two. Have at it."

As they headed toward the buffet, I glanced over to see Kyle and Amy coming toward us. Amy looked lovely in a sky blue gown that hearkened back to the prom days of the seventies. It fitted snugly in the bodice, then flowed out in a pouf of chiffon and underskirts. Kyle washed up pretty good in his navy suit, though he looked uncomfortable. I had the feeling he'd rather be in his uniform or in jeans.

I nodded to the extra chairs. "Care to join us? Dorian and Killian are at the buffet." They sat down, but Amy seemed ill at ease, twisting a handkerchief in her hands. Frowning, I asked, "Is something wrong?"

Amy glanced at Kyle, who nodded his head, then said, "Have you seen Lisa around anywhere?"

I motioned to the throng of partygoers. "Isn't she out there? I assumed she'd show up here, and to be honest, I was going to read her the riot act. She took off this afternoon and left us high and dry. I had to scramble to take care of the last four makeovers."

Amy sighed. "I don't know if she's here or not. I've been looking, but there are so many people it's hard to sort through them all. She didn't come home to get ready, and I assumed that she went back to your place with you and your aunt. Did she say where she was going?"

I shook my head. "No. She did leave a note, but I don't have it with me. She's probably going to show up late. I'll bet she's at home getting ready now."

Kyle patted Amy's hand protectively. "That's what I said, but this woman is such a worrywart." He turned to her. "I told you, Lisa will be fine. You're just playing the older sister. Give her time to show up, and I'm sure she'll have a good reason for why she's late." He flashed me a smile, and for once, he looked truly happy.

"So, you two enjoying the dance?" I asked, making room as Killian returned from the buffet. He slid in beside me and slipped his arm around my waist, drawing me in for a kiss. I lingered on his lips for a moment before resolutely pushing away.

Amy shrugged. "It's very pretty here, but I'm not used to big parties. I think I'd be happier at home with a movie and popcorn." She blushed, as if remembering that her date was sitting right next to her. "I mean, I'm happy to be here, but . . ."

Kyle ignored her stumble. "I know exactly what you mean, and I feel the same way. I had to put in an appearance, being the chief of police, but as soon as it's decorous, we can leave and go back to your place."

Killian suddenly pushed back his chair as Dorian returned to the table. He held out his hand and looked at me. "Dance?" I excused myself and followed him out to the dance floor. As we found a place on the floor, he whispered, "I had to get away from Dorian. No offense, but I don't think I like your friend very much. He was going on and on about how I should marry you and make an honest woman of you. I think I offended him when I told him to back off, that we'd make our own decisions."

One thing I'd give Killian—he didn't mince words, and he didn't play games to keep the peace. He called things as he saw them. But that wasn't what bothered me. What ticked me off was the fact that Dorian would go on a tangent about the marriage issue when he knew how I felt about it.

"I'll talk to him tomorrow. He's being an ass lately, and his mama's to thank for that. Now, are you going to dance with me, or are we just going to stand here?" I held out my arms, and Killian gave me that slow grin again, and the rest of the night was a blur of movement and sound and lights and his hot body pressed next to mine.

❧

By the time we got home, Auntie and Kane—whose car was still in the driveway—were nowhere to be seen. I assumed they'd gone to bed. I led Killian up to my room after we raided the refrigerator and made sure that the Menagerie was tucked in for the night. Everybody was curled up asleep, even old Delilah who raised one eye to blink at us as I gave her a little scritch on the head.

Killian closed the door behind us, and I turned, ready

to finish the night in style. The Gala had been lovely, and the music was still pounding in my blood. I flipped on the stereo, taking pains to make sure it wasn't loud enough to filter through to Auntie's room a floor below. The house was well insulated though, and I could usually get away with pumping up the volume to a decent level before she complained.

I turned. "Unzip me?"

His hands ran the length of my back, making me shiver, as he found the zipper and slowly lowered it. "Get undressed," he said roughly, his fingers resting against my lower back. "I want you. Now."

Sucking in a deep breath, I slid out of my dress, hanging it up before turning around to face him, naked, and loving every minute of his scrutiny. His eyes narrowed, and his lips curled ever so slightly. Then, two steps, and he caught me up in his arms and laid me back on the bed, still in his tux and tails. I tilted my head back as his lips pressed against my neck, leaving a trail of kisses down to my breasts, my stomach, and lower yet. I gasped, moaning softly.

As he moved to take off his jacket, I stopped him. "No, leave it on. Please." I gazed into his eyes, and he knew exactly what I wanted. What I *needed*.

"Please, what?" he demanded, reaching for my wrists.

"Please, *sir*," I said, as the winds picked up. A clatter of rain thrashed against the window, but the world outside faded as we met in that ancient dance of power playing against power, deep within the night.

≈

The phone rang at seven thirty the next morning, and I shot up in bed, glaring at it for a moment before fumbling for the receiver. "Yeah, who is it and what do you want? It better be good at this time in the morning," I said.

Killian mumbled something next to me and turned over on his side. I gazed down at the lanky drink of water in my bed. He was muscled but lean, and a thick mat of red hair dappled his chest. His red was natural, that much I'd found out a few months earlier, much to both our delights. It was hard to believe that we'd only been dating since late August. It felt like we'd been together for a couple of years. We fell into synch without even blinking. And we didn't have to talk to cover the silence, one of the nicest parts of the relationship. He could be reading while I worked out, and neither one of us felt the lack of conversation.

The voice on the other end of the phone was not who I'd expected to hear. Actually, I had no idea who to expect. The only people I could think might call me at this time in the morning after a late-night party were Elliot—which he might actually be stupid enough to do—or Barbara. And only Barb if she were in trouble.

To my shock, however, it was neither one. Kyle's voice rang out loud and clear, and I had the feeling he and Amy had gone home early as planned. I didn't remember seeing them leave, and we had closed down the place at two AM.

"Persia, you awake yet?" He sounded impatient, and I growled in the phone.

"Obviously, since I'm talking. However, a moment ago, I wasn't. What's up? We didn't get in till two . . . I have had about three hours of sleep altogether." I reached for my water bottle and chugged own a mouthful of warm Dasani.

He cleared his throat. "I won't ask what you were doing for the other two hours," he said. "I don't think I want to know. Anyway, I'm calling to ask you if you ever saw Lisa at the Gala. I'm at Amy's. Lisa never came home last night, and we couldn't find her there. Do you know who she was going with?"

"Yeah, she said Mitch Willis." I frowned. "Do you think that maybe she stayed over with him?"

"What about that note you mentioned? When she left work early?"

Oh yeah. I'd forgotten. "Hold on, let me get my purse." I slipped out of bed and into my robe. Well insulated or not, the house still got cold, and central heating didn't always do a great job when a storm came through. A glance out the window showed another dreary, rain-soaked day. The sky was that silver-gray that was so common on the coast, and I had the feeling that we'd seen the last of the sun until spring, unless we lucked out. There were no birds to be seen, nor squirrels. Everybody was hiding out until the downpour lightened up.

I fished the note out of my purse and opened it, picking up the phone again. "Here we go. Here's what she said . . . 'Persia, I had to take off for the rest of the afternoon. I'm sorry I didn't tell you myself, but I knew you'd be upset. Please believe me, this is very important and relates to what we were talking about at the pool yesterday. Don't be mad, please. I wouldn't put you on the spot if I didn't have a really good reason. See you tonight, and I hope to have good news to tell you then! Lisa T.' That any help?"

"What did you talk about at the pool?"

I bit my lip. She'd told me in confidentiality, saying that even Amy didn't know. "I'm not sure I should tell you. What if she comes home? She was keeping a secret from Amy, and I know she wanted to wait to tell her about it until she was certain that it checked out."

Kyle cleared his throat. "How about you tell me, and I'll look into it. If it doesn't pan out, or if she comes home, I'll let her be the one to tell her sister about it. I have a nasty feeling about this, Persia. I don't usually go on hunches, you know but . . . Amy's terribly upset. I've never seen her like this. She's sure something happened."

After thinking it over for a moment, I decided that it couldn't hurt. After all, I didn't have anything specific to tell him. "Okay, but remember, if Lisa finds out, you made me tell you." I ran down what she'd told me as generically as possible, then let out a long sigh.

"That's it?"

"That's it. No specifics, no nothing." Pausing, I lowered my voice to avoid waking Killian. "Kyle, what are you thinking? You really think Lisa's in trouble, don't you?"

He didn't answer for a moment, then in an equally low voice he said, "Yeah. I don't know why, but I think she is. And I haven't a clue about where to look, so if you think of anything else, let me know."

"Do you want me to come over?" I asked. "I don't know if I can do anything, but maybe together we can think of where to look for her."

"That might be a good idea," he said. "But wait a bit. Amy's taking a little nap. She was up most of the night, and I made her drink some chamomile tea and try to rest."

I glanced at the clock. "I'll go back to sleep for a couple hours and be over about ten, then. That be okay?"

"Sounds good. Bring Killian, if you like. He seems a good sort, although I think he's a little too much of a city boy for my tastes," Kyle said.

I laughed then, despite myself. "Well, then maybe you shouldn't date him."

As I hung up, I wondered just what had happened to Lisa. Chances were, she had just stayed overnight at Mitch's house. But Kyle's worry preyed on my mind—he wasn't given to hysterics. If he thought something had happened, then maybe it had. Whatever the case, I crawled back into bed and curved my body around Killian's. He mumbled in his sleep again, and I closed my eyes. Lisa was probably okay, I told myself as I began to drift off. In fact, she'd probably be home by the time we got there.

Chapter Five

Killian and I decided to skip breakfast, as appealing as Auntie and Kane's waffles looked. He needed to go home to prepare for his meeting on Monday, and I was on my way to Amy's. Kyle hadn't left any messages, so I assumed Lisa hadn't returned yet.

On the way out to our cars, Killian pulled me into his arms and gave me a long kiss. I held on to the feeling, not wanting him to let go. "I won't see you until tomorrow night or Tuesday," he said. "Wish me luck with the meeting."

"You've got it, sweetheart. And more. Call me when you get back to let me know what they said. And thanks for Betsy Sue's number!" I watched his Jag speed off, then followed in my Sebring. At the corner of Briarwood and Statehouse Drive, he took the left turn that would take him the most expedient route to his condo, which overlooked Hampton Bay. I kept going straight. Amy and Lisa's father had owned a house on Driftwood Lane, the house they were trying to save from the hands of the bill collectors.

As I pulled into the driveway, I saw Kyle's police cruiser there. I grabbed my purse, hopped out of my car, and headed for the door. The rain had slowed to a drizzle, misting over the island with a ghostly feel. The smell of woodsmoke from surrounding houses filtered down, a smoky reminder that we were nearing winter. I rang the bell and waited for a moment until Kyle opened the door and ushered me in.

I'd been over to Lisa and Amy's several times. The house was a good fifty years old, a simple three-bedroom, two-bath rambler. The kitchen and living room were large in the way that they often were in older homes, and the furniture was a good thirty years old. Lisa had told me that they planned on selling it all and replacing it once they had their financial affairs under control, but for now a retro-seventies feel, complete down to the green shag carpeting on the floor and the paneling on the living room walls, permeated the house.

Amy was sitting at the kitchen table, a coffee cup in her hand. She glanced up at me and blinked. I could see the lack of sleep in her eyes. She was similar to Lisa in looks, though Amy's hair was strawberry blonde, and she kept it pulled back in a ponytail. Where Lisa wore makeup and low-rise jeans, Amy's face was almost bare, and her dress was a generic shirtwaist that had probably come from Sears or Kmart. She flashed me a wan smile that disappeared almost before I had a chance to return it.

I slid into the chair next to her. "No word yet, I take it?"

Kyle held up the coffeepot, and I shook my head and pointed to the plate of Danish sitting on the counter. "No thanks. I wouldn't mind one of those, though, if that's all right."

As he handed me the plate and a napkin, his cell phone rang. He stepped into the other room to answer it.

Amy bit her lip. "Lisa may seem like a wild child," she said, "but she's never stayed out without calling before. At least not since we moved back to Gull Harbor. I know something's wrong. I just know it."

"Does she have any favorite clubs? Nightspots? Are you sure she didn't show up for the dance last night?"

"Nope, she never made it there. There was a message on the phone this morning from Mitch, her date. He asked where she was and why she hadn't called to tell him that she'd changed her mind. Kyle is trying to track him down—he didn't answer his phone when we called him back."

"Did you check Lisa's room to see if the dress she was going to wear is still here? That might pinpoint the time a little better. If she never came home to change, then it will give us some idea of when she disappeared." I leaned back and looked around at the kitchen. There were touches of Amy all over—needlepoint samplers and copper molds on the wall—but very little to remind me that Lisa lived here, too.

"I don't know." Amy shrugged. "We couldn't afford to buy anything new, so I have no idea what she'd been planning on wearing. We didn't have a lot of free time to sit around discussing fashion, not with all that's been going on lately."

Feeling rebuked, I concentrated on the Danish. When Kyle came back, both Amy and I snapped to attention. But the look on his face didn't lend itself to comfort.

"One of my boys found Lisa's car," he said. Amy gasped and instinctively reached for my hand. I held tight, bracing her as I wondered if Lisa was in the car. If so, then something must have happened, or Kyle would have just said, "We found Lisa." But he was quick to put our immediate fears to rest.

He held up his hand, shaking his head. "Don't go to pieces on me. She wasn't in it. The car's locked, in a parking lot down by Lookout Pier. Let's take a ride down there and see what we can find out. Do you have a spare key to her car? We'll want to get inside."

"Yes, I do," Amy said. She retrieved the key, then set her phone to forward to her cell, just in case Lisa called home, and we took off. Amy rode with Kyle, and I followed behind in my car.

⸙

Lookout Pier was on a sand spit, much like Lighthouse Spit, but was off the beaten path and didn't attract as many tourists. While the walkway that ran out over the bay was well traveled during the summer, hardly anybody used it during the winter months. For one thing, no restaurant or coffee shop had sprung up next to it yet, so the joggers and early morning walkers didn't have a retreat from the weather or a place to grab coffee after they'd gotten their fill of exercise. For another, Lookout Pier was harder to get to. The bus ran directly to Lighthouse Spit but stopped a good walk down the road from Lookout Pier. So unless arriving by car, it wasn't an easy jaunt.

As I eased into the parking lot behind Kyle, I noticed a pale blue Honda Civic in the corner of the parking lot. As I climbed out of my car and pulled my jacket tighter against the wind that was whipping up whitecaps out on the water, I saw that another police car was parked near the Civic, and two officers whom I recognized by face but not by name were sitting inside. When they saw Kyle walking over, they jumped out of the patrol car. I took my place beside Amy, and she gave me a grateful smile.

"What have we got?" Kyle asked. "This is Lisa's sister, by the way. Amy Tremont." I could tell by the emphasis in his words that he was tipping them that a relative was listening, just in case they'd found anything darker between the time they called him and now. "You boys remember Persia Vanderbilt? She's Amy's friend." They nodded at me, and I nodded back.

Amy produced the key, and Kyle took it, cautiously opening the doors. Nothing inside looked like a struggle had taken place. While they searched the car and trunk—

which was thankfully devoid of any sign of violence—
Amy and I walked over to the water's edge. She stared at
the dark waves crashing against the surf.

"What was Lisa doing here?" she said. "She's terrified
of the water. She'd never come to a beach without a
damned good reason."

"I agree." In fact, I'd been thinking the same thing. I
could barely get her to walk around a swimming pool
with lifeguards nearby and me by her side. I glanced back
at the cops. One of them—Kyle had introduced him as
Tim Grady—was walking along the pier. The wooden
plank leading out to the main walkway was open to the
water, which swelled just feet below it. During the summer, jet skiers could pull up to it and clamber onto land
easier that way.

I looked at Kyle, who was gazing out at the water, and
had a nasty feeling which way his thoughts were headed.
He caught me staring at him and walked over to where we
were standing.

"There's nothing in the car to indicate what she'd been
planning. Her purse and keys are gone." He shaded his
eyes and looked at the pier again. "I think we'd better get
a search and rescue team out here pronto."

Amy paled and shook her head. "Lisa wouldn't walk
out on the pier—there's no way she'd ever set foot on it.
She's too afraid."

"Afraid?" Kyle asked, frowning. "Afraid of what?"

"Lisa has hydrophobia, Kyle. She's terrified of water. I
can verify that, because I've been working with her to help
her overcome her fear. She wouldn't have willingly gone
for a walk on the pier any more than you'd catch me walking down the aisle in a white dress. Seriously, get that
thought out of your head and find some other clue to go
on." My eyes narrowing, I gave him a shaded look. Kyle
was a good man, but he lacked foresight and tended to
latch on to the easiest answer that entered his mind.

He arched his eyebrows but merely said, "Nevertheless,

we'd better get SAR out here now. Who knows? She may have decided to tackle her fear head-on. People do that, you know." As he strode back to his cruiser to call for a team, Amy turned to me, her face a mask of white.

"He didn't hear a word we said, did he?" she asked incredulously.

"Amy," I said, stepping cautiously around the potential landmines inherent within the conversation, "Kyle is a good man, and he's good at his job. I suppose he has to check out the most obvious possibilities before excluding them." I bit my lip, wondering how far to go, but decided that was enough for the moment and might actually give her some hope.

By the time the search and rescue crew arrived, we were all soaked through. The rain had turned into a steady drizzle, saturating the air and everything exposed to it. Three teams of young volunteers arrived, and Kyle set them to scouring the pier. A dive team soon followed, and I led Amy back to my car, where we sat protected from the cold while they did their work.

"This isn't happening," she said. "It can't be. Lisa didn't drown; I tell you, she wouldn't go near the water."

I thought about the storm the night before and how it had raged while we were at the Gala. Whatever reason Lisa had for coming down here, I knew it wasn't a walk on the pier. No sane person would brave weather that bad for a walk, and she wasn't exactly firing on all cylinders when it came to open water. No, she must have had a different reason for showing up here. Could she have been meeting somebody? But who?

Obviously, by what she'd written in the note she'd left me, Lisa expected to learn something about their father's money. But that could mean many things. She might have been planning on talking to somebody, or just digging up information at the library for all I knew. Or perhaps she'd never meant to come here at all. Maybe somebody brought her here. There could be a dozen reasons why her car was found in this parking lot, but most of them didn't offer any comfort.

I turned back to Amy. "Did Lisa have any enemies? Anybody who was really mad at her?"

Amy shook her head. "Not that I know of. She broke up with a guy a few months ago that she'd been seeing for about three months. His name was Shawn Johnson. I don't think it was a bad breakup, but I could be wrong."

Just then, Kyle tapped on the window. I rolled it down, and he poked his head inside. "Hey, we're going to be awhile here, sifting through stuff. Do you mind if I keep the keys to her car so we can run it in to the station to thoroughly check it out for evidence?" Amy shook her head. I could tell she was both afraid and uncertain what to do next.

I spoke up. "Kyle, why don't I take Amy home now? You can call her if anything shows up, and it won't do any good for us to be out here waiting. I honestly doubt if you're going to find anything near the water."

Kyle glanced at Amy's face, then nodded, a grateful look in his eyes. "If you would, that might be best. I'll call as soon as I find out anything," he told Amy. "Will you be okay if Persia takes you home?"

Amy nodded, and I could tell she was just letting us direct her like a marionette at this point. I gave Kyle a little wave and eased out of the parking lot, speeding back to Driftwood Lane. Amy was silent, and I didn't interrupt her thoughts.

When I pulled into the driveway, I turned to Amy as she put her hand on the door handle. "We'll find out what happened to her, Amy. Maybe she just took off on the spur of the moment with a friend. Sometimes people do things out of character. I know it won't do any good, but please, don't worry too much until we know for sure what's going on."

Her lips twisted in a painful grimace, she squinted, and I saw a single tear glinting at the corner of her eye. I had the feeling Amy relied more on Lisa than the other way around. "Would you like me to stay with you for awhile?"

She pushed open the door and slid out. "No, but thanks, Persia. I appreciate the offer. I'll call you when we find out something."

Feeling helpless and wishing I could do more, I gave her a little wave as I headed back home to Moss Rose Cottage. Where the hell was Lisa? And why had she left her car on a beach—one of the few places I knew she wouldn't be caught dead?

&

Kane was gone by the time I walked through the door. Auntie was reading the newspaper over a pot of tea. I fetched a cup and saucer from the cabinet and slid in opposite her at the table. The curtains were open, showing rough water cresting against the shoreline. The rain had backed off, but the wind was still cold. So much for parties and galas, I thought. Thanksgiving was coming up, and we should be planning dinner, but right now that was the last thing on my mind.

"What happened, Imp? You look worried." She poured me a cup of tea, and I squeezed a slice of lemon over the cup, stirring gently. A plate of Barbara's Russian tea cakes sat next to the teapot, and I bit into one, savoring the melt-in-your-mouth taste of nuts and powdered sugar.

"Lisa's missing." I hadn't even told her about having to take over Lisa's station yesterday, I realized. I hadn't wanted to spoil the mood of the dance. With a sigh, I launched into the events of the past twenty-four hours. At first, Auntie was indignant when I told her about Lisa's note and the extra work, but her irritation quickly turned into concern when I concluded with the locked car on the beach and the fact that nobody had seen Lisa since she'd walked out of Venus Envy's doors the day before.

"Heaven's mercy." Auntie stared at her cup, frowning. "Do you think she's okay?"

It was a question that I really didn't want to consider. It was one thing to say that I didn't think she'd gone anywhere near enough the water to drown, but quite another to say that I thought she was okay. I'd put on a game face for Amy, but now, alone with Auntie, I let down my guard.

"Honestly? I don't know, but considering that they've found her car and it was locked, that everything of importance seems to be gone from inside it, that it was found in an area that Lisa would never think of going by herself . . . it doesn't look good, does it?"

"Could she have been carjacked? Did she have anything valuable with her?" Auntie finished her tea and reached for the teapot.

"Well, I gave her my old Marc Jacobs handbag a couple of weeks ago. That could be worth up to three or four hundred on eBay, but honestly, I doubt if Lisa had anything else that was worth much, except the car itself, and *that* we found."

Taking my tea, I stood up, walking over to look out the windows at the fading afternoon. "Add in the fact that she was investigating something as touchy as the loss of her father's money and . . . I don't know. Nothing adds up. Maybe she really did run off for the weekend with some guy like I suggested to Amy and Kyle. It wasn't her current boyfriend though, because he called last night and left a message, asking where she was and why she hadn't called to cancel if she wasn't planning on going to the dance with him."

"If she did step out with someone, then she'll return home and feel bad about how badly she scared her sister." Auntie sighed, then said, "Imp, there's nothing you can do right now. However, this brings up an uncomfortable discussion regarding Venus Envy. With Lisa missing, we have to hire someone to take over her station until she comes back." She gave me a look that told me she thought I was going to protest.

"Oh hell, I hadn't even thought of that," I said. "It almost feels like turning traitor, doesn't it? After all, Lisa's missing, and we don't know if she's okay or lying in a ditch somewhere, dead."

"Imp, this is one of those uncomfortable times when your personal feelings are going to feel at odds with owning a store. Sometimes, you have to push worry to the side, at least when it comes to business. The shop won't wait for us to find Lisa, wherever she might be."

"Yeah," I said after a moment. "I know you're right." I let out a long sigh as I rummaged in the refrigerator for something to eat. All I'd had for the day was a Danish over at Amy's and a few of the Russian tea cakes. Sugar might taste good, but it wasn't about to cut it for the rest of the day. I found a leftover container of lasagna and popped it in the microwave, then poured myself a glass of orange juice. As the food heated, I turned back to Auntie, who was waiting for my answer.

"What if we call Maxine and ask her if she wants a temporary job?" Maxine had come in second for the job when we interviewed. She'd almost had it, but Lisa's experience was a little better. "I already called Betsy Sue, Killian's former receptionist. She's going to help Tawny at the counter." I retrieved my lasagna and a fork and sat down at the table, digging into the cheesy dish.

Auntie folded her newspaper and propped her elbows on the table. "Persia, I'll make a businesswoman out of you yet. Good idea. I'll tell you what, I'll call Maxine, since you called Betsy." She pushed herself out of her chair and headed toward the den. "And Persia, why don't you take a break for the rest of the afternoon? You've been working so hard. Go read a book or work out."

I glanced down at my feet, where Beauty was curled. "Have the dogs been walked yet?"

When Auntie said no, I whistled. Their toenails clattered on the kitchen floor as they rushed in. They crowded around, looking excited but minding their manners.

Beauty, Beast, and Pete were generally well behaved, with only a few lapses.

"Where's your leash? Find your leash!"

They ran off toward the utility room, then came scurrying back, each one holding a leash in its mouth. I ruffled Beauty's head as I attached her lead, then Pete's, and then the Beast's. The Beast was some bizarre mix with a face only a mother could love, but he was all heart.

Pete was getting up in years for a dog, and I'd noticed he was slowing down a bit over the past month or so. Time for a vet check.

And Beauty was our beautiful, delicate black cocker spaniel who knew what her name meant and reminded us with every winsome glance that she was the fairest of them all. I slipped on a suede jacket, a pair of gloves, and then, leashes and dogs firmly in hand, we headed out the door and down the porch.

The clouds were roiling overhead, and a sniff of the air told me we were in for it later. I was born with a heightened sense of smell, which both helped and hindered my work. Some days I was overwhelmed by the multitude of scents floating past my nose, and other days it was as if I could discern to the smallest ingredient that went into a blend. Most gifts were double-edged swords, when I thought about it.

Once we crossed Briarwood Drive and the path leading through the rocks and driftwood that littered the upper part of the shore, I took the leashes off and let the dogs run. They were well trained; we could trust them not to run in the road, though we never let them out unsupervised unless they were in the backyard, which was thoroughly enclosed.

Beauty and Beast went bounding down the shore while Pete walked sedately by my side. He was aging; I could feel it. I also knew that it would tear Auntie up when he crossed the Bridge. I knelt beside him and ran my hands over his sides, checking him out for any suspicious lumps or growths—anything out of the ordinary—but he seemed right as rain. Still, a vet trip wouldn't hurt. My guess was a mild case of arthritis.

"What do you think, Pete? You think that Lisa went for a walk on the pier by herself?" I looked down at him, and he barked once. "I don't think so, either." An array of twigs and branches dotted the shore, and I chose one at random and threw it as hard as I could. Pete looked up, and I nodded. "Go get it, boy. Take your time." He trotted off, slower than either Beauty or the Beast, but looking as proud as he always did when he brought back his quarry.

During the summer I'd taken to coming down to the beach early in the morning and spending thirty minutes meditating in the early light of dawn. I even brought my yoga mat a few times and ran through my routine by the water's edge, the brine-soaked air invigorating me as could no other stimulant. I loved being outdoors, and winter was always a struggle with my inner beach bum.

The waves rolled in with a veiled sense of threat, daring me to come join their dance. I slowly approached the edge of the water, keeping a few feet away as the spray pelted my face. The waves encroached a little farther with each thundering roll. I held my breath as the surf kissed my feet and then, just before the next assault coiled around my ankles, I jumped back a couple steps, playing catch me if you can with the leading edge of the water.

"Did you come back for Lisa?" I whispered to the waves. "Did you come to finish what you started when she was a little girl? Do you know where she is?"

But the water remained silent, a relentless drive toward the shore. Feeling insignificant and powerless in the face of such a force, I turned abruptly and joined the dogs. We played a few more rounds of fetch, and then, with one last glance at the bay, I whistled to the dogs, fastened their leashes, and headed back to the house. As we crossed the road, I noticed that we had company. Barbara's car was in the driveway. Had I forgotten a date for dinner? Or was

she just dropping by? Jogging lightly, I took the stairs two
at a time, the dogs beside me, and opened the door.

As we entered the house, I unhooked the dogs, and they
took off for the kitchen in search of a snack. I slid out of
my jacket, hung it in the hall closet, then followed the
sound of Barbara's voice. She was sitting in the kitchen
with Auntie, a stricken look on her face. Her makeup was
smeared, and she was holding a crumpled tissue in her
hand. Auntie looked up at me and shook her head, warning me that whatever had happened, it wasn't good.

"What's wrong?" I sat down next to Barb and took her
hand in mine. Our friendship had outgrown the need to
pussyfoot around each other.

She pressed her lips together, and tears streamed
down her face as I glanced over at Auntie, who silently
pointed to a single suitcase standing near the table. Oh
hell. Not *that*.

"Barb, what happened? Talk to me, *chica*." I shook her
hand a little bit, and she gasped and wiped her eyes.

"I left Dorian. I couldn't take it another minute. That
mother of his is a tyrant. She's turned him into a jackass,
and I won't put up with them ganging up on me." Barb
broke down again, and I slowly let go of her hand as she
folded her arms on the table and rested her head on them.

"Barbara asked if she could stay with us for a little
while, and I told her that of course she's welcome here."
Auntie looked pained. Barb and Dorian were family to
both of us, and this was quite a blow. But she hadn't been
privy to Barb's tale of woe with Mama Konstantinos.
Considering all the ups and downs Barb had been through
over the past year with her self-esteem, I wasn't all that
surprised. I slipped over to the stove and put the kettle on
to heat for some tea, then fixed a tray with the teapot and
some lemon, cream, and sugar. As I poured the steaming
water over the bags, the fragrant and familiar aroma rose
to tickle my senses.

Barbara sniffled and wiped her eyes. "Thank you, Miss

Florence. I know you both must think I'm crazy, but things have been so rough since Mama Konstantinos arrived. I've tried to make peace. I've bitten my tongue so hard it bled, but today was just the last straw."

I carried the steeping tea over to the table as Auntie fetched cups and saucers. "Talk to us, girl."

Brushing her bangs back from her face, Barb accepted the cup of tea. She fidgeted with the spoon, stirring in three spoons of sugar before she realized what she was doing. I silently took the tea from her and poured out the overly sweet brew, then rinsed out the cup and poured her another.

"We were eating breakfast. I always make sure Dorian has a healthy breakfast on weekends. He eats too much sugar and starch, so we have poached eggs, bran cereal, and fruit smoothies on weekends. Mama K started bitching at me about how I should cook a big, old-fashioned breakfast. I told her no, the doctor said Dorian needs to get his cholesterol down, and the last thing he needs is to overload his system with rich, sugary food—which she loves. She started ranting on about how I'm trying to run the house, and that Dorian has the God-given right to set the rules."

"Uh-oh." I could see the train wreck coming from a mile away.

"I blew up. Dorian walked in just in time to hear me call her a shrew and tell her to fuck off and keep her nose out of things. I tried to explain, but . . ." She looked up helplessly.

"Yeah," I said softly. How could you explain that? And Dorian, sweet man that he was, had an overdeveloped sense of family pride. I could just imagine what went down between them. It must have been a bad scene all the way around.

Auntie motioned me into the living room. "Set her up in the guest room and tell her to rest for a bit. She's overwrought and needs to calm down a little. I talked to

Maxine, and she's still looking for work, so she'll be starting Tuesday."

"Good," I said, distracted. I glanced back at Barb. "I suppose I should have a talk with Dorian—" I started to say, but Auntie cut me off with a sharp shake of the head.

"I wouldn't. It never pays to get in the middle of married folks' spats. Barbara and Dorian love each other, and they've been together for years. They'll work this out. But perhaps I will take his mother out for lunch this week and have a little chat with her. Sometimes the truth sets better coming from a member of your own generation." She sighed. "This is one reason I've never trod the path to the altar. I have no patience for the compromise that living with someone can require."

I grinned at her and gave her a big kiss. "You live with me and do all right." Before she could answer, I winked. "I know what you mean. And I take after you down to the core."

She stopped at the door to the den and turned. "I know, and sometimes I lie awake thinking about that, Imp. My way isn't a path that's right for everybody," she said. "Just don't feel you have to follow my footsteps in order to make me proud of you."

"Heard and noted," I said. "But Auntie, face it, you're my role model. And there's not a damn thing you can do about it."

With a chuckle, she entered the den. I turned back to the kitchen, thinking about Barbara and marriage and compromise. Yeah, I loved hanging with Killian, and we had an undeniable chemistry, but marriage? Not in the cards.

Chapter Six

*B*arbara sat on the bed and stared morosely at the floor while I unpacked her suitcase. She seemed to have lost all of her fight. I watched her in the mirror as she blew a few stray strands of hair out of her face. After I finished putting away the outfits she'd brought, I turned and slid onto the dresser, dangling my legs over the edge. My feet almost reached the floor.

"So," I said.

"So," she answered.

"So what are you going to do about the bakery? It's the holiday season."

She shrugged. "Let Mama Konstantinos help him and see just how smoothly the week goes. A few days of her complaining twenty-four/seven, and he's going to be on his hands and knees begging me to come back. I never thought he'd be so blind. I guess maybe the experts are right. Maybe we never really know the person we're living with." Her expression went from peeved to despondent.

I decided she needed to get her mind off her problems.

"You get dressed in jeans and a sexy top. We're going out for dinner, and then we are going to have a drink and go dancing at El Toro Caliente." The lounge had just opened a month ago, up on Pettigrain Peak, and was a spicy blend of salsa dancing, would-be lovers watching the bar, and drinks to die for. Cheesy? *No.* Sleazy? *Just a little.* And just what we needed.

⁂

"Are you sure about this?" Barb asked, hanging on to my arm as we slipped through the doors to the bar.

"Yes, so quit your worrying. We're going to have a few drinks, dinner, dance a little, and forget about our problems." I glanced around. El Toro Caliente was a damned good parody of a spaghetti Western saloon, right down to the giant cactus in the corner that had a chain around it to prevent drunken barflies from stumbling into the thorny arms of the gigantic prickly pear.

"My, my, my," I said, scoping out the place. Amid the requisite lounge lizards and girls looking to turn a trick, there were several handsome cowboy wannabes. Of course, most were techies out to shake off their chiphead images, but a few were downright cute. I reminded myself that I was playing on an exclusive field, one that I didn't want to lose, and sashayed over to the counter, Barb in tow.

I was wearing a pair of camouflage cargo pants that were actually Capri pant length, a sleeveless olive V-neck tank, a low-slung, wide, riveted belt, and I glammed up the whole look with a pair of rhinestone stilettos. Barb was wearing a pair of low-cut jeans and a pink turtleneck. She looked fresh-faced and almost too wholesome.

I slid onto a barstool and motioned to the bartender. "Two Cuervo Gold margaritas. Lime. And can we get some peanuts?"

He nodded, giving me the once-over. His eyes stopped

at my bluebell faerie tattoo, and he grinned. "Nice tat," he said. "Good ink."

"Thanks, I like her," I said, winking at him. Barb hopped up on the stool next to me, and before we knew it, we were on our second round of margaritas. A man in blue jeans a little too new to be used for any real dirty work sauntered over and asked Barb to dance. I gave her a little push. It would be good for her self-esteem. I could stand to blow off a little steam, too.

Which is how I found myself dancing with some biker dude who looked like he'd just gotten out of prison. He was surprisingly light on his feet and surprisingly polite. The Rolling Stones were blaring out of the speakers with *19th Nervous Breakdown*, and Dawg—that was the biker's name—and I brought the house down with our combo swing-jitterbug rendition. The song ended, and breathless, I leaned on the counter.

"Another round," I said, motioning to the bartender. He lined up two frosty marguaritas, and Barb, who had finally let down her guard and was laughing along with me, carried our drinks to a table near the mechanical bull. I slid into the chair and eyed the monster.

"Hmm, I wonder how hard that is," I said, sipping my drink. The lime cut through the thick taste of tequila with a tart bite.

The man on the bull suddenly went flying to the mat. His buddies were ribbing him, and as he shrugged off their jibes, the bartender shouted out, "Ladies ride free! Any woman in here tough enough to take on El Toro for a free drink?"

Barb poked me in the arm. "You could do it!" she said, snickering. "Go on, let's see you ride the bull!"

I gave her a thunderstruck look. "You have got to be kidding. You want me to get up there and make a fool of myself?" I stared at the silent, hulking, mechanical beast. It was just a machine, I thought, but then images of women ripping off their shirts and giving a bunch of drunks a cheap thrill raced through my head. "You just get that thought out of your head right now, Barb."

"Come on, Persia, you know you can do it. I can't; I'd be on the ground in seconds. Please? I want to see you ride El Toro. Show those men that anything they can do, you can do better." Her words were slurred, and I realized she was happily tipsy and ready to pick a fight with the world of men. Dorian's defection had loosened her inner hellcat, all right.

"Holy crap, I can't believe you want me to—" I stopped as the bartender sauntered up to us. "Yes?"

"I heard your friend there. Come on, give it a whirl, and I'll give you both two free rounds. You look like you got the muscle to handle the ride." His eyes slaked over my arms and I swallowed a sharp retort when Barb started to clap.

"Go on, Persia. Please? For me?"

I gave her a long look and shook my head. "You sure you want to see me humiliate myself in front of the whole bar?"

She grinned. "No, I want to see you blow their socks off."

"The things I do for you . . ." I grumbled but stood up and, amid a round of applause, headed toward the bull. Jesus, I'd ridden horses and motorcycles, but neither of those had put up a fight about it. It couldn't be *that* hard, though, I thought as I kicked off my stilettos and swung atop the beast.

As I braced myself, the room wobbling ever so slightly thanks to the two drinks I'd already had, a crowd gathered to watch. Most were men—the techies in cowboy getups, but here and there I spotted a biker or barfly. Three women were watching, too, arms linked around their dates' waists. Barb let out a loud howl, and her enthusiasm seemed to fire up the crowd, who followed suit.

The bull began to move, slowly at first, and I braced the sides with my knees, grateful for my long legs. If I'd been short, I would have already been struggling. The room began to blur as the speed increased. I held fast, gritting my teeth as the bull bucked me back and forth, feeling myself slide a little to the left, then a little to the right. I wasn't about to tear off my shirt, but a bloated sense of power—no doubt nourished by the tequila haze—swept over me, and I pumped my right fist into the air, letting out a war cry that echoed through the bar. The crowd went wild, cheering me on, and I made the ultimate mistake of any hero—I let fame go to my head, and my attention wandered. The next thing I knew, I was flying through the air, landing back-first on the mat. Dazed, I shook my head as Mr. Biker and the bartender picked me up.

"Are you okay, Persia?" Barb hustled over to me, carrying my shoes.

"Yep," I said, brushing myself off. "I think I'll live. I'm fine. Just lost my concentration there for a moment."

The bartender reappeared with two fresh margaritas, and we returned to our table. By the time I was half done with my drink I'd collected five phone numbers, none of which I planned on keeping, been offered a chance to join a wet tee shirt contest, which I politely declined, and been given a scathing look by one of the women who was holding on to her boyfriend's arm so tightly I thought she was going to break it off.

Barb was reaching that turning point between giddy and lugubrious, and I decided that our fourth margarita would be our last. There was no way in hell we could even think of driving home, so I called Auntie, and she drove out to pick us up. On the way home, both Barb and I were exiled to the backseat of Baby in case we decided we had to throw up. As I staggered up the porch steps, Auntie just shook her head and reminded me to set the alarm because, drunk or not, I was needed at the store the next morning.

Before I made my way up to bed, Barb motioned me into the guest room. "Thanks, Persia," she said. She was drunker than a skunk, but I could hear the relief in her voice. "I would have spent the evening moping and feeling sorry for myself. You helped me work off a lot of my tension. You're a good friend, you know? Not many people would ride a mechanical bull just to make their buddy happy."

I gave her a hug and headed for the door. "I'm glad that you enjoyed yourself. And if it took me playing cowgirl to cadge a smile out of you, I'm glad I did it. Get some sleep, Barb. Tomorrow will be better. Dorian will come to his senses—you wait and see."

And with that, I hauled my tired ass up to bed and passed out almost before I hit the sheets.

⁓

When my alarm went off, I woke up with a splitting headache. I squinted at the clock. Eight AM, and my tongue felt like it had grown a layer of moldy fuzz. I cautiously pushed myself to a sitting position. Delilah and Buttercup were curled up on the bottom of my bed in a tryst they'd never permit while awake. Buttercup had snuggled up with her head on Delilah's butt, and Delilah was curled around so that she was practically spooning Buttercup. I grinned. Posers, both of them.

As I stood, a wave of vertigo raced through me, and my stomach lurched. *Oh hell*, I thought as I raced for the bathroom. A few minutes and a whole lot of mouthwash later, my nausea let up, though a steady pounding still drove stakes through my head. I squinted into the mirror. My eyes were almost glued shut, and I ran a cold cloth over my face, blinking as I washed the sleep sand away from the corners. I looked like hell. With a sigh, I sat down on the bench near my claw-foot tub and began filling it with warm water and peppermint bubble bath. Maybe a long soak would help jog some of the cobwebs out of my brain.

As I dipped my toe in the water, then slid down in the big old tub, I leaned back and rested my head against the bath pillow. The water made me a little seasick at first, but it felt so good on my muscles that I soon relaxed. I wasn't used to drinking so much. Oh, I'd had my share of bouts, but it had been awhile since I'd tied one on.

Twenty minutes later, feeling more waterlogged than revived, I hauled my butt out of the tub, dragged on a comfortable jersey skirt and cashmere sweater, then slipped into my favorite pair of brown suede boots and zipped them up. Their insoles were so cushy that my blisters would be well protected.

Auntie was at the table. She gave me an evil grin when I poked my head into the dining room. "Breakfast's on the stove. Get yourself a plate and eat. You need something in your stomach if you're going to make it through the day."

I grimaced but obeyed. She'd fixed a stack of toast, along with well-drained bacon, a fluffy omelet, and a pot of strong, black tea. I helped myself to three slices of toast and a jolting cup of tea with lemon, then joined her in the dining room, where I slid into a chair with a faint groan.

"Tore it up last night, did you?" Auntie pointed to the tea. "Get that inside of you, but first eat a slice of toast because you better cushion your digestive system before you bathe it in tannins." She wiggled her finger, and I obediently bit into a slice of toast. "Let Barbara sleep in. After the emotional upset yesterday and the partying you two did, she's going to need some rest."

I chewed slowly, gauging my stomach's reaction to food. So far, it was behaving itself. "What if Dorian asks where she is?"

"Then we'll tell him. And we'll tell him to take a few days to think over what happened and cool off." She made sure I ate every bite of my toast, then handed me a big glass of water. I drained it dry and was happy to note that I already felt a little bit better.

"My car is still over at the bar. Can you run me over there so I can pick it up?" I asked.

She nodded. "Get your things, and let's go. We've got a lot to do today."

As we headed out to Baby, I glanced at Auntie. She didn't seem mad, but she wasn't overly friendly either. I knew that she didn't have anything against drinking, at least in moderation, so I doubted that one drunken binge had turned her against me. But if it wasn't that, then what was bothering her?

"Is everything okay?" I slid into the front seat and fastened my seat belt.

"What, child? Oh, yes. I'm just preoccupied." She started the ignition, which purred at a substantially lower register than usual. "Damned Kyle. Baby was just fine, but now listen to her—sounds like she's got a muzzle on."

I repressed a snort. "Baby's still Baby, she's just a little quieter."

"Well, I don't like being ordered around by somebody young enough to be my son," she said, and I knew that's what was eating her. That Kyle—whom she'd known since he was barely into puberty—could force her to do something she didn't want to do.

"You'll live," I said, grinning at her. She rolled her eyes and then pulled out of the driveway.

We chatted about our plans for the holidays until we reached the club, where Auntie pulled into the parking lot next to El Toro Caliente and I hopped out. Everything was in order, and nothing had been touched on my car. I followed her down to Island Drive and parked three doors away from Venus Envy. A space behind her, I hopped out of my car to bustle into the shop. As I walked through the door, I glanced in the back, hoping to see Lisa's face. We hadn't heard a word from either Kyle or Amy since I'd dropped Amy off at home, and while I didn't expect a minute-by-minute update, it felt like it had been a long time since I'd talked to them, even though we hadn't cracked the twenty-four-hour mark. But Lisa was nowhere in sight.

Auntie had already headed to the office, but stopped as Tawny popped out from the spa room, Betsy Sue in tow.

They were chatting like old friends. They'd met at the same beauty convention where I'd met Killian, but I had no idea if the two had maintained contact. Speaking of which, Killian should be at his meeting by now.

"Hey, Betsy," I said, giving her a little wave. "Glad to have you aboard."

"Persia, Miss Florence, thanks for taking me on. You don't know how much this means to me." She beamed, perky as ever, but there was something so unassuming about her cheerfulness that it never felt grating or annoying.

Auntie gave her a nod. "Come on, girl, come back to the office with me and fill out your paperwork. Then Tawny can finish showing you the ropes."

As they disappeared into the back, I turned to Tawny. "Has Lisa called?"

She shook her head. "No," she said, her expression serious. Both she and Seth knew that Lisa was missing. "Should I call her clients and reschedule?"

I pressed my lips together. "Yeah . . . tell them something came up, and that we'll call this afternoon to reschedule. Hopefully by then, Auntie will have gotten Maxine to agree to take over her place on a temporary basis."

Tawny looked like she wanted to ask more questions, but I shook my head and headed for my station. My morning was free from consultations, but I had to inventory my supplies and match them against what we would need over the next few weeks for the shop lines that I'd created. Not a good idea to run out of Peppermint Panda lotion during the Christmas season, not when it was currently our best-selling item. On the other hand, I'd cut down on how much Vermillion Verve I was making because it seemed to sell best during the summer months.

After I made a list of oils and other supplies I was running low on, I took a break to get myself a cup of tea. Seth had just finished up with a haircut, and he was shaking his head. I glanced at his client, a woman I didn't recognize, as she wandered out to pay Tawny. She was sporting a jaunty cut that made her look ten years younger than when she'd walked in the door.

"Nice job," I said. "You really know your stuff."

Seth snorted. "Yeah, but she's a real piece of work, that one." He sighed, then got the broom and began sweeping up hair. "I tell you, Persia, I hear the damnedest things in my line of work. Do you get that with your clients, too?"

Frowning, I dropped my tea bag in the garbage and took a sip of the hot drink. "What are you talking about?"

"Lisa and I were just discussing this last Friday." His voice dropped, and he stared at the floor for a moment. He and Lisa worked side by side on a daily basis, and I knew they'd developed a friendship. "Being a hairdresser or beautician, you hear the wackiest stuff from your clients. We get the lowdown on affairs, hidden scandals, PMS bouts, husbands who can't perform. I swear, some of my clients forget I'm just a person and not some psychiatrist."

I blinked. "My clients aren't quite the same. I guess I don't spend long enough with them to build up that kind of trust." As I glanced over at Lisa's empty station, a light-bulb went on in my head. "Listen, you say that Lisa gets the same thing?"

He nodded. "Yeah, we've talked about it before. Makes things awkward sometimes. For example, one of my clients is having an affair, and she told me about it, along with the name of her lover—God only knows why, but she did. Then, three days ago, I ran into her at Georgio's Restaurant. She was having dinner with her husband and his best friend—who happens to be her lover. You would not believe how uncomfortable I was. I had no idea what to say. Her husband looked so happy, poor schmuck."

"Jesus, that's a nasty situation," I said. "Do you think Lisa might have overheard something she wasn't sup-posed to know?"

"I don't know about that, but she gets the same thing."

With a shrug, he finished cleaning his station. "Sometimes we exchange war stories."

I finished my tea and headed to the front counter, where I tapped Tawny on the shoulder. She had just finished showing Betsy Sue how to run the cash register. "Where's Lisa's appointment book?"

"Over there. Why? You want it?" She made room for me to slip in behind her so I could grab the planner.

Betsy gave me an excited smile. She was blonde, perky, and her tummy showed a little rounded bulge. Killian hadn't been kidding when he said that she and Julius were expecting. "Persia, thanks so much for this opportunity. It means the world to me right now."

I winked. "So how's the bun? And how's Julius?"

She blushed, her hand dropping to her stomach. "I'm fine. This job will sure help take the stress off. I'm really starting to show now. Julius's thrilled, but of course, we were hoping to get married before the baby arrives. If Killian can get his funding, maybe we'll still have a chance."

"Well, you just take it easy, and Tawny will help show you what you need to know. And if your ankles start to swell, we can get you a stool to sit on behind the counter." I picked up Lisa's appointment book and returned to my station.

Seth's comments about clients spilling secrets made me wonder if Lisa had told any of her makeovers what she'd been planning on. I was flipping through Friday and Saturday's appointments when I was interrupted by the sound of my cell phone ringing from the muffled depths of my purse. I scrambled to answer and caught Kyle just before he was about ready to hang up.

"Any word from Lisa yet?" I asked after his "Hello" boomed into my ear.

He paused, and I heard him let out a long sigh. "No, we haven't. Amy's frantic. She's been gone two nights now, and I told Amy to file an official missing person report today. She's coming in this afternoon." By the sound of his voice, I could tell that there was some friction going on in lovebird city.

"You really do think she's dead, don't you?" I could hear it in his voice. He was ready to close the door based on where Lisa's car had been found.

Kyle cleared his throat. "Look at it from my perspective. Lisa's car was found at Lookout Pier. There was a horrible storm the night she vanished. Lisa can't swim. It adds up, yes, but I'm not going to mark the case closed, if that's what you're thinking. We'll treat this like any missing person case that we get."

"Have you told Amy you think she drowned?"

Another pause. Apparently he had, and apparently Amy hadn't taken it very well. "Yeah, I did," he said after a moment. "She's convinced that I'm going to just let it drop."

"But you aren't, right?"

My question had apparently pushed his buttons, because Kyle exploded. "God damn it, Persia, you *know* that I'll do everything I can to find out what happened to Lisa. I'm not writing the girl off, even if I do think she drowned. But you've got to understand, my department is swamped. With the budget cuts going on, I can't spare anybody for overtime unless it's an emergency."

He came to an abrupt halt, and I had the feeling that he was debating whether to tell me something. I let the silence hang and, after a moment, he spoke again. "I'm going to tell you something, but you damned well better keep it under your hat. Don't even tell your aunt, you understand?"

"Sure, I promise," I said, crossing my fingers behind my back.

"Persia, I have to lay off two of my men next month. Every person on my staff is necessary, but the city just isn't approving enough money to keep up with all the crap going on around here. It's like the city council is sticking its head in the sand. Gull Harbor's growing, and so is our crime rate. But they expect me to be able to cut corners and make do with less, even though they complain when we can't get out to calls right away because we're tied up somewhere else."

"Oh cripes, Kyle. That sucks. Who are you going to fire?"

"Lay off, not fire. They'll be able to get unemployment easier that way. And I don't know who yet. Grady's got a kid on the way. Shanna's a single mother. Roberts is nearing retirement; if I lay him off now, it's going to wreck his pension. And it goes on and on like that." He let out a sound like a strangled gulp. "I don't know what I'm going to do."

"I'm sorry. I didn't know. So a missing person case . . ."

"If Lisa was a kid, we'd be out there combing the streets. But she's an adult, and there's no real evidence that anything's happened to her, other than maybe falling off the pier. Mitch Willis hasn't heard from her, and he's got an alibi for Saturday night. For every hour we spend on her, we take our investigations away from other cases. Right now we're hunting down an armed robber, an ATM thief, a rapist . . . there were two car thefts over the weekend, and we've got one verified missing person who's seventy years old with Alzheimer's. He wandered away from his daughter's house last night in his bathrobe."

I leaned back in my chair and rested my head on the wall. Kyle was right, but he was also headed for a train wreck. He and Amy were obviously hitting it off. How was he going to balance his requirements of being the chief of police with the fact that it was his girlfriend's sister missing?

"Want some advice, Kyle?"

"No, but I'm sure that I'm going to get an earful." After a grunt, he added, "Okay, what is it?"

Unable to believe I was about to volunteer my time, I

blurted out, "Use me. Let me do some quiet investigating on the side. Amy likes you a lot, but if you slack off on the search for her sister, she's going to get real pissed real soon, no matter what the reason."

Kyle cleared his throat. "You think she really likes me?"

"Yes, you dolt, of course she does. It's obvious, if you'd take your head out of the sand. Listen, I was thinking that maybe some of Lisa's clients from this week might have a clue as to what she was up to. I was talking to Seth—"

"Seth?" He sounded clueless.

"Get with the program, Kyle. Seth's our hairdresser. Anyway, he told me that clients are very touchy-feely. They talk about everything with their hairdressers and beauticians. I was thinking maybe Lisa told one of her clients on Friday or Saturday what she was up to. I could go talk to them. Since Lisa worked for us and she's a good friend of mine, it wouldn't seem out of the ordinary for me to do that."

He was quicker to take me up on my offer than I'd expected. "You'd do that? Because her car checked out—no strange prints inside, no sign of foul play, no sign of anything out of the ordinary. And the sand didn't look like there was a tussle, though with the wind and rain that night, who knows?"

I blinked. "Sounds like I've just been deputized."

"More or less. No prowling, no getting yourself in dangerous situations . . . just ask a few questions if you would, while I try to figure out where to look from here. Oh, and Persia?"

"Yeah?" I glanced at the clock, thinking about my to-do list for the day. I'd just have to push a few of my errands back until tomorrow.

"Thanks." He hung up, and I stared at the receiver. So the department was in a budgetary fix that was impacting police services. It figured. People could be so shortsighted. Save a few taxes today but lose your shirt in the process. Wait until some of those city council members dialed 911 and came up with a busy signal. I decided to set Auntie to work on the situation, whether Kyle wanted me to say anything or not. She was persuasive. While I looked for clues to Lisa's disappearance, Auntie could start badgering the town leaders into coughing up more money for Kyle and his crew.

⚜

I made two calls: one to Barbara, asking her to come help us at Venus Envy if she wasn't going to work at the bakery for the day. As I suspected, she was happy to have something to do, even if it meant being right next door to the Baklava or Bust Bakery. I had the feeling she was hoping Dorian would see her and rush over to apologize.

The other call was to Amy. "Listen, I thought I'd go out and ask a few questions about Lisa. Sort of get a head start on things. I'm going to check out some of her clients from last week, see if she said anything to them about her plans. And what did you say the name of her ex-boyfriend was?" She told me, and I jotted down his name.

"Persia," she said, and I could hear the hesitancy in her voice. "Why are you doing this? Isn't this Kyle's job?"

I thought fast. "Kyle thinks I'd have a better chance of getting them to open up to me, since I'm one of the owners of Venus Envy, and friends with a number of our customers."

She murmured an assent, though I wasn't sure she was thoroughly convinced. When I hung up, I called Kyle back and filled him in on the excuse I'd given Amy so he wouldn't blow it when she came in to file the missing person report. After I finished, I picked up my notes and Lisa's appointment book and stuffed them in a spare tote bag I kept under the counter.

Auntie was sitting amid a pile of invoices and spreadsheets six inches high. She glanced up at me and saw that

I had my coat on and purse over my shoulder. She let out a little huff of irritation. "No, no, no! You aren't going out, are you?"

"For a little while. Barb's coming in to help, though. I'm going out to talk to some of the clients who Lisa saw last week. They might know something, and they'll be more willing to talk to me rather than to Kyle." I hesitated, remembering my promise to keep quiet about the layoffs. "Another thing . . . you might want to talk to some of your friends on the city council and tell them to loosen the purse strings on the police department."

"Why? What do you know?" Aunt Florence gave me that look that said she knew I knew something she didn't. And Auntie wasn't happy when she was kept in the dark.

I gave a little shrug but winked. "Just call it preventative medicine. I should be back before one."

With a sigh, Auntie waved me toward the door. "Go, but give me a call if you're going to be much later than that so I can rearrange some things I was going to do this afternoon."

"Thanks, Auntie. I won't be too long," I said, giving her a quick kiss. As I headed out the door, I wondered if I was wasting my time. Kyle thought Lisa was sleeping at the bottom of the inlet. Finding out something of value from one of her clients seemed like a long shot, but we had to start somewhere. And Kyle certainly wouldn't be able to follow up on all these leads . . . not as quickly as I could.

Braving the rain, I ran toward my car, closing the door in just in time to avoid being caught in a massive downpour that overwhelmed my windshield wipers. As I waited for the sudden surge of rain to back off, everything took on a bleak edge. My cell phone rang, and I answered, but it was a wrong number. As I stared at my phone, I wondered . . . Lisa had a cell. Had anybody called it? Surely, Amy had, but I still had to try.

My fingers were shaking as I dialed the number. The

ring on the other end told me that wherever her phone was, it wasn't in the inlet. I waited. One ring. Five, and it switched to voice mail. As I left a message, the downpour eased up. Would she get my message? Was her phone even with her? As I pulled out of the parking space, I found myself praying that Kyle's hunch was wrong.

Chapter Seven

First things first. I was going to drive home and change. My comfort clothes were beginning to feel baggy, and the hangover was starting to lift. I was also hungry, and the thought of a ham sandwich was beginning to sound appealing. From home, I could also call the names in Lisa's book and ask them if I could drop in.

As I walked through the door, Dodger, our silver tabby, and Nalu, our black shorthair boy, stopped short in the hallway, where they were playing tug-of-war with a loaf of bread. A little over a week ago, we'd found a loaf of partially devoured bread on the bathroom floor, and we'd blamed the dogs. Now I knew the identity of the real culprits.

"What the hell are you two doing?" I stomped over, shooing them away from the bag. They watched, all innocent-like, as I picked up the bread and examined it. Yep, teeth marks pointed the finger, all right. Dodger was good at climbing, where Nalu was a little too fat to scramble up on the counters. Dodger must have pushed the bread off to the waiting Nalu, and together they decided to make tracks with the booty.

"You twits," I muttered, carrying the bread into the kitchen. A couple of slices looked munched on, but otherwise everything seemed okay, so I dropped the remaining slices, minus two for my sandwich, into a Ziploc bag and threw away the old wrapper. The slobbered-on slices went in the dog's dishes, which no doubt Dodger and Nalu would pilfer as soon as I wasn't looking.

I fixed my snack, then sat down with the phone book, my sandwich, and a glass of tomato juice at the table. As I ate, I jotted down names and then hunted through the phone book for their addresses. First on the list from Lisa's Friday appointments was Heddy Latherton. Well, if Lisa had said something, Heddy would be only too happy to tell me. But she wasn't home, so I left a message on her voice mail and went on.

Barb had been her next appointment. I could talk to her after work. Third on the list was Karen Sanders. She answered on the first ring. When I introduced myself and asked if I could come over and ask her a few questions about Lisa, she quickly nixed that idea.

"I don't mind talking to you, but not at my house. Can you meet me at the Starbucks adjacent to Barnes & Noble in an hour?" She lowered her voice. "I just don't want to talk here at home. You can understand why."

Okay, obviously she thought I was privy to something I wasn't. Either that, or she was a drama queen. "Sure," I said, wondering what it would take to pry information out of her. "See you in an hour."

The fourth and fifth appointments were Donna and Enid Smith, elderly women who lived out on Ridgerock Road. They were sisters, regulars in our shop, and they loved company, so I was in like Flynn. I told them I'd drop by in a couple of hours, and they insisted I come for a late lunch. Feeling a tad guilty—they thought I was coming over just to be friendly—I agreed. I'd take them a bouquet and spend an hour or so dishing with them so I didn't appear rude.

Lisa's sixth appointment, a Candy Harrison, wasn't home either. I left my name and number.

I ran upstairs to change clothes—I'd dropped a spot of mustard on my skirt while fixing my sandwich—and slid into a pair of black jeans and a skintight black V-neck sweater. My stomach had calmed down since I'd eaten, and while I was still tired, I felt ready to take on the rest of the day. After making sure my mascara was good to go, I brushed my teeth, then headed out to meet Karen. The two-story Barnes & Noble was across the street from the mezzanine of Delacorte Plaza, connected by an enclosed walkway that stretched across one of the entrances to the mall.

The Barnes & Noble had a Starbucks coffee shop attached, and I stopped at the counter and ordered a grande tea before looking around. A woman raised her hand, and I recognized her. We hadn't officially met, but I'd seen her in the shop several times. She always struck me as a bit of a flake, but I put on a smile and took a seat at her table. She leaned forward, looking just a little too eager.

"Persia, I was so happy to hear from you today. You said you wanted to talk about Lisa?"

So much for social niceties, I thought. But hey, it would get me out the door that much sooner. "Karen, hello. Nice to meet you. Yes, I was wondering if you remembered anything Lisa might have said during your appointment."

"What's wrong? Is she in some sort of trouble?"

Hoo boy, here it came. Treading cautiously into the subject, I said, "No, probably not. But her sister hasn't heard from her for a couple of days, and we're trying to figure out if she went on vacation or something."

Karen's eyes glittered, and I realized I had a young Heddy Latherton on my hands. The town gossip, Heddy had a mouth that outweighed her common sense by ten to one. My aunt couldn't stand the woman.

"Let me think." She sipped her drink, which looked like some sort of green tea blend, and her eyes lit up with an unnatural glow. She leaned forward and whispered, "Lisa seemed high-strung and anxious to get done with the appointment. I thought there might be something wrong."

That could mean any number of things, including Lisa just wanting to get Karen out of her chair. In the two minutes since I'd sat down at the table, I'd developed an instant distaste for the woman. I usually tried not to make snap judgments but Karen rubbed me the wrong way, and I wasn't sure why.

"Did she mention anything about plans for the weekend? Maybe something with her boyfriend?" I sipped my tea and puckered my lips. Apparently the lemons had received a good dose of tang by the sourpuss faeries.

Karen blinked. She lowered her voice and in a conspiratorial tone said, "You know who I am, right? And why I wanted to meet here instead of my house?"

It was my turn to blink. I was beginning to feel like I'd walked in on the wrong movie, or a bad *X-Files* episode. "Uh . . . no. Why don't you enlighten me?"

"My sister is Yvonne Sanders. She was Shawn's girlfriend until Lisa stole him away. Yvonne would kill me if she knew I went to Lisa for a makeover, even though Shawn and Lisa broke up months ago." Karen sat back, an expectant look on her face.

I still wasn't altogether clear on what she was trying to tell me. "So, is your sister still mad at Lisa?"

Karen played with her Danish. "Lisa just swooped in and carried him off. Yvonne was crushed. I don't know if she'll ever get over it." She let out a tragic sigh. "I don't know if I'll ever have a great love like that. I like to think so, but it's so hard to meet people." She made a little shrug and gave me one of those basset hound looks, peppering my irritation with a tinge of compassion.

I looked her over a little more closely. Karen was wearing a baggy sweatshirt beneath a pair of overalls. It was impossible to tell what her figure looked like, and she sat as if she were uneasy in her body. Her hair was pulled back in a messy ponytail, and she had a Mariners baseball cap slung on backwards. Her nails were bitten to the quick, and her face was bare. She could be a pretty girl if she'd take a few pains with her appearance, but the truth was, she'd never be a classical beauty. It occurred to me that perhaps she didn't think she was pretty at all, so why bother trying? Self-esteem was a rare commodity in women. I idly wondered what she'd looked like after the makeover.

"Can you think of anything out of the ordinary that Lisa told you? Do you remember if she said she was going anywhere?"

Karen crinkled her nose, thinking. After a minute, she shook her head. "No, not really. I was too nervous to pay attention. I've never been to anything like the Thanksgiving Gala before. I guess I was thinking about that, mostly. And I'd never had a makeover before. I still can't believe what she was able to do to me, but I don't think I can ever learn how to put on makeup like that. It seems like magic to me." She sounded wistful and, once again, I felt sorry for the woman.

I gave her a wide smile. "Listen, there are a lot of good books and magazines on the subject. Start with Kevyn Aucoin's books and magazines like *Pout* and *Winsome* and *Allure*. Buy a good makeup mirror, and inexpensive drugstore cosmetics for practice, and when you find colors you like, get them in a good department store brand. I can tell you right now you'd look great in lilac and rose-colored eye shadow, and a dusty rose-colored gloss or lipstick. When you pick out foundation, pick one that matches your skin tone—don't go darker. And use a translucent powder."

She beamed and pulled out a notebook. "Can you repeat that? I think I'd like to give it a try. Yvonne's always been the pretty one, but maybe . . ." She stopped, biting her lip. I thought I saw tears glistening in her eyes.

"Maybe you can find your *own* beauty and stop comparing yourself to your sister," I said firmly as I reached for her notebook. I jotted down some suggestions and the titles of a couple of good books and handed it back to her. "Remember, people treat you the way you treat yourself. So stop beating yourself up, okay?"

"I'll try," she said, giving me a grateful smile. Standing up, she added, "Listen, don't tell Yvonne I went to see Lisa, would you? She'd be pissed at me."

I nodded and watched as she trudged out of the coffee shop and into the bookstore. She glanced around, and then asked a clerk something, and I saw that he pointed her toward the health and beauty section. What do you know? She was taking my advice.

I drained my tea, made sure I had my purse and tote bag, and headed out to the car. Along the way, Karen's remarks about Yvonne replayed in my mind. Could Yvonne have been so angry that she'd finally decided to lash out? It seemed a distant possibility, but nevertheless, we'd have to check it out. Because as it was, we were striking out, and every day that Lisa was missing reduced our chances of finding her.

⋅❧

I pulled into the Smith sisters' driveway at quarter to one and made a quick call to the shop. Tawny answered, and I asked her to tell Auntie that I'd be about an hour later than I'd expected. As I walked up the flagstone path to the house, Enid Smith stuck her head out the door and motioned me to hurry.

"You'll catch your death in that rain, girl. Get in here." She ushered me into the quiet two-bedroom ranch house that had been built in the early eighties. The décor was à la the *Golden Girls*: mauve and mint green with splashes of yellow. Wicker furniture abounded, and large potted palms and ferns. I'd been over to Enid and Donna's on several occasions, and each time, the whimsy and lightness of the house never failed to coax a smile out of me.

The sisters played mother to three Himalayan Siamese, all of whom were loud, sleek, and spoiled. They raced over to me when I sat down at the dining room table and milled around my feet. I reached down and tickled their ears and patted their backs.

Donna swept in from the kitchen carrying a tray of clear crystal dishes that contained what looked—and smelled—like lobster salad on croissant rolls. Both Enid and Donna were dressed as if getting ready for an afternoon tea, but I had known them long enough to know that this was their everyday getup. Neither would ever be seen in public with a single gray curl out of place or without a handbag that matched their shoes. They adored my aunt, but I knew they thought she dressed like a bag lady.

As she set the plates on the table, Donna prattled on about how good it was to see me. I leaned back, glad I'd come. Even if it did mess up my schedule, I enjoyed the Smith sisters' company and didn't get over here often enough. They were comfortable in their lives, and they made their guests feel comfortable in their home.

As we settled down to eat, and I flourished the peach-colored napkin onto my lap, Donna said, "Okay, Persia, we know you have something to ask us. You didn't just drop over here for a leisurely visit."

When I tried to protest—feeling vaguely embarrassed because she'd hit the nail on the head—she added, "Save it for someone you can snow." She was smiling though, and no sense of rebuke lingered in her words. "With the holiday season upon us, there's no way you'd have time to run around on a weekday like this. Your aunt must be stewing to have you back at the shop."

I gave her a wry grin. "Well, yes, she probably is. You know I love coming to visit, but you're right. There is something I need to ask you." I bit into the lobster salad and closed my eyes, reveling in the rich, sweet flavor of the flaked shellfish as it mingled with diced apples, celery, shallots, and water chestnuts, all blended together in a Dijon mustard dressing. The croissant matched perfectly with the salad. "Oh yum, this is so good," I added. "I had a sandwich about an hour ago, but I guess I was hungrier than I thought."

Enid poured lemonade all the way around. "So, what is it that you want to ask us?"

I decided just to plunge into my questions. "You were both in last Friday to see Lisa for makeovers. I'm wondering if she said anything about her plans for the weekend to you. Anything about where she might be going, or who she might be seeing?"

Enid looked at Donna, and they gave each other that little frown that people do when they're trying to remember something. After a moment, Enid shook her head. "Not offhand. What about you, Donna?"

Donna gave a little shrug. "Not really. She talked a lot about what she thought we should be using. It was very nice of her to take the time, but really, we just dropped in on the spur of the moment, and already have our own beauty routines."

"Almost thirty years, my routine's been the same," Enid said.

I repressed a smile. I had the feeling a lot of her routines had been the same for the past thirty years or perhaps longer. The Smith sisters were creatures of habit, and if you went shopping at the Shorelines Food Pavilion on Saturday mornings around nine AM, you'd always find them there buying their groceries for the week.

"Did something happen?" Donna asked.

"Lisa took off from the shop early on Saturday afternoon, and nobody's seen her since. She's probably fine, but she forgot to tell her sister where she was going, and we're just checking into things; making sure that nothing happened."

I glanced at the clock. Auntie would string me up if I didn't get back to the shop pretty soon. "I hate to eat and run, but Auntie's waiting for me. Lunch was lovely, and it was so good to see you again." On the spur of the moment—and because I knew Auntie wouldn't mind—I added, "What are you doing for Thanksgiving? We're holding a big get-together at our house for friends. Dinner and the whole shebang. We'd love it if you could come."

Enid looked at Donna, and they both nodded. "I think that would be delightful, my dear," Enid said. "We haven't formalized any plans yet, and dinner at Moss Rose Cottage sounds just perfect. Let us know what you want us to bring. We insist on helping out."

I gave them each a hug, patted the cats, and then headed back to my car, where I flipped on my Jane's Addiction CD. So much for any clues, but at least I'd been able to relax for a moment and enjoy a good meal with good friends.

❧

As I hurried into the shop, Auntie looked over from where she was arguing with a UPS man. Apparently, he'd given us the wrong package, and she was pointing out that Venus Envy was *not* the same shop as McBride's Auto Supplies. He winced as she shoved the box back in his arms and motioned me over. As I approached, the parcel deliveryman made a hasty retreat.

"I see you chewed him up one side and down the other," I said.

"This is the third time in the past month he's brought us the wrong package. I'm going to call and complain to his supervisors. He could at least read the labels before he brings them into the shop. I'm glad you're back," she said, not pausing between thoughts. "Did you find out anything?"

I quickly filled her in. "I'm waiting on two calls, and I'll talk to Barb after work. Where is she, by the way?" I asked, glancing around the shop. "Did Dorian come to his senses and apologize?"

"I wish. Barbara's in the back, doing laundry." We had a washer and dryer in the back of the spa room where we washed the towels used for facials and haircuts. Auntie had decided that taking them home was just too much bother, and so she'd found a good used set, and we did laundry a couple of times a week.

As I was wondering whether I should go over to the bakery and talk to Dorian—even though Auntie said not to, it felt like somebody had to do something—there was a crash as a rock came hurtling through one of the front windows. A second immediately followed, and a third. Glass shards sprayed like shrapnel, covering the floor and shelves.

"Good Lord, what's going on?" Auntie's eyes went wide as I pulled her away from the windows.

"I don't know," I said. "Get everybody toward the back. I'll call Kyle and then find out what's going on."

As Auntie hurriedly herded the startled customers toward the back of the shop, I pulled out my cell and punched in 911. I quickly told dispatch what was happening while watching to see that Auntie, Tawny, and Betsy managed to get everyone away from the front of the shop where they could be hurt by breaking glass. The officer taking my call told me that they'd send a cruiser right over.

No more rocks appeared, and I cautiously made my way across the glass-covered floor. Luckily, whoever decided to vandalize our store had only managed to hit one of the huge front windows. The other was still intact.

And then I saw him outside near my car, which now sported a broken windshield. Elliot leaned against a telephone pole, a drunken smirk on his face. As he idly tossed another rock toward my car, I lost it.

"You bastard! You're going down!" I raced out of the store, heedless of the glass. When Elliot saw me barreling toward him, he seemed to sober up pretty fast. Or maybe he was just aware of how close to death he was in that moment, because he turned to run, weaving erratically down the street. But I was faster, and within less than a minute, I tackled him, bringing him down on the sidewalk. I straddled his chest as all my frustration came pouring out like so much venom.

"Your luck just ran out, you fucking bastard!"

I broke his nose with the first punch and blackened his eye with the second. Before I could land a third, Kyle pulled up in his cruiser and jumped out to haul me off of Elliot while his partner dragged the object of my fury to his feet. I struggled, trying to escape Kyle's hold, and he finally shoved me against the wall that separated Venus Envy and the Baklava or Bust Bakery.

"Persia, get a grip!" His voice was harsh, but I could see a glint in his eyes that told me he was having trouble keeping a straight face. I struggled again, intending to give Elliot a kick in the balls as a parting shot, but Kyle managed to keep me from getting loose, and I finally relaxed.

"All right, all right, I'll keep my hands to myself," I said, gritting my teeth. Kyle let go, though he kept his eye on me as he did so. I turned to look at Elliot. While he had shattered our windows, I'd done a pretty good job of messing up his face, and I didn't regret my actions in the least.

"Oh Persia, what did you do?" Auntie's gasp came from the door of Venus Envy. The look on her face told me that she was having trouble making up her mind whether to yell at me or not.

"Now can I get my restraining order?" I asked Kyle, all the while keeping an eye on my nemesis.

His voice brusque, he said, "I don't think you'll have any problem with that now."

Elliot squinted at me, and I could swear I still saw a hint of a leer behind the swelling. His nose was a brilliant blue with black streaks, as was the skin around his right eye. His left eye wasn't looking too good, either, and I'd managed to split his lip. A little blood trickled down from the side.

"Man, that must hurt, huh, Elliot?" I asked, a snarky grin on my face. I couldn't help it. Nope, not sorry in the least.

"I want to press charges against her for assault!" Elliot struggled feebly against the officer who had a hold on him, but his look was pure spite.

"What? You're the one who brought this on yourself, you son of a bitch!" I was ready to fly at him again, but Kyle's hand on my arm stopped me.

"Sure, I broke your windows, you whore, but you won't listen to me. You won't pay attention to me! I had to do something." His whine grated on my nerves, and I wished now that I'd knocked him out.

Oh wonderful, Mr. Stalker had turned into a full-blown nut job.

Kyle frowned, then gave me a sideways glance. "Sorry, Persia, but you're going to have to come with me."

"What?" I backed away, astounded. "You're arresting *me*? But he shattered our windows and damaged my car!"

"Yes, and we're arresting him, too. But you shouldn't have hit him. Did he threaten you in *any* way? Was it self-defense?" Kyle added, and I knew he was trying to be helpful, offer me an out.

I stared at Elliot. As much as I wanted to lie and say yes, I couldn't. Auntie had brought me up better than that. I sighed. "I need my purse."

Kyle motioned to Auntie. "Miss Florence, can you get Persia's purse for her?" He motioned to the other officer. "Call for another cruiser and take Elliot to the hospital after you read him his rights. And collect the stones that

he threw through the window. Don't mess up any fingerprints."

I felt like I was back in junior high, getting into fights
again. And by the look on Auntie's face, I was due for a
scolding like I hadn't had since that time. I slung my purse
over my shoulder, listened to Kyle as he read me my
rights, and indicated I understood them.

As he put his hand on the top of my head to make sure
I didn't hit the top of the cruiser as I slid into the backseat,
it occurred to me that maybe, just maybe, I hadn't handled
matters the way I should have.

Chapter Eight

Having never had the pleasure of being arrested before, I was in for an experience. Oh yeah, the wrong seat in the patrol car, all right. I stared at the steel mesh that separated me from the front, thinking that, actually, with my temper, it was a miracle this hadn't happened before.

On the way to the station house, Kyle kept his words short and clipped. "Persia, I can't believe you did that. You bludgeoned the guy."

"You know how much that creep's gotten under my skin since last spring," I said. "He's damned lucky I didn't break more than his nose."

He glanced at me in the rearview mirror. "Yeah, and you're lucky you didn't, either. As it is, you're going to at least be paying some fines. The judge may take some pity on you, seeing how far Elliot's pushed you over the past few months, but still . . . Persia, you gave him a black eye and broke his nose!"

"I would have busted his balls, too, if you hadn't stopped me." I sighed and stared out the window. Jail wasn't my idea of the best way to spend the afternoon. And poor Auntie, she had to watch me get carted off. I leaned my head back, groaning slightly. "Damn it, it's all Elliot's fault. I take responsibility when I really screw up, but damn it, Kyle, that freakin' idiot had to know I was going to snap one of these days. He pushed too hard this time. Our customers could have been hurt by that shattering glass."

"I'm not disagreeing with you, and I guarantee that you'll get your restraining order, and Elliot will be doing some time. I'll talk to the judge. I'm just glad you've been keeping a tight record on how much he's been bothering you." He pulled into the driveway leading to the station. As he helped me out of the car, my hands bound behind me in the metal cuffs, he chuckled.

"What's so funny?" I glared at him.

"If I told you, you'd slap a harassment charge against me," he said softly, and I knew he was thinking something I didn't want to hear.

I grunted. "In the mood I'm in, I probably would. You just keep your thoughts on Amy, okay?"

"Whatever you say, Shifty. I've got to think of an appropriate nickname for you now. Maybe Sockeye, or Thinks With Fists?"

I growled but said nothing. He was enjoying this all too much. As we headed toward the door, I asked, "How long do you think I'll be in?"

"If Miss Florence—or you—can post bail, then you should be home for supper." He opened the door and escorted me in. The dispatcher's expression went from blank to shocked. We knew each other, and she wasn't used to seeing me in irons. Kyle led me to one of the desks in the main room, where he sat me down next to an officer I'd seen around but whose name I didn't recognize.

"This is Officer Shanna Reynolds. Why don't you tell her everything that happened." He glanced at the woman. "After you're done taking her statement, process her. Be gentle, though, she's a friend of mine." He grinned once more before heading back out the door.

"Well, damn," I muttered under my breath. "Today's pretty much been shot to hell."

Officer Reynolds gave me a thin smile and put a piece of paper in the typewriter. As her fingers moved over the keys, I told her exactly what had happened. She didn't say much, but as she tapped away, I heard my name and looked up. Winthrop Winchester was making his way among the desks. Auntie's lawyer—and mine—he was one of the best in the state. I glanced up at him as he stopped by my side.

"I want a restraining order against Elliot now. If I don't get it, I'm going to make certain he moves off this island." I was dead serious. Elliot had crossed the line for the last time, and I wasn't in any mood to give him another chance.

Winthrop nodded. "I'm on it. How long till you're done with her and we can bail her out?" he asked the officer.

Shanna Reynolds gave him a veiled look. "Another half hour."

He gave me a long look. "I'll get the ball started on the restraining order while you . . . finish your appointment here."

I behaved all the way through fingerprinting, which left a mess on my hands, and mug shots, which made me wish to hell I'd gotten more sleep the night before. If I had to have a picture taken that would last long after my death, then why couldn't I have bothered with a little more makeup? Grumpy and tired despite the wonderful lunch I'd had, I finally found myself released into Winthrop's waiting hands, not once seeing the inside of a jail cell.

He kept his peace until we were outside, heading toward his car. "You little idiot! I can't believe you did that," he said. "You worried your aunt sick and gave yourself a nice little record. Why couldn't you have just waited until the cops got there?" Blowing out a long sigh, he shook his head. "Don't answer that. I know what your aunt calls you, and she's right. You're certainly more impetuous than is good for you."

We slipped into his car, and I leaned back against the headrest, reveling in the softness of the leather. Which reminded me, my car was now unusable until I got the windshield fixed.

"What about Elliot? Did you get the order?"

"Yes, it's in the works and should be approved. Don't you worry about him. Florence wants to sue his butt off in a civil suit for damages, and you can take him to court for harassment. By the time we're done with that miserable loser, he'll slink out of town and hopefully never come back."

"I don't want his money," I said. "I just want him to get out of my life for good. But I suppose he should pay for the car and the windows—that's only fair." I stared at my hands. The ink had stuck to my fingers, and they were now a delightful shade of purple-black.

Winthrop glanced at me. "Don't touch the upholstery, okay? It costs a bundle to remove ink stains."

I let out a long sigh. "Okay, okay. So where are you taking me?"

"Home. Your auntie's there, waiting for you. She left Tawny and Betsy in charge of the shop. Your friend Barbara stayed to help out."

Great. Now I'd inconvenienced everybody. I just hoped Elliot hurt like hell. I couldn't help but relish the feeling of freedom that punching his lights out had given me. I'd been wanting to do that since he first showed up in Gull Harbor earlier this year, bent on making me miserable. I'd better enjoy it, I thought grimly, because Auntie was going to bite my head off.

As we pulled into the driveway, I let out a long breath. "So, do you think I'll end up in jail for this?"

Winthrop snorted. "I hope we'll be able to prevent that. By the time we get done laying out Elliot's background and his current habit of harassment, we'll have the judge on our side—and jury if need be. I might be able to convince him to drop charges, though." He turned off the engine. I didn't like the sound of this, because I knew what was coming. "If you go against your aunt's wishes and avoid a civil lawsuit, he'll probably jump at the offer to drop assault charges against you."

"But that's not fair—" I sputtered.

He waved away my protest. "Fairness has no place in justice. Trust me, I know. The fact is that he has no money, his job isn't worth squat, and he doesn't have any assets. A lawsuit would only serve to soothe your ego; it wouldn't do a damn thing otherwise except tie up the courts, cost you and your auntie a bundle, and take up time you could be spending on other, more interesting things."

I stared at him. He was serious. "But I want to pound Elliot into the ground so he can never bother me again!"

Abruptly, I realized that I was on the verge of having a temper tantrum and squelched it. Winthrop and Auntie didn't need me acting like a brat, although right now I felt about thirteen. Come to think of it, that was the year I'd gotten into my first fight after taking aikido for six months. Before that fight, I'd been picked on constantly. Afterward, nobody bothered me again. I'd sprained a boy's wrist and broken two of his fingers. Luckily, there were witnesses to verify that it had been self-defense, but I hadn't spared any feelings when he wouldn't quit grabbing at my ass. I'd nailed the sucker.

I raced up the steps, taking them two at a time, as Winthrop followed more sedately. As I opened the door, Beast came rushing up, happy to see me. He planted his feet against my shoulders and gave me a big lick with his floppy old tongue. I laughed for the first time since Elliot had gotten jiggy with the rocks and followed his hulking form into the kitchen.

Auntie was fixing dinner. Or rather, arranging takeout

on china. Yum, Peking duck, deep-fried prawns, pot stickers, and chicken fried rice. She looked up as I came into the kitchen and dropped the box of rice on the counter, rushing over to embrace me.

"Oh, Imp, I was so worried! I called Winthrop the minute that Kyle took you away." She pushed me back, staring at me.

"Where's Barb?" I asked, looking around.

"She called to say she'd be here in an hour or two. She's eating dinner out." Auntie sighed and brushed a stray bang away from her face. "What the hell did you think you were doing? Elliot could have hurt you—he could have had a gun!"

I shook my head. She was far more worried than she needed to be, but that was family for you. "I'm fine, Auntie, really. I didn't even have time to see the inside of a cell before Winthrop showed up. Everything will be fine. And you know perfectly well that Elliot's a wimp. By law, he can't carry a gun, and I'm sure he's too scared to touch one."

She sniffed, her mouth twisted in a worried frown. "Persia, I want to talk to you about that. I know you know how to shoot. As long as he's on this island, I want you to buy a gun, and I want you to get a concealed weapons permit. Elliot's gone over the edge. Maybe next time he won't play fair. Maybe he'll be sneakier."

Me? With a gun? I sat down, staring at the counter. On one hand, Auntie made a lot of sense, but could I be trusted with a weapon like that? I honestly couldn't answer that myself, let alone trust somebody else to know.

"Auntie," I said softly, "that's probably not the wisest move. Look at the way I went after Elliot. I know myself enough to know that I'm better off without one. I don't want to get locked up for shooting somebody."

Winthrop cleared his throat and sat down at the table, opening his briefcase to bring out a sheaf of papers. "Persia's right, Florence. Your niece is a wonderful young woman, but she's got a hair-trigger temper, and I'd hate to see her end up in a situation she couldn't get out of."

Auntie and I put dinner on the table, and I fetched another plate for Winthrop. As I took my seat, he raised one eyebrow. "So, have you made a decision about how we'll proceed? Are you still insisting on suing Elliot? By all means prosecute him, but if you want my advice, you won't take him to civil court."

"What are you talking about—" Auntie looked indignant.

I interrupted. "He's got a point, even if I don't like to admit it."

Winthrop explained to her what he'd told me. Auntie grumbled, but she was a smart cookie, and she immediately saw his point of view. "I don't like it, either, but Persia, I agree. Listen to Winthrop. We don't need you chancing a court case that might land you in jail, even though you were provoked."

Feeling backed into a corner from all sides—including my common sense, which I wasn't very happy about listening to at the moment—I gave Winthrop a nod. "See what you can do. Tell Elliot that if he drops charges, we won't sue his butt off. But I want that restraining order, and I want to see him in jail."

Winthrop shuffled his papers and slipped them back in the briefcase. "You're making the right decision, Persia. I know it doesn't feel good, but trust me—I have waged so many lawsuits that I can't even begin to count them, and at least half were a waste of time due to lack of assets on the defendant's side. It would cost you far more than you'd ever win."

He accepted a plate from Auntie. Winthrop seldom stayed for dinner, but I knew he ate out a lot with clients. I wondered how his wife felt about him being gone so often. He never mentioned her, and neither did Auntie, but I assumed he had one. I'd seen a picture of a woman and children on his desk when I was in his office.

My curiosity got the better of me. "Winthrop, are you married?"

Auntie snorted wine out of her nose. "Ouch! Persia, you take the cake."

Winthrop answered, smooth as silk. "Why? Are you interested?" he asked, a smirk on his face that made the towering lawyer suddenly seem *much* more intimidating than usual.

Red-faced, I rubbed my temples. "I just thought . . . we never hear about her, and I saw a picture on your desk—"

He let out a belly laugh. "Mrs. Winchester took the children and left for France fifteen years ago. I keep the picture there because I love my children and am proud of them. I should put up a current one, but it always occurs to me when I'm not there to do it. The photo also reminds me never to take anyone at face-value. Seemingly the epitome of propriety, my ex-wife was having an affair. When I found out and filed for divorce and custody, she fled the country with the children."

Shocked, I asked, "What happened to your kids?"

"Since she was a good mother, rather than put my children through a horrendous court battle, I decided to give her primary custody with the stipulation that I see them for a month every year. They're grown now, and two have returned to the States. They visit me quite often, actually. My other daughter stayed in France with her mother. I haven't seen her in five years, and she never writes or calls." He looked wistful, as if he'd missed out on the best part of his life. In a way, I suppose he had.

"I'm sorry," I said. "I didn't mean to pry."

"No apologies necessary. It was long ago, and life moves on. Now, back to your situation. We should have the restraining order by tomorrow. I'll pay a visit to Elliot and make sure he knows what he's facing. I'll impress upon him that if you file a civil suit against him, he'll be in debt to you for years."

"What about the vandalism?"

"He probably won't spend much time in jail for that, but with the restraining order, if he starts stalking you again, then we can go after him under the antistalking laws. I'll make sure he knows what the penalties for those are, try to nip any thoughts of that sort of behavior in the bud."

We ate our dinner. Auntie and Winthrop carried on a lively conversation while I sat deep in thought. The excitement of the afternoon had distracted me from Lisa's disappearance, but with the coming of nightfall, I couldn't help but wonder where she was. Was she alive? Hurt somewhere and unable to call for help? It was cold out. If she had taken a tumble into a ravine or gotten caught in some wooded area, she wouldn't be able to survive many more nights like we were having.

The ring of the phone broke through my thoughts, and I motioned to Auntie that I'd get it. Heddy Latherton was on the line, and I cringed. Even though I wanted to ask her about Lisa, I dreaded wading through the mire of gossip and chitchat to get there. Unfortunately, my reputation had preceded me, and Heddy was full of questions about my infamous afternoon.

"Oh Persia, I heard you were arrested for beating up your ex-boyfriend! Are you okay? I heard that you took quite a pummeling from him. He hit you with a rock or something? I can't imagine why Kyle would arrest you for fighting back in self-defense." She paused to catch her breath.

Grabbing the opportunity, I set the record straight. "No, Heddy, he didn't hit me with a rock. He broke one of the big windows at Venus Envy, and he also smashed my car's windshield. I lost my temper and broke his nose."

She gasped. "You're so brave! I'd have been terrified to do such a thing. Your aunt is a lucky woman to have such a brave niece."

Ever since Auntie and I'd staged a falling-out to allow me to dig up evidence at Bebe Wilcox's, Heddy had inexplicably become my champion and friend. Auntie couldn't stand her, and I had a feeling the sentiment was mutual, but Heddy stood up for me and had taken me into her more than ample bosom.

I wasn't sure I liked the honor; it meant I had to listen to her gab on and on, but it also meant that she still steered business our way, and she was always first stop on the grapevine if you wanted to hear the latest rumors making the rounds.

"Heddy, I have something I need to ask you, and I'd appreciate it if you'd think really hard about your answer. This is *important*." I let my voice linger over the last word. Heddy loved to be included in anything that might remotely be earthshaking.

She caught her breath. "Of course, Persia. You know I'm only too happy to help. What do you want to know?"

"You came to Lisa for a facial on Friday morning, right?"

"Yes, that's right. I come in every week on Friday."

"Did Lisa say anything about where she might be going or what she might be planning for the weekend? Anything that seemed out of the ordinary?"

The seconds on the clock ticked by as Heddy ruminated on the question. After a moment, she said, "Well, she did mention that she was thinking of looking for a job in Seattle if things slowed down after the holidays. Is that any help?"

My spirits sank. Heddy had a nose for gossip that was more sensitive than a bloodhound's. If she hadn't picked up on anything useful, maybe my idea was a wild-goose chase. "Thanks, Heddy. It's not quite what I was hoping for, but I appreciate your call."

"Is something wrong? I heard through the grapevine that Lisa's missing. Is that true?"

Great. Quid pro quo time, now. "Yes, she is. We aren't sure where she went or even if she's in trouble. That's what we're trying to find out. Maybe she took off with a friend for a few days and forgot to let anybody know." I gracefully wormed my way through the rest of the conversation and cut it short. As I hung up, Barb came through the door.

"Hey, Jailbird!" She took off her coat and hung it in the closet. "What's shaking?"

"What's shaking with you? Who did you have dinner with?" My heart leapt, hoping it was Dorian. Maybe they'd patched things up.

Barb winked. "A very handsome man, but get your mind out of the gutter. And out of the clouds, for that matter. It wasn't Dorian," she said, and a wistful look spread over her face. "In fact, other than when he came over to find out what was going on at Venus Envy this afternoon, I haven't talked to him since I left yesterday afternoon."

"Who was your dinner date, then?" I asked, a little suspicious. Barb had been running on low self-esteem for months now, though for the life of me, I couldn't figure out why. Hitting her forties had been a shock for her, rather than a time of empowerment, and she was feeling the lack of her youth. She'd always looked a decade younger than she was, but now her worries over aging were catching up to her. I had the feeling that stress over a few problems in her marriage was more of a culprit than her actual age.

"Ari. He's trying to play liaison."

Ari was Dorian's nephew, and he doted on Barb and Dorian. It made sense that he'd be doing everything in his power to convince them to make up. He'd come over from Greece wanting to widen his options, and Dorian put him to work. He was now one of the head bakers at the Baklava or Bust Bakery and had decided to make the family business his career. Dorian and Barb had promised him a partnership if he stuck it out for ten years and did a good job.

"What did he say?" I asked.

Barb gave me a smug look. "I guess Dorian confided in

him that Mama Konstantinos is being a real bear now that I'm gone. She's trying to tighten the apron strings, and without me there to take the heat, Dorian's getting it full force. I think he's remembering just why he left Greece in the first place. I'll bide my time," she added. "Give it a couple of days and see what happens. Meanwhile, you tell me what the hell happened today. I can't believe Kyle arrested you!"

Auntie and I bade good-bye to Winthrop, then she yawned and headed toward the stairs. "I'm going to turn in early and read in bed, girls. You get some sleep, and no partying tonight!"

We laughed and waved her off, then curled up by the fire, surrounded by the dogs, most of the cats, and Hoffman, who clucked and pecked his way over to jump up on the footstool, then on the sofa. He settled down next to me with a satisfied shake of the feathers.

As we relaxed in front of the crackling flames, Barb's cell phone rang. She glanced at the caller ID. "Dorian. Should I?"

"Oh, why not? You can always hang up if he gets obnoxious."

Frowning, she bit her lip, then answered the call. "Yeah, I'm here . . . Ari talked to you? He said what? Yes, that's right . . . Dorian, you don't know how rotten she makes me feel; you refuse to see it. No, don't come over. I said no!"

She stared at the phone and hung up. "Dorian's on his way. I told him no, but you know him. Let's talk about something else. So tell me, how was jail?" Barb asked, exploring the potato chip bag.

I shook my head. "Wouldn't know. Never saw the inside of a cell. I'm going to have to let Elliot off the hook on this one, at least in terms of civil court." I told her what Winthrop had said, and she blanched.

"Persia, Elliot's behavior is escalating. I'm worried. I

didn't used to think he was dangerous but now—who knows?"

Hoffman began to pick at his feathers, grooming himself, and I patted the big old bird on the butt. He gave me a sharp look, then went back to his bath. Across the room, Nalu perked up when he saw the rooster. Once in awhile he still attempted a coup on the critter, though Hoffman was handy with his beak and had never got more than a feather ruffled in one of their skirmishes. The dogs ignored the bird as if he was no more than a bug on the wall.

I considered the situation. Elliot, dangerous? Two weeks ago, I would have laughed her off, but today's escapade heightened his threat factor. "I'll talk to Kyle about him. Winthrop's getting a restraining order, but you and I both know that doesn't always work." My cell phone rang. "Hold on, be right back," I said, jumping up to get my purse. A glance at caller ID told me it was Killian.

"Hey, sweets, how'd the meeting go?" I asked as I punched the Talk button. I'd been too busy to worry about how he was doing, but now I held my breath, hoping to hear good news.

Killian whooped in my ear. "They love it! They're willing to buy in. I wish I could do this on my own, I don't like having partners, but their backing means I can start over now instead of waiting a couple of years to build up capital. So I'm back in business, baby."

I whooped along with him. He'd been working so hard to recover from Bebe's sabotage. "What's next, then? When do you open the doors?"

"First, I make a trip to New York after Thanksgiving. Until then, I'm going to be tied up with lawyers here. I'll be able to make it over for the holiday, but until then, I'm going to be swamped. You don't mind, do you?"

I smiled. We had agreed that we wouldn't be clingy, but lately we'd been asking each other, "Is it okay?" more than I wanted to admit. At this point, it wasn't spooking me, and I hoped it wouldn't become a problem.

"Not at all. You do what you have to. Are you staying in Seattle until Thanksgiving?"

"Yeah, that would be easiest. I can camp here at my brother's place, and it will cut out the ferry commute. I'll see you Thursday. I'll come early. Want me to bring anything?" He sounded positively giddy.

I laughed. "Just your cute little butt. Stay here Thursday night?"

"Of course. That will give me Friday and Saturday to pack. So how was your day?"

I had a feeling anything I said would barely register, he was so excited. "I punched out my ex and got arrested. Nothing out of the ordinary," I said. Before he could get another word out, I hurried to add, "Love you! See you Thursday," and hung up. I grinned at Barbara, who laughed. "Ten, nine, eight, seven, six . . ."

Ring. Yep, right on cue.

"What the hell did you say?" Killian was sputtering.

I snickered. "You heard me. I broke Elliot's nose after he threw a handful of rocks through one of Venus Envy's windows and got myself arrested. It'll be okay. Winthrop's sure he can work out a deal where Elliot will drop the charges. I'm fine, so don't go all hyper on me."

Silence. Then, "You take the cake. Life around you is never boring, I'll give you that. So, Elliot's in jail?"

"Unless he had the money to bail himself out, yeah. Honestly, I'm fine. Kyle had to take me in. He didn't want to."

"Sure he didn't. I still think he wants to get in your pants."

Hmm . . . jealousy? But Killian wasn't petty. "I doubt it, considering he and Amy are courting. So please, don't worry. I'll see you Thursday for Thanksgiving. Come early enough, and we can catch the morning show in my bedroom."

Killian grunted. "I'll be there by nine. You be careful.

And think about me tonight." His voice was husky. "I'll be thinking about you."

As I closed my cell phone, my stomach told me that I'd be thinking about him more than just tonight. He was the best sex I'd ever had.

Barb cleared her throat. "You two really click, don't you? So, he got the funding?"

I jumped up and danced around the room. "He got the funding! If things go right, he may be able to start his new business right after the new year. Betsy Sue and Julius will be so happy, but I'm not going to say a word for now until he tells them. It's his place to do so. Also, I don't want to jinx anything."

"This kind of news calls for a drink. You have anything around to make daiquiris? Strawberry would be delish!" Barb giggled. Although her reasons for being here were regrettable, I was suddenly glad she was. It was like having our own private slumber party. It had been a long, long time since I'd had a girlfriend sleep over.

"Let's go forage and see what we can find," I said. We wandered into the kitchen. I opened the freezer and found the frozen berries and ice while Barbara got out two daiquiri glasses. "I've got to get the rum. I'll be right back."

I went into the living room and crossed to the liquor cabinet. As I opened the glass doors, there was a sound at the front door. "Barb, I think Dorian may be here," I said as the kitchen phone rang. "Can you get the phone?"

"Sure," she called back.

I opened the door. Hell and high water—Elliot was standing there, a crazy look in his eye. His face was swollen, his nose bandaged, and his lip was split, and for a moment all I could think was that I'd done a damned good number on the jerk. And then reality registered that this wasn't a social call. I started to slam the door, but he shoved it open and backhanded me with a bone-chilling smack. At the same moment, Barb shouted something from the kitchen. I scrambled back, out of reach, before Elliot could hit me again.

"Barb! Call 911! It's Elliot!"

"I wouldn't do that if I were you," Elliot bellowed as Barb came racing into the living room, her eyes wide. He pulled out a revolver. I glanced at it and forced the panic down. If I screamed, it would only serve to enrage him.

Barb, on the other hand, began to shriek.

I thought I heard a creak on the stairs and turned to Barb. *"Shut up!"* I had to keep things quiet so Auntie wouldn't walk in on us.

Elliot let out a low chuckle. "Calm down, Barbara. We don't want you to have a heart attack. Or do we?" He sneered at me, and I looked into his eyes. They were a flood of flame and fury, and I knew that Elliot had lost it and that he'd come here to hurt me.

Chapter Nine

⊶ ⊷

"Elliot, put the gun down." For years, I'd been training women in my self-defense classes to deal with circumstances like this. Only now it was me, and I was on the end of a crazy man's gun.

Barb backed up, her eyes wide. "Oh my God . . . Elliot . . ."

"Just sit over there where I can see your hands," he ordered her. She obeyed without comment.

"Elliot, let her go. You want me. I know that, and you know that. Just let Barb go upstairs." I tried to avoid looking back at the stairs. I *knew* that I had heard Auntie moving around before Barb shrieked, but now it was still as a mouse.

"Shut up! *You* come over here," he said, motioning to me with the gun. I slowly moved toward him, hands held where he could see them, trying not to startle him in any way. The last thing I needed to do was set him off while somebody else was in the room. Hell, I hoped to avoid setting him off while *I* was in the room. "You . . . you mess with my head, Persia. You messed with me real good, and you shouldn't have! You deserted me when I needed you, and then you treat me like a piece of dirt!"

I took a slow breath and, keeping my voice as even as I could, said, "Elliot, you embezzled money. You lied to me. What did you expect me to do?" Maybe not the best answer in the world, but he wouldn't believe me if I turned tail now and pretended to still love him.

"You should have stuck by me. You should have waited for me," he said, his voice cracking. "You were mine, you were *all mine*."

I blinked. Not once had I made a firm commitment to Elliot, nor had he asked for one. Not once in all the years we were together had we planned out our future together. We'd taken things one day at a time. Apparently when his world shattered, so did his common sense. And he had only his own greed to thank for it. I couldn't feel sorry for him; he was too pathetic.

"What do you want, Elliot? Why did you come here? Why do you have that gun?" I sidestepped a footstool and kept inching forward.

He swallowed, looking dazed. I had the feeling he hadn't seen the dry side of sober in days, perhaps weeks. Elliot had always been weak, but now he was wallowing in self-pity. He wasn't sorry for what he'd done. He was just sorry he'd gotten caught.

He waited until I was near enough and then reached for my hand. I hesitantly held out my wrist. If I'd been alone, I would have taken a chance and fought him off. But with Barb present, I couldn't risk him shooting her by accident. Or out of spite.

Elliot grabbed my wrist and pulled me to him, glomming against me. He was breathing heavily, and from the smell of the stains on his shirt, he'd drunk more than his share of stale beer. He planted a wet one on my lips, and my stomach lurched. At one time, we'd had a reasonably good love life. Now, his touch revolted me.

"You come with me, baby. You're going to make it up to me for all the crap you've put me through. You just come with me, and your aunt and your friend won't get hurt." He waved the gun in Barb's direction. "Don't you go calling the cops. If that damned cop comes near me again, I'll shoot him."

Barb nodded, her lips pressed together in a thin line. As Elliot turned me toward the door, there was a sudden crash, and Kyle came rushing in from the kitchen, gun drawn. He took in the situation immediately and slowly took aim at Elliot.

"Drop the gun, Parker. Drop it now, and you can walk away from this," Kyle said. I could see the tension clenching his jaw, and he looked at me. I didn't dare let my guard down, didn't dare show fear, or Elliot would use that to his advantage. He was in back of me now, his arm around my waist and the barrel of his pistol pointed at my face.

"Put your gun down, Laughlin, or I'll shoot her. What have I got to lose? You arrest me, and I'm headed back to prison anyway." Elliot's voice had taken on a surreal quality, and I inhaled deeply. Sweat and musk and the ever-present beer mingled to create a stench that made me want to gag.

Kyle quietly lowered his gun and set it on the coffee table. He stepped back, his hands up. "Don't hurt her."

Elliot snorted. "Don't worry, that's not in my plans. Yet," he said, backing me up toward the door, his eyes trained on Kyle. I tried to gauge my chances if I resisted. Not good, not good at all. Elliot was at his breaking point. Another noise, and Auntie came into the room. Her face was streaked with tears, but she stood stiff, almost regal.

"Elliot Parker, you let Persia go. I'll go with you if you want a hostage, but you're not taking my niece." She spoke so softly that her words took a moment to register.

Kyle shook his head. "Miss Florence, go sit by Barbara. Elliot's in no mood to bargain."

"Good save, Mr. Police Chief," Elliot said. We reached

the door and were out on the porch. Kyle prevented Barb and Auntie from following. Elliot was breathing hard now, and I could sense he was both aroused and afraid. Not a good combination.

As we reached the steps, a noise to the left startled Elliot and he jerked. I took advantage and gave a brutal shove to his arm holding the gun, forcing it back at an unnatural angle.

Elliot shrieked as the gun went off, the explosion almost deafening me. The next thing I knew, somebody jumped from behind the porch swing and tackled Elliot, wrestling him to the ground. I leapt out of the way as there was another flash of light and thunderclap, and a shaft of fire grazed my shoulder. Crap! Had the jerk shot me?

As I rolled to the ground, trying to duck for cover, I heard the clink of metal on wood and in the glow from the foyer, saw the gun go skittering down the steps, firing once more into the dark night before it came to rest on the ground.

Elliot was fighting tooth and nail with his assailant, whom I could now see was Dorian. Dorian aimed one well-timed punch directly at Elliot's broken nose, and Elliot slumped, unconscious. Right about then, Kyle went racing past me down the stairs to collect the gun. He checked it, then looked at me.

"Miss Florence, call an ambulance. Persia's been shot."

Pain began to set in as I glanced up at the door. Auntie was standing there, her pale face staring down at me. She moaned gently, then turned to hurry back into the house. I gritted my teeth, trying to keep my composure. My shoulder felt like it had been hit by a flaming sledgehammer. Kyle motioned to Dorian. "Check her out while I cuff him."

Dorian started to kneel beside me, but Auntie reappeared, an afghan and pillow in hand. "Barbara's making the call," she said. "Dorian, get me another pillow, would you?" She examined me gently. "Child, how bad are you hurt? Do you feel faint?"

Kyle cuffed the unconscious Elliot as Barbara came running out.

"The ambulance is on the way," she said. Then Dorian was behind her, handing Auntie the pillow. His knuckles were bloody from where he'd connected with Elliot's face. Barb murmured something as Dorian opened his arms and enfolded her in a tight embrace.

Meanwhile, Kyle had taken over and was probing my shoulder. "I think it's just a graze," he said, gingerly poking around. "It's not bleeding heavily, though you'll have a nasty bruise. Looks like the bullet barely scraped you. In fact, although the abrasions look nasty, I'd say that some of the bruising was caused by your fall. Did you hit anything?"

I winced, pulling away from his fingers, and looked around. The patio set was right next to me, and one of the chairs had been knocked over. They were made of sturdy metal with plastic seats. I motioned to the overturned seat.

"Probably that. I jumped out of the way, the bullet must have winged me as it flew past, and I fell onto the chair. What a mess." I tried to stand up, but a wave of nausea overwhelmed me, and I sank to the ground again.

The ambulance siren pierced the night as it pulled into the driveway, and I closed my eyes, just wanting the chaos to end. Auntie knelt by my side with my head on her lap, and she kissed my forehead as the paramedics hurried up the steps. My one consolation, I thought as they began working on me, was that this little stunt should put Elliot away for a good, long time. Somehow, the fact that I'd broken his nose seemed very inconsequential at this moment.

❧

Three hours later, we were all back from the emergency room, except Elliot, of course, who was being kept in a guarded room at the hospital. His nose had been broken in a second place when Dorian tackled him. His right shoulder was strained—probably from when I shoved it away from me—and his right knee was swollen, though the doctors hadn't found any serious injuries in it. All in all, I thought, he'd best thank his lucky stars he was still alive.

Dorian and Barb were snuggled together on the sofa. His hand sported a bandage, and he'd fractured two fingers in the fight. My bandage was smaller; the bullet had only barely grazed my skin, but the abrasion burned. What really hurt, though, was the huge bruise right above my left breast and my left shoulder. The doctor said I'd torn a few ligaments in the fall. He gave me a shot of corticosteroids, prescribed some heavy-duty ibuprofen, and sent me home with instructions to rest for a few weeks. I'd be on my treadmill rather than weight training until it healed up.

Auntie was in the kitchen, fixing tea and cookies and whatever else she could think of, while Kyle leaned back in the recliner, looking as worn as I'd seen him in a long time.

I made myself comfortable in the rocking chair and leaned my head back against the cushion, wishing that I could start the evening over again.

"He's going to stay locked up this time, isn't he?" Barb asked. The phone call she'd taken just as Elliot barged through the door had been from Kyle, warning me that Elliot had managed to post bail. If he'd called five minutes earlier, or if Elliot had showed up five minutes later, none of this would have happened.

Kyle nodded. "I hope so. I can't believe he managed to scrape up bail money. This time we've got him, though. Attempted kidnapping, assault, unlawful possession of a handgun, possession of a stolen weapon, violation of parole . . . we'll be able to rack up the charges. I think Elliot's going to find himself in prison for a long time. My guess is he won't see the light of freedom for a good twenty years."

"Just keep an eye on him till he gets there. He's slippery," I said, frowning as I shifted in my seat. The moment I moved, pain shot through my shoulder, and I groaned.

"Will you sit still?" Barb said. She and Dorian hadn't said a cross word to one another all evening, and I had a feeling their feud was over. "You're going to hurt yourself again."

"I'm okay, honest." I stopped. "Well, I'm not, but I'm not going to die or anything like that." Turning cautiously, I asked Kyle, "So, on to our other big problem of the day. Any news about Lisa?"

He shook his head. "Nothing. She's been gone forty-eight hours now. The trail . . ." His words died away as he stared into the flames.

"The trail goes cold at forty-eight hours. I know," I said, feeling a mire of depression slipping over me. Thanksgiving my ass, this week was turning out to be one of the most painful in a long time. "How's Amy doing?"

"Not well. She expects me to be able to say, 'Oh, I know where Lisa is!' and run out and rescue her, but the truth is that we haven't got a clue. Lisa's ex-boyfriend, Shawn Johnson, was at the dance Saturday night. After the dance he and his girlfriend went out for drinks with two other couples—all easily verified. Lisa's current boyfriend is in the clear, too. He was waiting for her, and when she didn't show up, he thought she stood him up and went out to dinner with his roommates."

"Speaking of Lisa's ex-boyfriend," I said, "I talked to Karen, the sister of Yvonne Sanders. Yvonne went out with Shawn before he dumped her for Lisa. Karen said Yvonne is still pretty upset at Lisa and begged me not to tell Yvonne that she'd gone to Lisa for a makeover."

Kyle frowned. "Karen Sanders? You aren't talking about a tall girl, the plain type . . . are you? She wears overalls—"

"That's her," I said.

"I wouldn't put much stock in what she says." He accepted a cup of tea from Auntie as she set the tray down on the coffee table. "In fact, I'd be apt to think she's just looking for a little attention."

"Why?" I asked, taking a sip from the steaming cup that Auntie pressed into my hand. Celestial Seasonings' Lemon Zinger. The fruity flavor flowed down my throat, soothing my nerves.

Kyle bit into a gingersnap and licked his fingers. "Mmm, good. Thank you, Miss Florence."

Auntie smiled. "Anything to take the edge off, Kyle."

"And we appreciate it," he said, then continued. "Karen's quite a bit younger than you, I believe." He held up his hand when I started to laugh. "I kid you not. She looks in her late thirties, but she's only twenty-two or twenty-three. She grew up in Yvonne's shadow, and more than once she's been in to the station, telling us one outlandish tale or another. She's hungry for attention, and she'll do anything to keep you talking."

I'd wondered about that. As I thought back to our conversation, it made sense. She wasn't a drama queen out of vanity but out of loneliness. I suddenly felt the weight of the world descend on my shoulders. The pain and fear from Elliot's escapade, along with the worry over Lisa, all combined to knock me out with a one-two punch. I slumped back in my seat and let out a whimper.

Auntie was at my side in an instant. She immediately assessed my need for sleep and rest, and turned to Barbara. "Help me get her into the ground-floor guest room. She's exhausted, and I won't have her climbing the stairs tonight."

Dorian stood, motioning for Barb to stay back, and before I knew what was happening, he'd swept me up in his arms and carried me into the guest room as Auntie led the way. He didn't even seem to notice his injured hand.

I laughed, really starting to lose it. As he gently deposited me on the bed, I whispered, "You'd better start treating Barbara right and listen to her, or you're going to lose her. She's worth her weight in gold, you know."

He gave me a long look, and at that moment I could see what Barb saw in him. He was her protector, her guardian, her lover, and her companion. His eyes said it all. Dorian gave me a gentle nod.

"I know," he said. "I promise, I won't be such a stupid man ever in the future. Mama will stay at a hotel the rest of her visit. My wife will never be driven out of her home again."

I realized then that he understood how he truly could have lost Barb. Not just by her walking out on him, but during the standoff with Elliot. Elliot could have gone nuts and shot us all. He could have hurt Barbara or killed her, and then Dorian would never have forgiven himself.

Dorian's gaze told me all these things. I had the feeling that whatever problems lay ahead of the couple, they would work them out in a way that didn't require one person to stomp out of the house in order to make a point.

I started to tell him he was doing the right thing when the lights went out, and I slid into unconsciousness.

❧

When I woke, a rare glimpse of winter sun was glinting through the windows. Auntie was sitting by my side, watching me. I started to push myself up, but an ache a mile wide hit me in the shoulder, and I groaned, leaning back.

"Oh God, just don't ask me to stand up," I said. I'd no more spoken when I realized I had to go to the bathroom. "Well, hell. Auntie, can you help me up?"

"Of course, Imp." She helped me to my feet, and I shuffled into the bathroom and awkwardly fumbled my way through a bare basic routine. Toilet, brush teeth, wash face, stare at bloodshot eyes . . . yep . . . bare minimum. She tapped at the door, and I let her in.

"I need to change your bandage. They showed me how at the hospital. Sit down." As she prepared a strip of clean gauze and antibiotic spray, I eased my nightgown down over my shoulders. I didn't remember changing into it, so Auntie and Barb must have done it for me. My shoulder was stiff and hurt like hell, but not quite so much as I thought it might.

"I sure banged up my arm, didn't I?" I said, gingerly testing my range of movement.

Apparently Auntie thought I was trying to exercise it, because she scolded me. "Persia, you stop that! The doctor said you're to rest, and rest is what you're going to do. I don't want you ending up on the operating table. By the way," she added as she peeled away the bandage covering the abrasion on my shoulder, "there was a phone call for you this morning."

The tape holding the bandage on took a layer of skin with it when she pulled it off and I resisted the urge to yelp. "Who was it? And what time is it?"

"Candy Harrison. She said you left her a message. I told her you'd call back when you woke up," Auntie said and gently sprayed the bruised scrape with the antibiotic. The chill mist both hurt and soothed the stinging wound, and I wasn't sure whether to let out a sigh or an *ouch*. The abrasion hurt, but the bruising hurt worse. She fitted the new bandage over the top and taped it down. "It's nearly lunchtime. You slept deep."

"I wish I'd been awake to take her call." I cautiously stretched my neck. Damn, and I'd thought the fall from my exercise ball had left me stiff. This was ten times worse. "I ache. I can't sit still, or this is going to get worse before it gets better. I need a walk or something."

"After breakfast," Auntie said. "You need to take a hot bath first, and then you need to eat." She paused, then added, "Kyle called. There's still no sign of Lisa, so they're notifying the papers and putting flyers up. And he told me that Elliot's due in court this afternoon for the judge to set bail. Do you think he'll be able to pay it again?"

I shook my head. "Doubt it. This was a lot more serious. But he had been able to before, so I tempered my prediction. "At least I hope not."

While I eased myself into the bathtub in the downstairs bath, trying to keep my bandage from getting wet, Auntie went up to my room to get me some clothes. I stretched back in the tub, wondering if my talk with Candy would reveal anything helpful. I scrubbed myself with a bath puff and some rose-scented bath gel as my mind fluttered from thoughts of Lisa to thoughts of Elliot. How did I manage to get involved with so many troubled people? For once, I thought with a loud sigh, why couldn't things just run like clockwork?

As I steadied myself and stepped out of the tub, Auntie came in carrying a chocolate brown broomstick skirt and a loose red peasant top that I usually wore in the summer. It wouldn't constrict my movement or bind my shoulder, and if the abrasion oozed a little blood, it wouldn't show against the crimson color. My bra was more problematic, but there was no way I could go without one. My breasts were too big to be comfortable without support, and I had no desire to incur any more havoc than gravity had already wreaked on my boobs.

But Auntie brought me my front-hook sports bra, so I could easily slide it on like a blouse. Finally, I stepped into my skirt and pulled it up over my hips.

"This sucks. I don't have time to be incapacitated," I complained.

"Give yourself time to heal, or you'll be laid up longer than a month. Just take it easy and let people help you, Persia." Auntie hit on my sore spot, and she knew it.

"I don't like being vulnerable. Look at what it got me!" I followed her into the kitchen, where she opened the refrigerator and brought out the yogurt to go with the granola.

"Don't be so hasty, Imp. You'll heal, but you have to let your body pace itself. You're in good shape, so the healing process should be quicker for you than for some people. Just give it time, and don't rush it. Now, eat your breakfast." She poured my cereal and took the top off my yogurt.

"Auntie," I said after a few bites, "last night I thought Elliot was going to kill me. He had a look in his eye I've never seen before. He's gone around the bend." I paused, trying to find the right words. "I thought about what you said—about me buying a gun. Even if I'd had one, it wouldn't have done me any good. I couldn't have gotten to it soon enough. I can't wear it twenty-four/seven—that would be ridiculous. And if I did own one . . . I might have killed him. I was so angry and so frightened."

She nodded. "You know yourself best, Imp, and I respect your decision. You know," she added, "when Keola was murdered I went through a period where it was hard for me to leave the house. Once I moved back to the mainland, I cloistered myself in the penthouse I rented at a hotel in Seattle and stayed there for months. I ordered everything via delivery. The shock took a toll on me, and it took me a long time to get over it. I don't want that to happen to you. I know you've had a scare, so if there's anything you need, anybody you want to talk to, just let me know."

I pushed my chair back and wandered over to the windows that overlooked the ocean. The light was all silvery as the clouds kissed the water, and it was hard to discern where the water left off and the sky took over. As I stared at the waves that were foaming on the beach, my thoughts ran to Lisa again. *Where are you?* I thought. *Where did you go?*

The phone rang, and Auntie held it out. "Candy Harrison," she mouthed.

I took the receiver and said, "Hello? This is Persia."

"Persia, I got your message. Did I leave something at

Venus Envy when I was there?" Her voice conjured up images of a vacuous bleached blonde. Marilyn Monroe, only
a dumb and cheap parody.

"No, nothing like that. I wondered if you could meet
me for coffee or something? I'd like to talk to you about
our beautician, Lisa."

There was a brief pause, then she said, "Okay. Well, I
guess I could fit in a coffee break this afternoon. But
I don't know what I can tell you. I barely know the girl. I
just came in for a makeover."

We agreed to meet at two PM, and I hung up. Auntie
looked at me quizzically. I frowned. "Do you know anything about Candy Harrison? She's been in at least once
for a makeover."

Auntie cocked her head. "Her name sounds familiar.
Let me think a moment . . ." As she rinsed the dishes and
put them into the dishwasher, she stopped and snapped her
fingers. "I know! She's Annabel Mason's private nurse.
You know—the woman who chairs the Thanksgiving
Gala."

"Really?" I glanced at the clock. "I think I'll give Amy
a call. She's probably a nervous wreck by now." I had no
sooner dialed the number when Amy picked up. She was
sobbing.

"Oh Persia, Kyle just called. Somebody found a body.
Kyle's on his way. He thinks it might be Lisa. Can you
come over? I can't be alone right now, and I have to go
identify the body."

I stared at the phone. The day wasn't going to get any
better, was it? "I'll be right there," I said and hung up. It
was then that I remembered I didn't have a car; mine was
in the shop, its windshield shattered.

"Auntie, I need to go over to Lisa's right now. Can I
take the truck?" Auntie had a small Mazda pickup that she
used when she needed to haul something home like a
piece of furniture.

"Bad news?" she asked, pulling the key off the Peg Board.

Then she stopped and tossed the keys on the counter. "I just remembered. Trevor told me the truck needs brake work; it's too dangerous to drive."

I slumped. "Maybe bad news. And damn it, I didn't know the truck was out of commission."

She gathered her purse and jacket. "Get your things. I'll drive you over, then I'll go rent a car for you to use while yours is being worked on."

We headed out to Baby, Auntie making sure the doors were locked. Trevor came running up to the car as we were getting in. He leaned down to poke his head through my window.

"I just heard what happened. Persia, are you okay?"

I'd never seen Trevor look quite so worried. He was our main gardener and kept the gardens and acreage going. Lately, he'd been nursing hundreds of new rosebushes. We'd had to lay out almost twenty thousand dollars—or rather, Auntie had laid it out—to replace the entire rose garden we lost thanks to Bebe's sabotage. Trev was determined to make sure they were healthy and blooming by next year, even if we wouldn't have enough petals to gather for making the rose water that was so popular at Venus Envy. Trevor figured it would take two years before our new roses were up and running enough for us to make use of them.

"Well, I've been better," I said, wincing as I slid into my seat.

He shook his head. "That bites. If you need anything, let me know."

I gave him a little wave, and we took off. As we wound around the bend, I pulled out my cell phone and made a quick call to Kyle.

"I heard about the body. I'm on my way to Amy's now. She asked me to come over. Kyle, make damn sure that it's her. Don't assume, because I'm sure you're wrong."

"Persia, I have no idea if it's her. I've met Lisa a few times, but people look different when they're dead. And I didn't know the girl all that well. We can't match this woman's fingerprints to any records, and according to Amy, Lisa's never been arrested. If it's not her, then we'll start the long process of putting drawings in the newspaper and on TV. But it's better that we eliminate—or confirm—whether we have Lisa in that morgue before we go to all that trouble. And to do that, Amy has to come in to see if she can identify the body. If it's not Lisa, then she can rest a little easier. I'll pick her—both of you—up in about a half hour. How are you, by the way?"

"Okay," I said, hesitating. "Actually, pretty sore. My shoulder really got bludgeoned. By the way . . . speaking of psychos, I wanted to make sure Elliot's still in jail." I tried to sound lighthearted. "You haven't let him out, have you?"

Kyle's voice was soft when he said, "He's safely locked up. Persia, he goes in for a bail hearing today. The prosecuting attorney is recommending he not be remanded on bail. The DA is asking for five thousand dollars, but I guarantee he'll never get out that easy."

"When will he be in court?" I asked. "I want to be there."

"Not a good idea. I tell you what, I'll go down to the court this afternoon and call you the minute the judge sets bail. Will you let me do this for you?"

I paused. I had to meet Candy anyway. And the truth was, I really didn't want to see Elliot. Strike that. I wanted to see him tied to a pole, covered in honey, and skewered on an anthill.

"Thanks, Kyle. I appreciate it," I said. Maybe Auntie was right. Maybe I had to let people help me out once in awhile, instead of always being the one with the answers. I wasn't sure I liked it. The thought of accepting help scared me, and if I was honest, it hurt my ego. But then again, weren't growing pains supposed to hurt a little bit?

Auntie glanced at me as she turned onto Driftwood Lane. "You did a good thing, Persia. Sometimes, you have to let go." She pulled up in front of Amy and Lisa's house. "Here we are. I'd stay, but I'd better get you a rental car. I'll be back in an hour or so."

As I walked toward the door, I wondered just what the hell I was going to say to Amy. She opened the door, her face puffy and covered with tears, and I realized that more than anything she just needed a friend to sit with her. To be there and not to try to fix anything. I held out my good arm and, wrapping it around her shoulders, we turned and walked into the living room.

Chapter Ten

Amy's face was stained with tears and mascara drips, and she looked so fragile that I wanted to pull her into my arms and hold her safe, but my shoulder hurt too much for that, so I just gave her a squeeze as we walked into the kitchen.

"Kyle isn't sure it's her. He hasn't seen . . . her, so don't assume. Just wait until we know for certain." We sat down at the table where I pushed aside a box half full of tissues, a cup of cold coffee, and a half-eaten doughnut. "Is this all you've had to eat this morning?" I asked.

She shrugged. "I can't eat. Not now. What if it's her? What if we were wrong, and she did drown?"

Then we were both off base, I thought, but I didn't say anything. I pushed myself up from the table and cleared away her coffee cup and leftover pastry and put the kettle on for tea. There was a box of orange spice tea on the counter, and I poked around in the cupboards until I found two mugs and dropped tea bags into them, filling them with the steaming water. As the scent of orange peel and cinnamon filled the air, I opened her refrigerator and found a cup of yogurt and sat it in front of her with a spoon.

"This will be easy on your stomach. You need some protein. Try to eat a few spoonfuls, would you?"

She fretted but took the cover off and, glancing at me with a puzzled look, slowly began to eat. "What happened to you, Persia? You're hurt."

"Yeah, I got winged by a bullet last night. Apparently my ex-boyfriend decided making my life miserable just wasn't payback enough for the fact that I dumped him when he got busted and sent to prison for awhile. He showed up at the house with a revolver and a grudge."

I gingerly pulled the shoulder of my shirt down just enough to show her the bruise and bandage. She gasped.

"He's in jail, and I'm incapacitated. Auntie's off to the rental place to rent me a car, because Elliot also smashed up my windshield, as well as one of the shopwindows yesterday. I guess being hauled in by Kyle for vandalism pissed him off because that was when he brainstormed this little charade."

"I'm so sorry I bothered you," Amy said, paling even further. "I didn't know, or I wouldn't have asked you to come over—"

"Nonsense," I said, giving her a slow smile. "Your sister is my friend, and I care about what happens to her. And I honestly believe she's still alive somewhere. But on the off chance we're wrong about that, I want to be here for support."

Amy managed a small smile as she stood to answer a knock at the door. It was Kyle, come to take us to the morgue. I followed him as he wrapped his arm around Amy and led her out to the squad car. We both clambered in the back. It hadn't even been twenty-four hours since I'd been sitting in the back of this same car, cuffed for breaking Elliot's nose. So much had gone on since then.

We rode in silence as Kyle sedately drove through the

streets and pulled into the hospital parking garage. We took the elevator to the lower level, Amy, clutching her bag white-knuckled, had a look of pure terror on her face. I scooted next to her and put my arm around her shoulder and squeezed. She gave me a grateful look, and we silently stepped out of the elevator car and followed Kyle down the hall.

The doors to the morgue were gray metal, leading into a large room that was chill to the point of cold. A row of what looked like small, square lockers was built into one wall. No doubt to hold bodies, I thought. The room was lined with counters and cupboards, sterile white with an off tinge of blue. Blue was supposed to be peaceful, but here it just made the room seem a lot colder.

Covering the counter space were jars filled with strange-looking objects—I didn't want to know what—and sparkling clean surgical instruments lined up on a tray and files and charts. The air in the morgue felt muffled, like being inside during a heavy snowstorm—set apart from the rest of the world and immune to the noise and bustle going on outside of the doors.

Amy swayed, and I was glad I'd gotten her to eat something. I buoyed her up, sliding my good arm through hers to give her extra support. Kyle motioned to the technician, who was clad in a mint green lab coat and a pair of white scrubs. He blinked, then gestured for us to follow him over to one of the cloth-draped tables. By the looks of the shape under the cloth, it was obviously somebody's temporary resting place.

The figure beneath the sheet was still as ice, not a flutter of material from breath or heartbeat. The sheet was pristine, clean beyond bleaching, and I realized then that although I'd seen dead bodies a few times before, I'd seen them where they fell, not in this state—under observation, irrefutably dead.

Amy steeled herself, her body going rigid next to mine as the tech asked softly, "Are you ready?"

Kyle moved to flank her other side, and I saw that his arm was linked through her other arm. Together, we'd catch her if necessary. She held her breath, nodding, and the technician drew back the sheet.

The woman was about Lisa's age, with blonde hair in a similar hairstyle, but she wasn't Lisa. Even I could see that, although her face had been battered by rocks and waves. Her eyes were glassy, vacant, and I relaxed, wondering who the poor soul had been. She would remain a mystery for awhile longer.

Amy let out a sharp breath, almost swooning as she shook her head. Her voice trembled with both joy and tears as she said, "No, that's not her—that's not my Lisa."

I nodded to Kyle. "She's right, that isn't Lisa."

He motioned, and the tech covered the body again as we turned away. "I'm so sorry to bring you down here, Amy. You, too, Persia, but we had to make certain, and to be honest, I wasn't sure. I didn't want to make a mistake. We don't have any fingerprints on record for whoever this is, and nobody's been reported missing that's around this age except for . . . Lisa."

"I understand," Amy said, her face a blend of rapture and sorrow. "But what happened to this woman? Did she drown?"

"Looks that way, but as I said, we don't know who she is," Kyle said. "She was found up the coastline a little, but the currents have been strong, and we thought . . ."

"You thought that Lisa might have fallen in, and her body was swept up the coast," I said, trying to be of help. "Well, you'd better start putting out notices that you have an unidentified drowning victim."

"Yeah," Kyle said. "I'll call in a sketch artist today to get started, and we'll notify the papers and news stations."

We exited the hospital, and Kyle drove us back to Amy's. "I'm just going to drop you girls off, because it's almost time for Elliot's bail bond hearing. I promised Persia I'd be there," he added, speaking to Amy.

I swallowed hard. "Don't let the judge free him, Kyle, because—if there is a next time—I won't hesitate to do whatever I need to in order to protect myself. You understand what I'm saying?"

He nodded. "I'll do what I can, Persia," he said. And yet, I heard an inflection in his voice that told me he couldn't make any promises. We climbed out of the car and headed for the door. Auntie wasn't back yet, so I followed Amy inside. She washed her face and opened the cupboard.

"I'm ravenous all of a sudden. Lisa's not dead . . . or at least, we have more hope than we did an hour ago," she said, her voice faltering. "Two people couldn't drown in the same storm, could they? You don't think that she was with a friend and they were both swept off the pier?"

I shook my head. "No, not really. I suppose it could happen, but remember that your sister was terrified of water. She wouldn't be out there walking, especially on a stormy night. Now, fix yourself something to eat."

She nodded, slowly pulling out a can of soup. "Would you like some chicken noodle soup? It's Olianto's." Olianto was a new brand that had recently come out; excellent organic products that truly tasted like they were homemade.

"I'd love some," I said, feeling hungry, too. Nothing like looking death in the face to make you appreciate being alive. And life meant sustenance, which meant food. Amy opened the can and poured it in a saucepan, then set it to heating while she found the dinner rolls and popped four in the microwave. I asked her where the bowls and saucers were, and set the table.

As we ate the steaming soup and warm rolls, I told Lisa I was meeting with Candy Harrison, and that she'd been the last woman to get a makeover from Lisa on Friday. Amy looked surprised.

"Candy? I can't believe Lisa would give her a makeover," she said.

"Why? Candy sounded like a bubblehead, but I didn't get the impression she was bitchy."

Amy blinked. "Don't you know who Candy is?"

"A nurse, my aunt told me. She works for Annabel Mason." At Amy's snort, I frowned. "What? What am I missing?"

"Candy worked for our father before he died. She was his private nurse during his last months. I'm not a big fan of hers—God knows she's annoying, but she does seem to know her job. But Lisa took an instant dislike to her for some reason. I'm surprised she even agreed to stay in the same room with Candy."

I put down my spoon. Now, this was an interesting turn of events and the first potential lead we'd had. "Are you sure? How odd. Candy told me she barely knew Lisa."

"Oh, she knew her all right. I ran interference. I'm not sure just why Lisa disliked her so much. Lisa likes almost everybody, so it was a shock when she was so rude to Candy. Let me know what she says," she added, picking up her spoon again. "I can't imagine it was a good meeting."

As I was wondering just what to think about the matter, a noise interrupted my thoughts. Amy peeked out the window. "Your aunt's here, and there's another car behind her."

I bustled outside to find Auntie standing near Baby, while a young man in a suit climbed out of the driver's seat of a brand-new dark silver Acura RL. He handed me the keys, and I saw a temporary license plate taped in the back window.

"Auntie—" I started to say, but she beamed.

"I know your car was getting old, and since we're almost at the end of the year, this was on sale. So, happy early birthday, my girl. You mentioned wanting to get one of these." The look on her face was priceless, and I rushed over to give her a hug, grimacing when I got a little too happy and hit my shoulder against her.

"Oh, Auntie! I love it—it's wonderful, and the color I wanted, too!" I skirted the car, beaming. No more convertible, but no more chancing rain or breaking down as often, either.

"What about Lisa?" she asked, interrupting my thoughts as she handed me the new insurance papers.

Amy answered for me. "It wasn't Lisa they found, so we're back to square one." She looked at me, though, and I knew she was thinking about our conversation about Candy. Maybe the nurse would be able to shed some light. Maybe Lisa had gotten in a huff and took off over something they argued about.

"I'm glad to hear that, my girl," Auntie said. "I was so worried when Persia told me. We'll find her yet. You just wait and see."

"I want to believe that," Amy said faintly. "I have to believe that. Persia, are you going to finish lunch with me?"

I glanced at the car. It would be here when I finished eating. "Yeah, I want to ask you some more about Candy." I turned to Auntie. "Thank you again, Auntie, it's perfect. The perfect gift! I never expected this."

She smiled then, a broad, infectious grin. "I know, Imp. I know. That's why I love buying things for you. You never *assume* I should get you anything, so it's always fun to see your face. Now, finish what you have to do, and be careful when you drive. With your arm sore, your reflexes will be slow. Just take it easy and promise me you'll be careful."

I promised and headed back inside with Amy as Auntie climbed into her Baby and drove the salesman back to the lot.

⋖•

After I finished eating, I spent a few minutes familiarizing myself with the inside of my new car. Auntie had gotten it registered for me, there was a bottle of water in the cup holder, a jack and spare tire in the trunk, and assorted goodies in the glove compartment. I glanced at the clock. Time to head out to meet Candy.

The coffee shop where we'd agreed to meet was almost full, but it was easy enough to pick her out in the crowd. She looked just like she'd sounded on the phone. Platinum bleached blonde hair pulled back in a puffy ponytail with little-girl bangs covering her brow, a figure that had been either enhanced or treated to the finest uplift support system in the world, fringed lashes reminiscent of Tammy Faye Baker, and garish red lipstick that didn't suit her coloring at all. She should have used a peach or a dusty rose.

What didn't match were her clothes. She was wearing a linen sheath that had to have come out of a Seattle boutique, and she was wearing Jazmin Royz, an expensive perfume that was only available in a few specialty shops throughout the U.S. Made with real jasmine oil, the perfume cost over three hundred dollars per quarter ounce and was made in limited quantities. And she was wearing the actual perfume. Jazmin Royz didn't come in an eau de toilette spray.

She eyed me as I sat down, little in the way of friendliness in her eyes.

"Persia," she said, looking me up and down with an appraising eye. It wasn't a question. She blinked, and I had the sudden desire to swat her because her eyelashes reminded me of a centipede.

I nodded. "Candy? I wanted—"

"I know, you wanted to ask me about Lisa Tremont. First, you should know that I used to work for her father. And second, you should know she doesn't like me very much." Candy spilled everything out in a whirl of words.

My turn to blink. "Oh?" I wondered if she remembered she'd told me she barely knew who Lisa was. I decided not to say anything and just hear her out; if she thought I suspected her of lying, she might be more cautious about saying anything. "May I ask why?"

Candy preened. "A lot of women are jealous of me.

Maybe she thought her daddy liked me more than he liked her."

The way she said *daddy* made me cringe. I stared at the woman, wondering just what it took to inflate an ego to that size, because regardless of what she thought, Candy was no sex goddess.

"And why would she think that?" I asked softly. There was something off-putting about the woman, and I couldn't put my finger on it, other than I found her coarse and cheap despite the clothes and perfume, like a rhinestone set in twenty-four-karat gold.

She darted a glance at the clock. "Oh, no reason. You know how some girls get around beautiful women. They're insecure over everything."

I leaned back in my chair, staring at her, wondering what the hell was going on in her head. Candy gave me a superficial smile.

"So what did you want to know about Lisa?"

"First, why did you go to her for a makeover, knowing she didn't like you?" Something was out of place, and I wanted to know what.

"Because she's the best on the island. Even if we don't get along very well, business is business. And I wanted to look good for a date Friday night." She shrugged. "Besides, Lisa needed the money."

"Did Lisa say anything about what she was going to do this weekend? Anything about plans she might have made?" I was pretty sure I was talking up a dead-end alley, and it didn't take long to prove me right.

"I wasn't really paying much attention. I was just there to get my makeup done, and that's all. She did my face, I paid her, that's it. After all, we aren't exactly the best of friends." She stood up, gathering her purse. "I have to get going. Nice meeting you," she said.

As I watched her sashay out of the door, I wondered just what kind of man would date Candy Harrison. Whoever it was, I didn't think I'd like him.

۰ِ

When I walked into the police station, I caught Kyle as he was eating a sandwich. I fingered the dieffenbachia that was sitting on a low table.

"A little late for lunch, isn't it? And if you don't repot this plant, it's going to die. I bet you haven't put it in a different container since you bought it, have you?" The poor thing was root-bound, four feet high and trying to grow.

"I didn't get a chance to eat because I was at Elliot's bail hearing, and I don't know anything about taking care of the plant. Shanna waters them. I'll leave a note for her. How tall will that thing get, anyway?" He put down his BLT and wiped his fingers on a napkin.

"As tall as the ceiling, and then you'll have to prune it. Just don't let anybody chew on it. This is a dumb cane. Also known as a mother-in-law's plant." I grinned.

"What happens if I eat it?" he said, sounding genuinely curious.

"Your throat and tongue will start to burn, you won't be able to talk, and if you get enough of the toxins, you'll die because your throat will be so swollen that you won't be able to breathe. So graze on something else if you get hungry," I said as I sat down and crossed my legs. "Okay, tell me, what did the Albatross get for bail? And can I send him a leaf or two of your plant to add to his salad?"

He raised his eyebrows and took a sip of his Coke. "I'm going to overlook that last comment. Elliot was assigned a two-hundred-thousand-dollar bail. Unless he comes up with twenty thousand from a bail bondsman, or finds somebody who'll take a chance on him, then he's stuck. So quit worrying." As he pulled out a bag of chips, my stomach rumbled. "He'll be transferred back here from the courthouse later on this afternoon. We're short on men this afternoon, so they're holding all the prisoners there until court recesses for the day."

"Can I have a few of those?" I asked, pointing to his chips.

He poured a handful on his napkin and passed me the rest of the bag.

"I talked to Candy Harrison today. She was the last of Lisa's appointments on Friday. Something's strange about that girl, Kyle. I don't trust her, and I don't like her."

"Why not? And who the hell is she?"

I gave him a rundown of my encounter with her. "Can you check to see if she has any sort of record? Yvonne Sanders, too. I think Karen was making a mountain out of a molehill, but you never know."

Kyle licked his fingers, dried them on his napkin, and jotted down a couple of notes. "Sure thing. I'll call you this evening with the information. Amy and I'll be out putting up posters about Lisa. It's time we went fully public. She wanted to earlier, but I thought for sure Lisa would be home by now. I'm still convinced . . ." He shook his head. "Never mind. Listen, where did you go to get your windshield repaired so fast? My truck got a ding in the windshield, and it's turned into a crack. I need to get it fixed."

I shrugged. "I didn't. My Sebring is still in the shop. Auntie bought me an early birthday present. I'm now driving an Acura RL—the one I had my heart set on buying next year. I'm going to get the windshield fixed on the Sebring and sell it."

With a cough, Kyle said, "Can you ask your aunt to adopt me? I'd like a new car, too." He grinned. "Miss Florence has a heart of gold, and you two seem like you're getting on fine. I'm glad for you, Persia. And I'm glad for her. I think she missed having you around, but she cared about your independence too much to say so. This is better, having you back in Gull Harbor."

For a moment, I was worried that he was going to start up again about wanting to date me, but the look in his eye was friendly rather than romantic, and I relaxed. "It's been good for me, too. I adore my aunt, and I can always zip over to Seattle on the ferry if I want to spend some time in the city. And . . . I wouldn't have met Killian if I hadn't come back. Hey, he got the funding for his new company!" I beamed, wanting to tell somebody besides Barb.

And Kyle didn't let me down. "Good deal," he said. "Good for him! That Wilcox woman sure did her share of damage, didn't she?"

I nodded. "Yeah, she did. Okay, I'm going to get moving. My arm's hurting, and I think I'll go home and rest. Call me with what you find out about Candy and Yvonne."

As I left, Kyle was busy organizing his desk. I happened to glance at one of the picture frames on the bookshelf behind him that looked new. Amy's smiling face shone out from the silver frame, and I let out a contented sigh. Kyle had finally found someone, and I hoped for his sake that it lasted a long, long time.

*

Auntie had gone in to work by the time I got home, and I puttered around the house, straightening up the kitchen and clearing out clutter in the living room. We needed a housekeeper, that was for sure. I should just call Maids Are Us and have them send somebody over.

As I wiped down the shelves and plants, Nalu came up and rubbed against my legs, and I tickled him with the Swiffer duster. He batted at it a couple of times, then sauntered off to find a cozy place for a nap. I settled myself at the dining room table with a notepad, pen, and Lisa's appointment book. Time to make a list of her appointments on Saturday and talk to them.

I jotted down names and phone numbers until the sound of a wash of rain against the floor-to-ceiling windows startled me. I glanced outside. The clouds had thickened; they were dark and pregnant with rain, looming over the ocean as they made their way across Port Samanish Island. Thanksgiving would be wet and gloomy, as usual.

I finished my list and started another, this one of chores

we needed to finish before Thursday, which was Thanksgiving. Clean the bathrooms, pick up the turkey—which we'd ordered fresh rather than frozen—make the pumpkin pies, buy dinner rolls from Barbara's bakery, make the cranberry sauce. Since Auntie always decorated for Christmas the day after Thanksgiving, we'd haul out the decorations and have them ready to go.

While I was thinking about Christmas, I put in a call to Sawyer Jefferson, who owned a tree farm on the other side of the island. Auntie used artificial trees, but she bought fresh swags and wreaths. I ordered one hundred feet of evergreen swags and three huge wreaths. While I was thinking about the holidays, I called the butcher and ordered a standing rib roast for Christmas, along with a large goose.

As I hung up, the doorbell rang, and I followed a barking Pete to the door. Bran Stanton was leaning against the doorjamb.

"Hey, come in!" I hadn't seen Bran in over a month, though we expected to see both him and his sister Daphne for Thanksgiving. Bran and I'd been an item earlier in the year, until I met Killian. We'd kept our relationship light, though, and had remained friends with no animosity or ill will.

He kissed me on the cheek and sauntered into the room, lanky as usual, with his long ponytail neatly held back by a coated rubber band. Pete barked loudly and sniffed at his pocket. Bran had been in the habit of bringing over dog treats when we were going out, and apparently he hadn't forgotten his furry friends, because he pulled out three Milk Bones and whistled. Beauty and Beast raced in, and he handed out treats to three very happy campers.

"What's up?" I said. "Do you want some tea or coffee? Something to eat?"

"I'd love some juice, if you have it, and something sweet. I'm giving up coffee for awhile." He followed me into the kitchen as I poured the juice and fixed a plate of assorted cookies.

"Giving up coffee? Did hell freeze over?" I grinned at him and motioned for him to carry the tray into the living room. We settled on the sofa, on either side of a snoring Buttercup. Bran petted her for a moment, eying me as I winced and reached for my shoulder, which chose that moment to twinge with a vengeance.

"Are you okay? You look like you're in pain."

I cleared my throat. "Uh . . . yeah, kind of. Actually, I got winged by a bullet and fell over one of the chairs on the porch. Tore a few ligaments, nasty bruise, bad abrasion. The usual," I said, grinning.

"Bullet?" His face was deadpan, but I could tell he was bursting to ask what happened. "Who, might I ask, was on the other end of the gun?"

"Elliot." I filled him in on everything that had happened over the past few days. "Kyle and Amy are putting up posters about Lisa this afternoon, but he's convinced she drowned."

Bran frowned and leaned back, closing his eyes. He was the town's urban shaman, and more than once had come up with accurate information through whatever psychic channels he frequented. I fully believed in his powers, though I didn't know how they worked. Auntie had been disappointed when Bran and I broke up, until she got to know Killian. Now she was happy they were both in my life, even though Bran was just a friend now.

"I don't think she's dead, Persia. I just don't get that sense, for what it's worth." He shrugged. "All I can see is silver . . . something about silver . . . that's it. So your friend is missing and your ex tried to kill you? Sounds run of the mill for your life," he said with a small grin. I smacked his arm with my good hand, and he caught it, bringing it to his lips. He kissed it lightly, then let go. "I can't say that I don't miss being with you, Persia. You're delightful, you know, and I wish Killian didn't object to sharing. But I'm glad you're happy. Victoria and I set our relationship aside for awhile."

I frowned. He and Victoria had been having an on-again, off-again affair for years. I'd known about her from the beginning, but Bran had focused on me while we were together. That they would set aside their relationship when there was nobody else in the picture seemed odd.

"What happened? Did she meet somebody else? Did you?" I folded my legs in the lotus position, wincing. Between my exercise ball breaking and Elliot's little adventure, I was stiff as a board. I'd need to stretch out before bed if I didn't want to get any worse.

"No, that's why I came to talk to you. I won't be here for Thanksgiving. Daphne will, though. And it also explains why I'm giving up coffee."

Curious now, I leaned forward. "What are you up to, Bran Stanton?"

He burst out into a hearty laugh. "Believe it or not, I've been chosen as a contestant for *Castaway: Amazon Adventure*. I fly out tomorrow to the Amazon to try to win a million bucks!"

Speechless, I could only stare. Part of me envied him, part of me wanted to smack him for not confiding in me sooner. I was about to say something when the phone rang.

"Persia," Kyle's voice came crackling over the line. "I've got some bad news."

"Is Auntie okay? Did you find Lisa?" My words tumbled out one over another as I froze, scared to hear his answer.

"No, no . . . Miss Florence is fine as far as I know, and we haven't heard a word about Lisa. No, this has to do with Elliot." He sounded like he was dragging each word out with a pair of pliers.

"Just tell me. What the hell happened? Did they lower his bail? Did he manage to make bail?" I held my breath, waiting.

Kyle cleared his throat. "Uh . . . no, and no. The thing is . . . well . . . see . . . Persia . . . Oh hell, I'll just come out and say it. Elliot managed to escape when we were transferring him back to the jail from the courthouse. He's on the loose, along with a couple of other prisoners, and we have no idea as to where any of them are."

Chapter Eleven

⋙ ⋘

I dropped the phone with a little cry. Bran leaned forward, concerned, as I scrambled for the receiver.

"Persia? Are you okay?" he asked.

I shook my head, holding up one finger. "Kyle? You still there? Sorry, I dropped the phone. Please tell me this is a bad joke," I said, even though I knew he'd never joke about something as serious as this. Kyle wasn't a prankster, and he wasn't a sadist, either.

"I'm sorry, Persia. I don't know how this happened. Officers Dryer and Reed were taking three men, including Elliot, out to their prowl cars. One of the men pretended to trip. When Dryer reached down to pull him to his feet, he managed to get hold of her gun and took her hostage. The men forced Reed to unlock their cuffs, then cuffed both Dryer and Reed to the outside of the car and gagged them. Then they all took off." Kyle sounded like he was strangling.

I stared at Bran, just shaking my head. "How on earth . . . how did he get hold of her gun? Why didn't you have more than just two officers there, since there were three prisoners?"

"Remember, I told you about the budget cuts? We're overextended, and we just don't have enough manpower." Kyle was terser than I'd heard him in a long time. I had the feeling he was embarrassed as well as worried.

"Well, did those men take your officers' guns?"

Another sigh. "Yeah. Elliot could be armed. Persia, be careful. Do you want somebody out there keeping watch? I'll assign someone, the budget be damned."

"No, you just keep everybody looking for them. I'll make sure my doors are locked and get Trevor out here with his dog to patrol the acreage. Auntie's going to be pissed royal over this one, so you'd better expect a row."

Kyle let out a garbled yelp. "I hadn't thought about that. You're right. I'm about to feed the TV station a bulletin to run as breaking news. Maybe somebody will spot Elliot and call in."

"Good idea. Who else escaped? Were they all dangerous?"

"Yeah," he said, breathing softly into the phone. "One of them, at least. One's a burglar, so I doubt if he's much of a threat to the public. The other though . . . he's a serial rapist. We've got to catch him before he leaves the island."

"Christ, Kyle. That's bad," I said, staring at Bran. With a sigh, I said, "I guess this means you won't have a chance to find out anything about Candy or Yvonne?"

"Already checked our files. No local records for either one, but I can't guarantee that means anything outside of Gull Harbor. And I sure don't have time to focus on that now, with this mess that's come up. Stay safe, Persia. I'll talk to you in a little while." He hung up, and I stared at the phone as the dial tone buzzed in my ear.

"Great. Just great." I was one degree below boiling.

Bran tapped me on the knee. "What happened?"

I looked at him, thinking that if I told him Elliot was on the loose, he might volunteer to stay and stand watch. But that would put a crimp in his plans, and how many chances would one be given to be on a TV reality show? I bit my lip, wavering. Finally, I just shook my head.

"Nothing I can't take care of."

"There was talk of guns?" Bran prodded.

"Yes, but nothing to get worked up over. I'm just still tense from the past few days. Nothing to worry over. Hold on a minute," I said, unfolding myself from the sofa and hurrying to the door. I peeked outside, but there was nobody in sight, so I hurried down to my car and made sure all my doors were locked. Trevor was riding by in one of the little carts Auntie had bought for him and our part-time gardener, Sarah, to make their jobs a little easier.

"Trev!" I waved him over. He started to ask how I was, but I brushed away his question. "This is important—listen to me. Elliot escaped. He probably has a gun, and nobody knows where he is. The cops are looking for him, but until they find him, will you keep an eye out? If you see him, don't engage him or put yourself in any danger, just call Kyle immediately. Understand? And then call me on my cell phone or the house phone."

"Oh shit, that's not good." Trev was earnest, if he was anything.

I gave him a soft smile. "No, Trev, it's not good. I only hope that things get better before they get worse. I'm going to make sure all the house doors are locked. You take your keys with you, and lock all sheds when you go in or out. Tell Sarah to do the same. We don't want him hiding in one of our outbuildings."

"Will do, and I'll bring Kali with me tomorrow." Kali was a huge hunk of dog flesh who was a lovely girl but trained as a guard dog. "I'll give the outbuildings a thorough check and lockdown before doing anything else this afternoon. And Persia, I'll carry my baseball bat with me." Trevor kept a baseball bat in his truck for trouble.

"Good deal," I said, though the thought ran through my head that a bat wasn't much good going up against a gun.

I headed back to the house, locking the front and side doors. Then, hurrying into the kitchen, I bolted the back door and the sliding glass doors out to the deck. While it was unlikely that Elliot could manage to climb up onto the deck that overlooked part of the backyard, better safe than sorry.

After I finished, I called Auntie at work and told her what had happened. She was, as I had expected, outraged.

"I can't believe they screwed up like that! If it's all because of a lack of funding, I'll light this town on fire so fast that the city council won't see me coming. Maybe it's time I ran for office. Nothing gets done around here until somebody gets hurt, and only then do they decide to make changes. It was that way when we were trying to raise money for a local hospital ten years ago, and it's still that way. I'm going to contact Winthrop and ask him what it would take for me to run in the next election."

I grinned. Auntie on the city council. Now, there was a thought, and she could probably do it, too. She had more spark than a live wire, and whatever she wanted, she usually got. I'd gotten my sense of drive and ambition from her, and if I was half as active as she was by the time I was her age, I'd count myself lucky. I glanced back in the living room. Bran was reading a magazine.

"Bran came over to visit. I'm going to go talk to him for awhile because he's leaving and won't be back for several months. I'll tell you about it tonight."

"Imp, you make sure the doors are locked tight," she said.

"Already done."

"Listen to me, girl. Go into my den. In the hutch next to the Renoir print, you'll find a china teacup with a key in it. That key opens the lower left drawer in the credenza. There's a pistol in there, and ammunition. I want you to go load it and keep it with you."

I gulped. Auntie had a gun? That was a new one to me. "I just hope to hell I don't have to use it."

"We can only hope. But if Elliot breaks in, you don't want him killing you before you can put up a fight. Carry it with you around the house." She sounded so confident that I almost gave in, but then my common sense came crashing back.

"Auntie, I don't want to wear a gun around the house. Any number of accidents could happen, and none of them are pleasant to think about."

"Persia, sometimes life isn't fair, and it's not always fun. Deal with it."

Finally, to quiet her down I agreed to at least find the gun and put it somewhere easy to reach. I quietly hung up and peeked around the corner into the living room. "Be right back, Bran."

He waved, engrossed in some article. I hurried into the den, and sure enough, there was the key she'd been talking about. I unlocked the lower left drawer in the old walnut credenza and there found a lady's pistol, delicate, with a pearl handle. I examined it, then shook my head. I didn't want the responsibility. I loved my martial arts lessons and could bring down a grown man if I had the advantage. I could use my body as a weapon, but I wouldn't carry a gun.

I put the gun back in the drawer and locked it, replacing the key in the cup. "Not this time, Auntie," I whispered to myself and rejoined Bran in the living room. He was finishing up my last column in *Pout*, and now he set the magazine down, grinning sheepishly.

"I like your work, Persia. You do a good job, and you know what you're doing. You don't give stupid advice, and your column doesn't come off pedantic or boring. So, what were you doing while I was reading? And don't lie—I know something's up. I'm not budging till you give me the lowdown."

I gazed at Bran, wondering just how much to tell him. Finally I said, "Do you promise to leave here when you need to, to go home and get ready for your flight, and to head out without another thought?"

He held up two fingers. "Scouts' honor."

So I told him about Elliot's escape and my worry that Elliot was going to try to come back to kill me. Bran listened to everything quietly, as he always did, without jumping in with a testosterone-driven frenzy to right all wrongs.

"So he could be anywhere on the island?" Bran asked.

I nodded and turned on the television to the *Northwest Cable News*, a twenty-four-hour news show that covered the news of the Pacific Northwest states—Washington, Idaho, and Oregon. Sure enough, the PR person for Gull Harbor's police department was talking with a reporter.

"Elliot Parker, Thomas Wynn, and Lonnie Carver managed to overpower their guards and escape while being transferred from the courthouse to the police station today. Consider these men armed and dangerous. Wynn is suspected of raping four women, Parker was under arrest for assault and attempted murder, and Carver just pleaded guilty to three counts of burglary. If you see any of these men, call 911, but do not try to apprehend them or get in their way . . ."

The report went on as they plastered a picture of Elliot and his buddies up on the screen. Elliot's mug shot was replete with broken nose, black eye, and bruises covering his face. They must have decided that the bandages obscured the view, because they posted another picture of him—this one a better shot. I grimaced as I stared at his face. What had I ever seen in him? How had I missed the weasel within that seemed to be his second skin?

Feeling a poor judge of human nature, I muted the sound and glumly picked up Buttercup, depositing her in my lap. She struggled, barely awake and surprised to be a sudden object of affection, but I held her fast and rubbed her down. She finally rewarded me with a purr, and I glanced up at Bran, who was staring at me with a quizzical look.

"Where's your boyfriend? You should call him, or he's going to freak once he hears that report."

Oh hell, I hadn't thought of that! I picked up the phone. "Thanks, Mr. Feel Good. Just what I needed to add to my worries—make the boyfriend feel bad. Yes, this is a such a *good* thing. Maybe we should invite Martha over to make us a macaroni salad and a centerpiece made out of Froot Loops and old banana peels." I punched in Killian's number and waited patiently. His voice mail came on, and I left a message to the effect of, "I'm still alive, don't worry, I'll see you soon."

Bran stayed until Auntie arrived home, with Kane in tow. He came bearing gifts—a shotgun. She reassured me that he knew how to use it. Not sure whether that made me feel any better or not, I graciously offered to fix dinner.

"You can't cook. You should be resting."

"I was going to phone for pizza," I said, a wry grin on my face.

"Then by all means, the kitchen is yours," she said.

I ordered three large pizzas, one Hawaiian style, one with sausage and mushrooms, and the third with pepperoni and extra cheese. Kane and Auntie sat at the table playing cribbage, while I lounged in the living room with a book. When the doorbell rang, Kane insisted on getting it, his shotgun right behind the door. He paid the delivery boy and locked the door firmly behind him as Auntie carried the pizzas to the table. I joined them.

"So, can we talk about something other than the fact that Elliot's still out there?" Kyle had called a few minutes before with the news that they'd managed to catch the serial rapist, but the Albatross had slipped the net, and they had no idea where he was.

"Let's talk about Thanksgiving and the holidays," Auntie said. "I noticed your list here, and added a few things to it. We're definitely calling in Maids Are Us to-morrow and having them thoroughly clean the house."

As we brainstormed plans, I tried to block out the thought that Elliot was out there somewhere, gun in hand and a grudge in his heart.

❧

Thanksgiving morning dawned overcast and cold, but without any rain. I'd managed to keep my nerves under control and spent Tuesday and Wednesday at the shop with Auntie, while Kane stayed at our house keeping watch. Killian had called, wanting to know if he should postpone his meetings and come back to the island early, but I told him no, that we were okay and I'd see him on Thanksgiving. He reluctantly agreed.

By Thursday morning, there was still no sign of Elliot, and no sign of Lisa. I didn't know which was more worri-some. Lisa had been missing since Saturday night, and the weather had been nasty. If she was in a ditch somewhere, I wondered how long she could last until help arrived.

Bran's reassurance that he thought she was still alive kept me hoping, though, and I broke down and told Amy what he said despite Kyle's insistence that I keep my mouth shut. I knew Kyle was trying to ease Amy into the thought that Lisa might be dead, but that didn't seem right. Not until we knew for sure. Without hope, what was there? Neither Amy nor I could figure out what Bran's reference to silver might be, but it gave us some-thing to go on.

My alarm rang at five thirty, and I heard Auntie and Kane already stirring on the stairs. I peeked over the rail, just to make sure that it was indeed the two of them, and was rewarded with bright smiles and a cheerful "Morning, Imp! Happy Thanksgiving!"

"I'll be down once I've taken a bath," I said. I gingerly went through my workout for the day, eschewing anything that might pull my shoulder but concentrating on leg and neck exercises. I cautiously stretched my arms, taking care not to engage any of the injured muscles to the point of pain.

After a hot bath, I fumbled into my bra and panties and slid on a pair of black jeans and a cranberry-colored tank that was formfitting but not too tight. It was embellished with embroidered leaves of bronze and rust and was perfect for Thanksgiving. After brushing my hair, I slid on a velvet headband to keep it out of my face, slipped into a pair of loafers, then hurried downstairs.

Auntie was stuffing the turkey while Kane was fixing breakfast. The smell of fried eggs and sputtering bacon whetted my appetite, and I planted a big kiss on the top of Auntie's head, then a quick peck on Kane's cheek.

"Morning, you two," I said, eyeing the food with the same focus the Beast gave to his dog dish every morning. "Should I feed the Menagerie?"

"All taken care of," Kane said. "And Trevor's already here. He and I did a quick walk of the grounds to make sure there's nobody out there. Can't be certain, of course, but we took his dog Kali with us, and she'd be barking if anybody strange was hiding out there."

Kali was a German shepherd–chocolate Lab mix who was not only brilliant but who had been professionally trained. She made me want to get another dog, one specifically trained to keep an eye on the place. In September, we'd made the decision to fence in most of the acreage but had only gone as far as to buy the supplies. We were waiting for early spring to do the actual work, when it would be easier to see the property lines. Now, I wished we hadn't been quite so lackadaisical about it.

I opened the door on to the deck and wandered out to peek at the water. Restless today, she was, as always, but I didn't smell a storm on the horizon, and it looked like it might even clear up. The wind was bracing, colder than usual and filled with salt-sea tang. I inhaled deeply. When I lived in Seattle, the smog and noise were enough to drive me nuts. I preferred the sound of the wind and water and the call of the gulls.

As I returned to the dining room, I saw that Auntie's hands were full of dressing and turkey innards, and Kane was wrestling breakfast onto plates. I made sure the place-mats and napkins were clean and then helped him carry the food to the table. Auntie told us to go ahead without her—she'd eat as soon as she finished stuffing the bird—and so Kane and I took our places and dug in. The bacon was maple flavored, and the eggs were perfect. I pulled out the backgammon set, and Kane and I busied ourselves with playing a couple of games over the food. I won the first, he won the second, and by the time Auntie sat down with her plate, we were well into the third.

After breakfast, I busied myself picking up around the house. It had been awhile since we'd done a thorough cleaning, and I vacuumed and scrubbed the guest bath-room till it shone and even hauled out the duster, chasing the cats around with it and playing bat-bat games until they were so excited they rampaged into the kitchen.

Auntie popped her head around the corner and, shaking her head, said, "Imp, would you quit riling up the natives? Delilah's so fluffy she looks like a walking fuzz ball, and Nalu just jumped on the counter and tried to get into the food. Now, either finish dusting or put away the toy." But I could see the smile lurking behind her stern eyes.

The smell of baking pies filled the house with cinna-mon and nutmeg and pumpkin, and in a fit of decorating frenzy, I lit every candle in the living room and dining room that were cat-proof, and started a fire in the fire-place.

By ten AM the house was full. Kyle and Amy were there, both looking a little ragged around the edges, and Daphne, Bran's sister. Trevor's girlfriend had gone back East with her family for the holiday, so he joined us for the day. The Smith sisters arrived carrying a basket of goodies including homemade fudge and rum truffles.

Killian showed an hour late and looking decidedly worried. Even though I'd insisted that I was fine, he was still wavering on going back to New York, but I quashed that idea.

"You have to. This is the future of your business we're talking about. I've got Auntie and Kane, and Kyle and Trevor . . . I'll be okay, babe. I promise you, I'll be careful." We were snuggled up in my bedroom, hiding out for a little while. Kyle, Trevor, and Kane were watching football, while Auntie held court in the dining room with the women.

Killian curled an arm around me and kissed me gently on the lips. "I couldn't bear it if something happened to you, you know."

"I know," I said softly, playing with his shirt. "Do you think you could avoid hurting my shoulder?"

He slowly unzipped my jeans, sliding them down over my hips. As he pressed his lips to my lower stomach, he said, "I don't think that will be a problem." He undressed me gently, one piece of clothing at a time, and then laid me back, trailing kisses over my body, over my face.

I leaned up on my elbows, watching as he undressed, taking in every detail. He was lean and muscular, and the hair all over his body was shockingly red. Killian had one long scar on his left thigh where he'd been hurt during a motorcycle accident when he was fifteen, and another on his upper left shoulder from when he was twenty. He'd gotten in a fight with a guy who had a knife. Killian may have been stabbed, but the guy with the knife lost the battle and ended up in the hospital with a broken shoulder. Killian was as good a martial arts student as me, and we sparred at least once a week.

I pointed my stereo's remote and flipped the switch, and Nine Inch Nails came blasting through the room. Lowering the volume so it wouldn't disturb anybody downstairs, I leaned back and waited, breathless, as Killian hovered over me, his gaze lingering on my body with eyes that reminded me of a starving wolf staring at dinner.

"Let me in." Killian's voice curled around me, making me woozy with desire. All the tension of the past few days threatened to swamp me in one giant wave, and there was only one way to break through to the other side.

And so I opened the door.

⁂

Killian and I took a quick shower and then dressed and joined the rest. Nobody commented on our absence, though I caught Kyle staring at me with a veiled grin. I ignored him, wanting to enjoy the day as much as I could. Not a sports fan, Killian joined the women and soon had both Auntie and the Smith sisters involved in a lively game of canasta. Amy had joined Kyle in the living room, and so I walked over to Daphne, who was staring out the window at the gloom-filled day.

"How do you feel about Bran running off to the Amazon?" I asked.

Daphne and Bran were twins. Their parents were British transplants and had named both of their children after literary figures. Bran's full name was Branwell Heathcliffe Stanton, while Daphne Rebecca Stanton bore a double legacy from Daphne du Maurier. Daphne ran a bookstore and was engaged to a history professor from the UW who was currently on a university exchange over in London. When he returned, they planned on marrying, and he'd take up teaching at the Gull Harbor Community College.

She considered my question before answering. That was one thing about Daphne—she never spoke without thinking, and when she did, you had the sense that her mind was made up about the subject.

"I think it will suit his nature. He's been adrift since tourist season came to a close. He missed some of it because of his broken leg, and he's feeling antsy. I can tell."

She winked at me. "And then he has to get over you, of course. This should help him along. I don't know what I'll do if he actually wins. There won't be any putting up with him, then."

I laughed. "In the first place, Bran doesn't need to get over me, and you know it. We're still friends, and I adore him, but we both knew there was no future in the relationship. However, I agree with you. If he wins, we'll never hear the end of it. Want to take bets on how many episodes of the show he lasts before being voted off?"

She let out a chuckle. "We should do it, though we can never let him know, or he'll hold it over our heads for the rest of our lives." Daphne gazed at the restless water as it churned, frothing at the shore. "So you haven't found any sign of your friend, have you?"

I shook my head. "No, and she vanished Saturday. Amy's frantic, and I'm heartsick over it. I know she didn't drown, Daphne. She was terrified of the water, and people just don't act against their nature when they have that strong a phobia. There has to be some clue down there on the beach where her car was. Something to tell us what happened."

"I assume Chief Laughlin's already combed the area?" she asked, but she didn't sound all that confident.

I stared at the ocean, wondering if we'd see any bad storms this year. Once in awhile, the water crested so high that it washed up the spit of beach and over Briarwood Drive. Moss Rose Cottage was high enough up a slope that we didn't have to worry about getting flooded, but sometimes Auntie had trouble getting in the driveway and had to take side streets and come in through the back part of our acreage.

"I suppose so. I think Amy wants to form a search party, but I know she's conflicted." I lowered my voice. "She wants to believe that Kyle is doing everything he can—and he is—but what he can do and what she thinks he can do are two different things."

Daphne gave me a quick, firm nod. "How long until dinner?"

I checked with Auntie and returned to Daphne's side. "A good two hours or so. Why?"

"I was thinking that you and I might go down to the beach and have a look around. I don't have Bran's gifts, but I have some semblance of second sight. And maybe we'll find something that the police missed."

I jumped at the chance. At least we'd be doing something, and I couldn't stomach sitting through a football game or another card game right now. Auntie wasn't happy that I was going out, but I took my cell and told her that I'd call every half hour to let her know that Elliot hadn't got hold of me.

As Daphne and I headed to the door, Amy suddenly appeared behind me. "I heard you're going down to the beach. I want to go."

As we gathered our coats and headed out to Daphne's car, I caught Kyle staring at us with an unreadable look. I gazed back at him, willing him to wish us good luck. He might believe that Lisa had drowned, but he couldn't prove it. And until he did, we had to believe there was still hope.

⁂

The landing at Lookout Pier was soaked through from the cresting waves, and I stood against the rail, staring out over the open water. Where was Lisa? Where had she gone? There was no sign of a weak railing, or that anybody had broken through any part of the rail. Add to that, the railing was a good four feet high. You just didn't fall over something like that without doing something stupid, like climbing up to sit on the edge. Granted, there was the open spot the jet skiers used to get aboard their machines, but that just strengthened my conviction that Lisa hadn't even considered walking out here.

I wandered back to Daphne, who was looking around

the beach, and Amy, who was searching the parking lot where Lisa's car had been found. Shading my eyes, I gazed at the surrounding area. Houses lined the cliffs that overlooked the inlet and Lookout Pier. Had somebody in one of those houses seen something? Had Kyle even checked? Suddenly, Amy gave a shout. Daphne and I ran over to her side.

She was holding a silver bracelet. "Silver!" she said, looking at me meaningfully. "You said your friend mentioned something about silver. This was Lisa's."

It was an allergy alert bracelet. I snapped my fingers. "Lisa does wear one of those, doesn't she?"

"She's allergic to bees, and she always carries an epinephrine pen and wears her medic alert just in case she's stung by a wayward bee and goes into anaphylactic shock," Amy said.

Sure enough, as we turned the bracelet over, we saw that it was engraved with the words "Lisa Tremont, Bee Allergy." The catch looked like it had been broken, as if the bracelet caught on something and had been abruptly yanked off of Lisa's wrist.

"Where did you find this?" I asked.

Amy pointed to the patch of weeds we were standing next to. Daphne fell to her knees, and we joined her, combing the area. I was looking at one of the long logs used to indicate the end of the parking space, when I caught a glimpse of something shiny. Cautiously, I reached beneath the log and pulled out a sample-sized bottle of hair spray. I was pretty certain it was Lisa's brand.

As I stared at the bottle, I realized that we were directly in front of where we'd found her car. The hair spray could have easily rolled under the log if she'd dropped it while standing beside her car. Trying to make sense of everything, I pulled out my phone and called Kyle. If Lisa had drowned, what were her bracelet and hair spray doing in the parking lot?

Chapter Twelve

Kyle showed up, along with Killian and Kane. The three *K*s I thought with a nervous giggle. For some reason, finding proof that Lisa had stood right here, next to her car, brought everything home. She hadn't just gone for a walk on the pier. Something had tugged on the bracelet hard enough to rip it from her arm. She had to know it had been yanked off, and she'd never just ignore the loss of it—which meant something prevented her from retrieving it.

I surveyed the area. My gaze went, once again, to the houses on the hill. Somebody up there surely had seen something. I walked over to Kyle, who was talking in low tones to Amy, and tapped him on the shoulder.

"Who lives up there? Do you know?"

Kyle glanced up at the row of mansions and expensive town houses. "In answer to your unspoken question, no, we haven't questioned people yet. That's Millionaires Row, if you didn't know it. Informally, of course. Most of the people who own those homes are so rich they make your aunt look middle class. And most of them were at the dance Saturday night, including Annabel Mason, who owns the big house in the center of the bunch."

Annabel Mason again. I stared at the house he pointed to. *Mansion* truly described the place. It was at least four stories high and looked like a modern-day Parthenon from here, made from gleaming white stone. I had the feeling that around front, there would be Grecian pillars supporting the roof of a portico.

Beside me, Amy drew in a sharp breath. I glanced at her. "What is it?"

"Oh, just that Candy Harrison works for Annabel," she said, and I could tell she was struggling to keep her voice neutral.

That's right—Candy Harrison did work for Annabel. That little fact had slipped my mind for the moment. "What do you really think of Candy? I know that Lisa didn't like her."

Amy shrugged. "I don't think much of her, to be honest, but she did watch over Father during his last months." She blushed and hung her head. "I have the feeling . . . well, he was a man, sick as he was, and I suppose he'd want somebody around who was pretty, though she seems kind of . . . slutty to me." Her voice lingered over the last, and I raised my eyebrows.

Could Candy be right? Did the Tremont sisters dislike her because they thought their father had been involved with her? My logical side argued that the man had been suffering from cancer, for God's sake. He probably didn't have the energy to do anything, let alone play chase the nurse around the bed. But logic didn't necessarily play into situations where strong emotions were involved. Lisa and Amy hadn't been able to come home to live until a month or two before their father died. Could guilt be a factor in their dislike of Candy?

"What did your father say about her?" I asked.

Amy's chin quivered, but her voice remained calm.

"He liked her. He said she made him laugh, and I suppose, in the end, that's all that mattered," she said tightly, then shrugged and turned back to Kyle.

I walked a little ways toward the base of the cliff. The drop-off was steep, and the side of the cliff was barren except for some scrub trees. It was only a matter of time until the wind and rain eroded the soil enough for one— or more—of those houses to come tumbling down the side as so often happened here in rain-soaked western Washington. People never learned, I thought. They didn't pay attention to mistakes from the past, and they went right on glibly believing that they would be the exception.

Abruptly, I decided that I wanted to know more about Annabel Mason and the woman she'd hired as her nurse. I turned and headed back to Daphne's car, thinking that it was time to pay a visit to Winthrop and see if he could help me find out anything.

Kyle was struggling with whether or not to call in volunteers to search the area today or let it rest until tomorrow. "It's Thanksgiving, and Lisa's been missing almost a week," he told me, out of Amy's earshot. "Sure, the bracelet and hair spray mean she was here, and maybe she didn't go out on the pier, but it doesn't tell us where she is, and I doubt if the beach is likely to yield up anything else of value. One more day—"

"One more day might mean the difference between life and death, Kyle," I said, irritated.

He stared at me point-blank. "Has there been a ransom note?"

I blinked. "What?"

"A ransom note? Has there been any call from kidnappers?"

Sucking in a deep breath, I shook my head. "Not to my knowledge."

"Then she hasn't been kidnapped for money. And if somebody did snatch her, and it wasn't for money . . ." He let his voice trail off, but I knew where he was going, and

I didn't like it one bit. He was thinking of Gary Ridgway and Ted Bundy and all the other predators who had frequented our state, luring women into their traps. Those women weren't kidnapped for money, and few of them made it out alive. Some of them had never been found.

"No," I whispered hoarsely. "Nobody here would do something that horrible—"

"Bebe Wilcox tried to kill you to protect her burgeoning cosmetics empire. Colleen Murkins and Debbie Harcourt killed Lydia Wang for far less than that. Hell, Elliot came to your house with a gun and was probably going to rape you and then shoot you. And he's still out there, so you damned well keep your eyes open and don't do anything stupid. Don't go anywhere alone. Don't think that you can always protect yourself, because maybe one of these times it won't be true. And don't tell me shit like this doesn't happen in Gull Harbor, Persia. You know it does."

Kyle's lips were pressed together in a tight line, and I realized he was as frustrated over Lisa's disappearance as the rest of us. I'd assumed he had just written her off to drowning, but apparently he wasn't quite so blasé as I'd thought.

I let out a long sigh. "You're right. Things like that happen everywhere. What if she's hurt, though? What if she wandered off and fell? Maybe tripped somewhere out of the way? There are ravines up there between the houses. What if she went hiking up there for some reason and fell? She could still be alive, but not for much longer with the weather the way it is."

Frowning, I could see that I had his attention. "It's a long shot," he said. "It doesn't make sense for her to have gone rooting around a ravine on a blustery night like Saturday. And it doesn't account for the broken bracelet."

"It makes more sense than someone who's phobic of water to go wandering alone out on a stormy pier when she can barely skirt a swimming pool with dozens of people around." I felt a surge of hope. Maybe I was right, maybe I wasn't just clutching at straws. Lisa had been afraid of water but not of going out in the woods. A ravine between two million-dollar houses wouldn't seem threatening, would it?

It was enough to jog Kyle into action. He got on his phone and asked for search and rescue volunteers to come comb the beach. Within twenty minutes, three men and two women stood there. Kyle showed them the bracelet, hair spray, and explained the situation. Amy gave them a picture of Lisa.

"Okay, if you would search the ravines around here, and any place where a wounded woman might drag herself to get out of the rain. Be careful, though. We don't want anybody hurt over this."

As they split up into two groups and hit the beach, we walked back to our cars. Daphne, Amy, and I rode back together; the men rode back with Kyle. On our way home, Amy lightly touched my arm.

"Persia, thank you," she said.

"Thank you? For what?"

"For making Kyle look again. For convincing him that my sister's worth the trouble. For believing that maybe, just maybe, she's still alive out there and needs us. I appreciate it."

I gazed into her eyes and saw the conflicting emotions. She liked Kyle, she wanted to believe that he was doing everything he could. But it was obvious that Kyle believed Lisa was dead, and he didn't have the manpower to mobilize an island-wide search.

I patted her fingers awkwardly, wincing as my shoulder gave a little twinge. "I think she's out there waiting for us. We just have to find her."

"Yeah," Amy said. "She's still alive. She's probably just hurt and can't make it to a phone."

Daphne remained silent as we pulled into the driveway and headed toward the house. The smell of turkey and cinnamon and sweet potatoes filled the air, and my stomach rumbled. As we climbed the stairs, she paused, motioning for me to wait until everybody else had gone inside.

"I told you that I have a little of the sight—not nearly as much as Bran, but some. Persia, the girl is still alive. I don't know for how much longer, but her bracelet—when I was holding it, I could sense her. I thought you'd like to know what I felt."

My heart leapt. For some reason, coming from Daphne, the words gave me more goose bumps than when coming from Bran. Perhaps it was because Daphne seldom said anything frivolous. Or maybe it was because she seemed so much more assured in her world, rock-solid and steady. Whatever the reason, I believed her.

⁂

Dinner was wonderful, if a little subdued. Auntie and Trevor had fitted the extra leaves into the dining room table, and it stretched long enough to handle a dozen guests or more. I brought out the good china—Auntie's Old Country Roses set—and set the table with Daphne's help. The Smith sisters had polished the silverware, and now everything gleamed as Auntie turned on the stereo and put in a CD of *The Planets*. Strains of classical music filtered out as we sat, ten at the table, while Kane took over the job of carving the turkey.

Amy was a trouper. She tried her best to keep lively, to keep from bringing down dinner, but when we were well into pie and ice cream, Kyle's cell phone rang, and she jumped, her face a mask of mingled hope and fear.

Kyle moved off to one side to take the call, while I poured hot tea and coffee for those who wanted something to drink with their dessert. We were a subdued lot until he returned, shaking his head.

"They didn't find much else, although in the scrub brush near the edge of the parking lot—toward the road, not the water—they did discover an eye shadow case. What brand did Lisa use?" he asked.

I knew that one, even before Amy. "Lisa preferred Shiseido."

His eyes lighting up, he asked, "Do you by any chance know what color she wore?"

"That's easy. We were discussing our favorite colors last week. She'd just bought a new duo . . . let me think . . ." I drummed my memory for the name of what she'd shown me. Amy looked blank. She didn't pay much attention to makeup. And then I remembered. "It was called Pomona Lime, I think!"

Kyle spoke quickly into the phone and began to nod. "Yes, yes, that's it. That belonged to her. Hold on and I'll be right over." He folded his phone and shoved it into his pocket. "I'd better get over there. They discovered a—what did you call it—"

"Shiseido," I said.

"Yeah, a Shiseido Pomona Lime eye shadow compact near the entrance of the parking lot. Looks like it was dropped in some scrub bushes. I'm going over there, and we'll call in a few more searchers . . . give the place another thorough going over. If she was dropping her makeup, maybe somebody had hold of her and she was trying to leave a trail."

He looked ready to jump for joy. This was probably the best news he'd heard in days. "Amy, do you want to come with us?"

She was already out of her seat and gathering her things. "Miss Florence, Persia . . . we hate to eat and run but . . ."

"Oh for heaven's sake, just go!" Auntie tsked. "You think I'm going to worry myself over you leaving early? There might be more to discover; you both need to be there. Persia, did you want to go, too?"

I shook my head. "Actually, I want to give Winthrop a call. He'll just love working on a holiday, but I need to look up a couple of things, and he's the one who can tell me how to find out what I want to know." I turned to Kyle and Amy. "You'll let us know if anything else surfaces?"

"Of course," Amy said, kissing me on the cheek. "Thank you, Persia. Thank you, Daphne. Without the two of you, we wouldn't have found her bracelet and hair spray and now, the eye shadow. You don't know how much I appreciate all of your help."

"Thank us when she's home, safe," Daphne said.

I saw them out, then quietly stood there, staring out the door. Auntie and the Smith sisters were clearing the table, Trevor doing his best to help. Somewhere, Lisa was out there. And so was Elliot. One, I prayed we'd find safe and healthy. The other, I prayed we'd find before he found me. Sighing, I looked up at Killian, who was standing behind me. He wrapped his arms around my waist and rested his chin on the top of my head, gently rocking me back and forth.

"I hate to do this, but I can't stay the night after all. I have to pack and get ready for my trip."

I turned in his arms. "I wish you didn't have to go, but I want you to fly back there and seal the deal."

"Promise me you'll be on your guard. That jerk is out there, somewhere, with a gun. I don't want to get a call in the middle of the night saying that he's broken in, or that you're in the hospital . . . or worse." He leaned down and pressed his lips to mine, and we were kissing then, deep and long, as his hands sought my back, my ass, my breast.

I didn't care if Auntie or Kane saw us, or Daphne, the Smith sisters, or Trevor. I didn't care about anything except making sure we got in a last kiss. With everything that had happened this past week, I wasn't feeling too confident. And truth be told, I was more than a little nervous about him flying back East. But I didn't want him to see my worry. He had enough on his mind already.

"I'll be okay," I said, pushing him back. "I'm going to be fine. And we'll find Lisa. And Elliot will make some stupid mistake that will give him away. Everything's going to work out. It always does." Even as I said the words, I knew that I didn't believe them, but I had to pretend, for both our sakes, that they were true.

Killian reluctantly hugged Auntie good-bye, shook hands with Trevor and Kane, and waved to the Smith sisters and Daphne. He slid on his jacket and, with one last kiss, was out the door.

I raised my hand, wishing he could come back, wishing that Thanksgiving had been a better holiday. We'd been straining to pretend everything was okay, yet it wasn't. I waved as Killian pulled out of the driveway.

As I returned to the living room, Auntie shot me a look that told me she knew exactly what was on my mind. She bustled over and put her arm around my waist, whispering in my ear as she bundled me off toward the kitchen. "Killian will be home in a week with the money to start his business. And we'll find Lisa, never you worry about that."

As soon as I could, I headed to the den, where I put in a call to Winthrop. As I'd predicted, he wasn't exactly overjoyed to hear from me on a holiday, but when I explained what had happened, he relented.

"After all, it's not as though I've got family here for the holiday," he said, and I immediately thought that we should invite him over for Christmas, if he had no other plans. "What do you need, kiddo?"

"As much information on Annabel Mason and Candy Harrison as you can dig up, especially Candy."

I could hear him jotting something down, then he said, "Got it. This will give me something to do this afternoon, as if I didn't have enough work. By the way, any word on Elliot yet?"

"No," I said, automatically glancing toward the window. "Not a word. He could be anywhere. I can only hope he managed to catch the ferry and leave the island."

"Let's hope they catch his ass and beat it raw,"

Winthrop said. "I'll call you when I've dug up anything good about these two."

As I hung up, the gloom seemed to settle around my shoulders, but I knew Auntie was trying to hold the day together, so I plastered a smile on my face and rejoined everyone in the living room. Kane and Trevor returned from their scouting mission, reporting that sightings of Elliot had been negative, and we tuned into an old movie—*Holiday Inn*—as the rest of the day passed without incident.

By nine PM, we'd seen everyone out. Kane had to go home for the night, and since Elliot hadn't reared his ugly head, we decided to just lock the doors and keep a close eye on the place. With the thickness of the doors—they were the ones that had originally come with the house—we felt fairly secure that we'd be okay. After everyone left, Auntie and I sat in front of the fire, talking. She'd made turkey pitas for us for dinner, thick with cranberry sauce and cream cheese and slivered almonds, and we were eating on TV trays as we prepared to watch *An Affair to Remember*.

"Tomorrow we'll get the Christmas decorations up, Imp. Tawny and Betsy Sue will handle the store. I made sure that we wouldn't be offering any hair, makeup, or fragrance consultations."

"How's Maxine working out?" I asked. I hadn't paid much attention to our second choice for Lisa's position.

"She's fine, but Lisa's got a touch to her work . . . I do hope she's safe, wherever she is. Trevor's coming over tomorrow to help us decorate. His girlfriend won't be back until Sunday."

I nodded, my mouth full of sandwich. As she readied the DVD, I swallowed. "Barb and Dorian have patched things up. At least we can thank Elliot for that." A glance at the fire told me it needed more wood, which I pointed out to Auntie. My shoulder was still bruised and aching. She piled another log on the flames, while I poured two glasses of white wine.

The phone rang as we were readying ourselves with tissues and the remote. Auntie answered, then handed it to me. It was Winthrop.

"I've got some notes for you. I'll type them up and e-mail them to you, but here they are in a nutshell."

"I'm listening," I said, taking a drink of wine to clear my throat.

"As you know—or may not know—Annabel is married to Lloyd Mason, who is a good fifteen years her junior. He was a lawyer until he retired early upon their wedding, but I can tell you he wasn't a very good one. I ran up against him in court a couple times and trounced his ass without so much as a blink."

I digested this bit of information. "Does he have money?" I asked, wondering if he'd married Annabel for her money or for love.

"Nothing to account for on his own. But he doesn't have Annabel's money, either. I happen to know that he agreed to a fairly stiff prenup agreement. That's common knowledge, actually, so I'm not violating any confidence there." He sounded so serious that I almost laughed but didn't. It was his job to maintain dignity and a manner befitting Gull Harbor's best lawyer, and I understood that.

"Okay, anything else about them?"

"Just this—and again, this is common knowledge. Your aunt could probably tell you the same thing. Annabel is in poor health. She has been sickly most of her life. Apparently she hired Candy Harrison to be her private nurse after the Tremont girls' father died. Her own nurse, one Julia Jones, moved to Seattle to take a job at a luxury spa."

So Annabel really did need a nurse to help her out. "What about Candy? What did you find out about her?"

Winthrop's voice was thoughtful, almost musing.

"Miss Harrison is a busy young woman. She's been around the block a few times. I made a couple of quick calls and found out that she was working at a private nursing home in Olympia. I don't know why, but she was fired four years ago and has been working in private home health care ever since. Two years ago, she went to work for Tremont when he found out he had cancer and would need help at home. She moved on to Annabel when Tremont died."

I frowned. Not exactly what I was expecting, but then again, I hadn't known what to expect. I didn't even really know what I was looking for. Just something to give me a handle on a woman whom Lisa seemed to detest.

"Oh, one other thing," Winthrop said, "before I go back to my book and brandy."

"Yes?" I waited, expectantly.

"Candy drives a high-end BMW. A little red two-seater job. Not exactly the sort of car a working girl can afford without a little help."

A BMW? I thought back to our meeting. "She also wears expensive clothes during her off-hours and a perfume that's extremely hard to come by."

Winthrop let out a little cough. "Interesting, to say the least. Well, that's all. Tell Florence I send my regards. Let me know what you come up with." He hung up, and I stared at the silent phone.

Let him know what I come up with? Hell, I didn't even know what I was hunting for. I ran everything past Auntie, and we brainstormed what we knew.

"The thing that strikes me is this: Lisa's father had money that he supposedly gambled away. Candy has an expensive car, clothing, and perfume. Could she have stolen money from him?"

Auntie shook her head. "Be cautious with your accusations, Imp. It sounds to me like Tremont might have become fond of her. Those could be . . . gifts, which she'd have every right in the world to accept, even if it didn't look good to outsiders. Or payment for favors other than her nursing skills. You can't go around accusing people of stealing just because you don't know where they got their possessions."

I frowned and drained my glass. "You're right, of course. And Amy seems to think that Candy and her father may have been involved. That would fit with what you just said. And it wouldn't be the first time somebody played sugar daddy to a tarty young woman in exchange for a little nooky."

"No, indeed," Auntie said. "They don't call prostitution the world's oldest profession for nothing. And even if it was a sugar daddy relationship, as you put it, that's not exactly against the law. People have been using sex to exploit others for years. Look at television," she added, offering me the bottle. "Look at the magazine you write a column for."

I let out a long sigh and refilled my glass. Auntie made valid points—all of them. And even if Candy had somehow squeezed money out of Tremont, that didn't explain Lisa's disappearance. I was grasping at straws and couldn't focus anymore. The day had been too long and too chaotic. I pushed everything to the side and raised my glass.

"Here's to all that's right with the world. To our little family," I said, patting Hoffman on the head. The rooster let out a sound that I could almost swear was a purr. He'd been hanging around the cats too long. "To having Killian and Kane in our lives. To Venus Envy. And to you, Auntie. I sure do love you."

She blushed and lowered her eyes. "Don't forget yourself, Imp. To you. When I took you in twenty-seven years ago, I had no idea what I was in for, but I knew that you were my niece and that your mother would have wanted it that way. Your father has no idea what a wonderful daughter he's missed out on. But I've appreciated every minute you've been in my life. I couldn't imagine life without you, which is why I worry so much."

"I know," I said softly as she started the DVD. The wind rattled the windows, and somewhere upstairs, I thought I could hear the gentle fall of footsteps. Auntie glanced at me and pointed to the ceiling.

I raised my glass again. "And let's not forget, here's to the Cap'n, who keeps a watch over our hearth and home. Cap'n, if you'd keep a watch out for that scuzzball Elliot, I would most kindly thank you, sir."

The footsteps paused, then started up again, lightly crossing the ceiling. They paused by the landing at the top of the stairs, then vanished. I leaned my head back then and laughed. All might not be right with the world, but at least things in our home were as they should be, and we were being watched over. Of that, I felt certain.

Chapter Thirteen

The next morning, Auntie hauled my ass out of bed early. I woke to her gently shaking me. "Persia, get up. We have a lot to do today. Come on, breakfast is ready."

I squinted at the clock. Seven AM? Ugh.

"Auntie, isn't it a little early?" I started to say, but she put her hands on her hips and frowned at me until I struggled out of bed. I blinked as she held out my robe and helped me into it. The smell of breakfast filtered up the stairs, and I was pleasantly surprised to find no turkey in sight on the breakfast table.

She'd made omelets and bacon, cinnamon toast, and orange juice. As I eagerly dove in to the food, a noise on the deck startled me, and I pulled back the curtains. Trevor gave me a weak wave from where he stood on a ladder. His tool belt was slung low across his hips, and I thought that his girlfriend was a lucky woman. He was sure a cutie. I pulled open the door and peeked out to find him hanging icicle lights around the eaves of the roof. It looked like he'd been at work a good hour or so, by the string of lights already in place.

I glanced back in the dining room. Auntie was off in the kitchen, pouring coffee. "Run, run for your life before she has you putting up the tree!" I grinned at him, and he laughed.

"Trust me, the trees are next on my list. I know exactly what the entire day is going to be spent doing. First the lights, then I set up the trees for Miss Florence, then I start decorating the yard. You'd better be prepared, sore arm or not. You'll be working all day, even if it's only to address Christmas cards."

Auntie had not only one Christmas tree, but three. One for the living room, one on the second floor landing, and this year she insisted on putting one up in my study. I was free to decorate as I wished, as long as I did so. The living room tree was a huge artificial fir, over twelve feet high, and it would be a vision in burgundy, gold, and ivory. The tree that went on the landing was a flocked blue spruce almost nine feet high, and would be decked out in blue, crystal, and silver. She kept the two color schemes in separate rooms to prevent a "Fourth of July" look.

I snorted, but secretly, I was excited. I'd spent too many holidays with Elliot, ignoring the passage of time. He hated decking out anything except himself, and he'd never celebrated anything that didn't have to do with some monetary windfall. I might be more of a Buddhist than anything, but Christmas reminded me of my childhood.

No matter where we were, on December 25 I could always count on finding myself in a holiday-bedecked room, with Auntie and Eva by my side. The score to the *Nutcracker* would be playing as we ate scones and drank tea for breakfast, and then we'd open our gifts.

Among other presents, Auntie always gave me a new diary and a new perfume I'd never smelled before. When I was young, they were light scents, suitable for a young girl. As I grew older, they grew more complex. I'd traveled

the world, not only with Auntie, but through those per-
fumes, which smelled like the incenses of India, the flower
shops of France, the spice factories of the Middle East.
After presents, we dressed and went to the local soup kitchen,
where Auntie and Eva and I would serve Christmas dinners
to those in need before going home to our own dinner. I'd
gotten a firsthand look every year at what it meant to have
nothing but the clothes on your back. It had impressed
upon me the importance of being grateful for what I had.

I hadn't thought of those traditions in years. As I mused
my way through the past, it occurred to me that I'd stored
my diaries in the attic under the watchful eye of Cap'n
Bentley. Were they still there? And what else would they
tell me that I'd forgotten over the years?

"Hey Trev, want breakfast?"

"I ate at home, but it sure smells good," he said, climbing off the ladder. I fixed him a plate as Auntie returned to
the table.

"Trevor, good, I wanted to run through a few things
with you. Sit down and eat while I talk." She consulted a
notepad. "Let me see, you'll need to go pick up the
wreaths and swags that Persia ordered. I just talked to the
tree farm, and they're ready. Do that before you finish the
lights. Oh, and when we put the lights on the tree and
mantel, I want you to hook them up to The Clapper system to make it easier to turn them on."

"I don't know if that's a good idea," I said, mumbling
through my breakfast. "We clap at the Menagerie a lot."

"Well, I want to give it a try. If it doesn't work out,
we'll change it. After you set up the trees, then finish the
lights, and we'll start hanging the swags and garlands.
Thank heavens we decorated Venus Envy at the beginning
of the month. While you go collect the greenery, I'll do
the dishes and vacuum. Persia, I need you to go shopping
for me."

"Shopping? On the day after Thanksgiving? Are you
nuts?" I gaped at her. "I thought that's why we stayed

home from work and foisted the day off on Tawny and Betsy Sue."

She snorted. "Don't be ridiculous. This is my decorating weekend, so I always take Friday off to get the bulk of it done. Now listen. I want you to buy candy canes for the Victorian tree and two new strings of twinkle lights," she said, then paused, thinking. "In fact, why don't we just replace all the lights? They're getting old, and I'd rather be safe than sorry."

"How many strings should I get?" I alternated between writing a list and eating.

She considered the question, then said, "Get twenty long strings, ten clear and ten multicolored. I can always find a place to put the extra if we have any. I also want two thirty-foot lengths of gold garland. And we need spray snow for the windows. I have the stencils. You need decorations for your tree, too. Whatever you see that you like."

My tree. I had no idea what to get, but I obediently wrote down "decorations." "What about the dining room? Don't you want a little tree for the table, too?" I was joking but I saw a gleam in her eye and wrote down "Tabletop tree" before she could say a word. "Got it," I said. "Anything else? Any food?"

"Hershey's kisses in holiday colors, seasonal candy. We'll need new wrapping paper, several types. Get something pretty. We have a lot of gifts to give out, so don't be stingy. Ribbons, bows, package labels, tape."

Feeling like I was one of Santa's elves being sent on a treasure hunt, I finished up my breakfast. Auntie had apparently already eaten. After I dressed and was ready to head out, she stopped me again. "Don't forget to drop into the shop and see how they're doing, would you, dear?"

I nodded. "Not a problem, Auntie," I said, sighing. Trev hadn't been kidding. It was going to be a long day.

By the time I reached Venus Envy from where I'd had to park two blocks away, I was breathless from the sudden chill that had descended overnight, and my breath froze in little puffs as I pushed my way into the shop. The store was so packed I had to squeeze my way through the crowded aisles. Considering we tried to keep the shop open and airy, that meant we were having a good old-fashioned holiday rush. Good for business, rough on nerves. Tawny and Betsy Sue looked run ragged, but they had smiles on their faces. Auntie was paying them each an extra hundred dollars for the day's work. Tawny motioned me over.

"Persia, can you take a deposit to the bank? We've already collected a lot of money," she said, lowering her voice. "I don't want to make just one run today." She glanced around at the customers who were swarming the aisles, looking for gifts for their loved ones. Auntie insisted on playing classical music and instrumentals during the holidays as opposed to the endless jingle of Christmas carols, and it seemed to soothe some frazzled nerves. Everyone was behaving politely, and there weren't many harried expressions that I could see.

"The Rest in Lavender line looks like it's going fast, and there are only five bottle of Rose Milk Lotion left on the shelf," I said. "Which means I'd better come in early on Monday and get started on more, you think?" I watched as Betsy Sue expertly wove customers through her checkout line, chatting them up as she bundled them off. She had a knack for retail work, all right.

Tawny nodded. "Business has been great. I got here this morning at eight AM and there were already ten people waiting at the door." We'd decided to open early and close late all weekend. "It's been nonstop ever since. I have the feeling people are splurging more on the smaller gifts this year, which bodes well for us."

She pointed to one of our regulars, who looked rather confused. "I'd better go help Mrs. Willet; she's probably looking for the Chamomile Cat catnip, and I moved the pet products to a different shelf." She dashed off as I secured the deposit envelope in my purse and headed for the door.

The bank was only three blocks away, so I walked rather than try to find another parking spot. The weather had definitely taken a turn for the chillier. A cold, crisp breeze ran through the streets, buoying along the shoppers that scurried from shop to shop. Island Drive was luminous, with trees in giant wooden planter boxes lining the street. The city had turned on the Christmas lights, and now the bare branches glittered with multicolored twinkle lights. Wreaths hung from the lampposts. They, too, were shimmering with lights.

I glanced at the sky, which had taken on a soft glow. Damned if it didn't feel almost cold enough to snow. We usually never got more than a few inches, but now and then a storm came through and left Gull Harbor bathed in white, if only for a few days. I sniffed and smelled the faint traces of snow on the wind. The Olympics, over on the peninsula, were probably in for it before nightfall.

A bell ringer from the Community Action Council was standing on the street corner, and I dropped a five dollar bill in the bucket, smiling as I eased my way through the throng of people crossing the street. Gull Harbor was, for the most part, a friendly place, and the majority of people were polite. As I passed by Sargent's Gift Shoppe, I waved at Kaycee Jones, an older African American woman who was painting a mural on their window. Kaycee was at least sixty and one of the town's preeminent artists. Every holiday her seasonal paintings adorned most of the shops in town, including ours. She was due to come paint our murals early the next week.

Kaycee was a regular at Venus Envy, buying everything in our Rose-Gardenia line, and twice a month she came in for a facial. She waved back, brush in hand, and went back to the snowman scene she was painting.

At the bank the line straggled toward the door, and I resigned myself to a long wait as I stepped in back of an older woman wearing a fur coat. She glanced over her shoulder and quickly turned, breaking into a soft smile.

"Why, Persia, how nice to see you." It was Annabel Mason, looking tired but cheerful. In the light of day, I could see the wrinkles lining her face, although like all women who were a little plump, the lines hadn't fully settled into her skin. But her eyes gave her away. They were the eyes of a woman who had endured a lot of pain but who persevered despite her ailments.

I glanced around, surprised that nobody had come to sweep her into a private office. Auntie might be up there on the financial ladder, but Annabel Mason was worth millions, and usually banks catered to their prized clientele.

She saw my expression and laughed. "Oh, I'll wait my turn. I'm not royalty, after all." Her words trilled off her lips, cascading like honey, and I wondered if she'd ever been a singer. At the very least, she could have made a fortune on voice-overs.

I mustered up my courage. "Ms. Mason, I was wondering—"

"Please, call me Annabel."

"All right. Annabel, I was wondering what time you arrived home after the Gala on Saturday night."

She squinted, thinking. "I wasn't feeling well, and I made my excuses early. I was hoping that people wouldn't notice. Lloyd and I left around ten. Why? Did something happen that I should know? That nobody told me about?"

"No, no," I hastened to say. "The Gala was perfectly lovely. It's just . . . when you got home, I wonder if you happened to look out the window of your house that overlooks Lookout Pier. And if so, did you notice anything unusual going on down in the parking lot?"

She blinked. "Oh my dear, I don't believe I even went near the window. No, I was so tired that I went straight to bed. You can ask my husband, though. Lloyd's a night owl and often stays up long after I've retired for the evening. I'm leaving town until tomorrow right after I straighten out a little problem with the bank, but you're certainly welcome to go over to the house and ask him if he might have seen anything. He often sits with a whiskey and soda and watches the water. Was there a problem down at the pier?"

I was about to explain when one of the tellers interrupted us, rushing over to Annabel's side. "Mrs. Mason, I'm so sorry. We didn't see you in line! You should have come right over to my desk. What can we do for you?"

Annabel gave me a little smile that said, *What can you do?* As she followed the attendant toward a private office, I heard her say, "I want to know just what this means. My husband's account can't be overdrawn again!"

The line inched forward, one person at a time. As I waited my turn, I thought about what it might mean to be trapped in a body that just didn't want to cooperate. Auntie had said something about Annabel having a heart condition, and I hoped for her sake that it eased off, whatever it was. She was one of the most genuinely unassuming women I'd met in a long time.

⁂

After depositing Venus Envy's take, I dropped back in at the shop and put the receipt in the safe in Auntie's office, then stopped by the Baklava or Bust Bakery. Dorian looked up from the counter and gave me a sheepish grin. He motioned me over.

"Persia, I want to thank you for what you said the other night. You're right. I neglected the feelings of the most important person in my life, and I will never forgive myself. I promise, I won't do it again. In fact," he looked around, making sure Barb was out of earshot, "I wanted to ask your help. I want to buy Barbara a present. What do you think I should get her? I'm torn between a new food processor and a new vacuum."

I stared at him. Barb hadn't been kidding when she'd confided to me that Dorian had the imagination of an amoeba when it came to gift giving. I cleared my throat. "Dorian, sweetie, listen to me. Barb doesn't clean. You have a maid to do the housework. If you want to buy a new vacuum, buy it for the maid. And a food processor? Barbara's in the kitchen all day here at the bakery. Why on earth would she want a kitchen gadget for a gift?"

He blinked, and I could see the wheels in his head turning.

"Think! You have a brain. Why not start buying her gifts she'll treasure? Like . . . oh . . . a diamond necklace? An amethyst ring? Maybe even just a dozen red roses— long-stemmed and from the florist, not the grocery store, along with a box of her favorite chocolates?"

Dorian looked downright embarrassed. "Oh good God, I can't believe it. I've turned into one of *those* husbands." He shook his head as he came around from behind the counter to sit at one of the tables that was still empty. Most were taken with customers munching on doughnuts and bear claws and coffee, but the morning rush had dwindled off, and there were a few free spots.

"So, you think she's right? That I'm not romantic? I know she talks to you about these things. I guess I didn't understand what she meant. Sometimes it takes a sledgehammer to hit the brain, you know?"

Not sure if I liked being compared to a sledgehammer, I just nodded.

"Persia, does she still love me?" His voice took on a frightened edge, and he stiffened, awaiting my answer.

I patted his hand. "Dorian, she adores you. She loves you so much, but you have to loosen up. You have to start treating her like a woman, not just your business partner. Quit taking her for granted, and stop putting your mother first. Barb's compromised a lot for you over the years. Now, it's your turn."

He thought over what I said, then let out a shuddering sigh. "I understand. I promise you I'll do better. And now, I'll call her for you. You two should go out to lunch." Before I could say a word, he bellowed out, "Barbara, Persia's here." Turning back to me, he said, "Please, don't tell her about our conversation? I want to surprise her."

Again, I patted his shoulder. "I promise. Just you get your ass in gear and do it sooner rather than later. Okay?"

"You have my solemn word," he said, returning to the counter as Barb emerged from the back, swathed in a huge white apron and covered with flour. "My petite love, my pretty wife, go with your friend and spend the afternoon having fun. Ari and I can run the bakery. Go shopping, and make reservations for dinner wherever you like. Mama will eat with Ari tonight, while we go out. I'll even put on a suit."

Barb, looking decidedly surprised, though happy, hastened to the back, returning a few minutes later clean and apron-free.

"I'll drive," she said. "You rest. You still look like hell."

I welcomed the offer. My shoulder was still hurting, though the pain had calmed down a little. We climbed into her Pathfinder. A month ago, Barb had decided that the way to add more adventure to her life was to buy an SUV, but I knew she was looking in the wrong direction. I could only hope that my little talk with Dorian would help solve the problem.

We headed to A Christmas Carol, a Christmas-themed store that carried just about anything a person could want for the holiday season. During the spring, they put up their Spring Dreams sign and sold gardening and picnic supplies. During summer they called themselves The Beach Hut and sold everything a tourist could want while on vacation. And during autumn they dubbed their store The

Halloween Tree and sold Halloween- and Thanksgiving-themed items. The owners did quite well, and every season there was a host of new toys and knickknacks and decorating items from which to choose.

"So, how's it going at home?" I ventured, hoping that I wasn't treading in dangerous water.

She shrugged. "Mama K leaves day after tomorrow. Early. She's so pissed at me that she hasn't said a word directly to my face since I came home. She only ate Thanksgiving dinner at the same table as me because Dorian threatened to take her back to the hotel if she didn't. And she's mad at him. Oh, Persia, I'm not sure what he said to her, but whatever it was, she's spitting nails over it. Tomorrow we'll have a family dinner together before taking her to the airport early Sunday morning."

"Wow," I said as I scrambled out of the car. "Sounds like *such* a good time. I can't understand why you're not enjoying her visit more." I tried to hold back a snicker, but she just waved at me.

"Thanks, hon' chile. I needed that. So, what are you buying here?"

As I opened the shop door, a group of demented cats warbled out "Jingle Bells" from the radio across the room. Grimacing, I examined my list. "What don't I need? Lights—lots of lights. Garland. Decorations. Candy canes."

"After this, you want to go to Macy's? I hear they're having an incredible sale." Barb's eyes lit up like a kid eyeing the cookie jar.

With a fleeting thought to how my hopes to avoid the shopping mobs were crashing at my feet, I gave her a bright nod. After all, what holiday season was complete without a little manic butt kicking through the sales aisles?

An overpriced and hectic half hour later, we loaded my bags of goodies into the back and then headed for Macy's. Barb was intent on the cashmere sale that was going on, and I knew that she wouldn't rest until we'd tried on every sweater in the store. I steeled myself as we pushed through the doors. The crowds were thick, and I could smell the rising panic as shoppers wrested dresses and jeans off the racks, shouldering their way through to the dressing rooms.

Women thronged through the aisles, and beleaguered-looking husbands darted glances toward the door, filled with the hope of escape. Oh, a few men took part in the frenzy, but I had a feeling most of the eager beavers were down in the toy and tool departments, jousting with levels and hammers rather than with Levi's and hangers.

Barb was an expert in jab and grab. *Jab* being shove an elbow into the person standing to your immediate right, and *grab* being snatch what they were holding and run away before they screamed bloody murder.

Unfortunately, she was determined that I learn the drill. She pointed out a salmon cashmere sweater that was well out of her reach on an upper shelf. To get to it, I'd have to elbow my way into a crowd swarming the lower shelves. I was no wallflower, but the thought of facing the piranhas daunted even me. However, Barb's pleading look spurred me on, and I decided to make her proud. I took a deep breath and waded in.

The first few women near the back parted, allowing me to join them. Maybe this wouldn't be so bad after all. But then I ran into a wall of flesh. The chick had to be four inches taller than me, and a good thirty pounds heavier, all of it muscle. *Bodybuilder*, I thought. Had to be.

"Excuse me," I said. She wasn't after the same sweater, so I thought she'd let me through, but then she turned around, and I saw a look I hadn't seen since I'd been present at a Rolling Stones concert where a decaying Mick Jagger threw one of his shirts to a group of screaming women in the audience. The chick's eyes were on fire. Steroid city. It had to be.

"What the fuck do you want?" she said.

"I'm just trying to get that sweater up there," I said, pointing. "Do you mind letting me grab it and get out of here?"

"Just wait your turn, bitch. I'll get out of the way when I'm good and ready." She snarled at me and I started to back away, not wanting to cause a scene, when one of the other women next to me whispered, "Jeez, who peed in her Cheerios?"

Unable to help myself, I snorted. "Santa Claus, maybe?"

Miss Muscle heard me—or thought she did—and whirled around. "What did you say about me? You said I look like Santa Claus? You think I'm fat?"

I blinked. Twice. I'd woken the sleeping giant and was in danger of being run down by the female equivalent of a Mack truck. "No, no, that's not what I said! I'm sorry— you didn't hear me right—"

"Oh, so now I'm hearing things?" The next thing I knew, Miss Muscle took a good swipe at me, barely missing me with her open palm. Her nails were dangerously long, and I reacted instinctively, my foot meeting her midsection. She flew back, landing against the shelf I'd been trying to reach.

In a mockery of slow-motion comedy, the shelves shuddered and then slowly began to topple forward. Within seconds they came tumbling down, hundreds of sweaters buffering the impact as they crashed to the floor, taking out a table of jeans on the way.

Somehow, maybe via some quirky Christmas miracle or maybe just thanks to a little old-fashioned luck, nobody managed to get hit by anything other than a flurry of cashmere and denim.

The entire floor of Macy's came to a shuddering halt at the sound of the thundering crash. In the midst of the absolute silence that followed, Barbara's nervous laughter rang out, followed by a growing din as frenzied shoppers began whispering.

I eyed Miss Muscle, who was staring at the mess with a confused expression on her face, and decided that the better part of wisdom was to tiptoe away. Turn tail and run wasn't usually my forte, but I had no desire to face the salespeople who would have to clean up after my little spat. Miss Muscle had started it; let her finish it.

I grabbed Barb by the arm and quietly but firmly steered her toward the door. "Put down those cardigans and let's scram. You can buy them somewhere else. We'll go to Lana's, and I'll buy you any goddamn sweater you want."

She started to protest, but one look at my face convinced her that I meant business. She dumped her sweaters on one of the tables that was still standing, and we edged our way to the door. At that moment, I saw the store security guard descending on the scene of our little fiasco. Miss Muscle looked ready to blow steam in his face.

"Move!" I pushed Barb out the door, and we raced for the car. I looked back to see if anybody was following us, but we lucked out and made it into her Pathfinder without being stopped. As Barb stepped on the gas and we squealed out of the parking lot, I leaned back and started to laugh.

"It could only happen to us, babe," I said, pushing my hair back out of my eyes. "Only to us."

Barb snickered. "Don't you know that's why I love hanging out with you?" she said as we sped down the road. "You're one laugh after another, Persia."

I gave her a goofy grin and snorted. "I know. Trust me, babe, I know."

Chapter Fourteen

After our mishap at Macy's, Barb returned to the bakery and I took off to finish my errands. A few flakes of white had fluttered past, and I had the feeling we'd be in for more by evening. Barb was excited. She loved snow. Actually, I had to admit that I was excited, too. Though I was a sun bunny at heart, it was hard not to feel a surge of joy when the first snow hit.

I decided to stop in at the police station on my way home. Kyle was in and saw me right away. He looked tired, downright haggard, in fact, and I wondered what the hell had happened.

"Any word on Elliot?" I asked as I sat down. The fact that my ex was out there on the loose wouldn't shake itself loose from the back of my mind. He could be anywhere, and that was what scared me.

A grim look in his eyes, Kyle shook his head. "Nope, not a word. Not a sighting. You be careful. We set up roadblocks, but we couldn't keep them up indefinitely, and there's always the possibility that he slipped through them. The State Patrol has his picture, and every county in Washington has an APB on him, so we're looking, but he's one man in a big state." He shifted a stack of papers on his desk and leaned back, resting his head on the back of his chair.

"I take it today hasn't been particularly good," I said, knowing the answer to my next question before he answered. But I had to ask. "No sign of Lisa?"

He let out a long sigh. "No. No sign of her, nothing. And no leads other than what we found in the parking lot."

I stared at my hands. "I feel so guilty."

That brought him upright. He leaned forward and rested his elbows on the desk. "Why on earth should you feel guilty?"

Shrugging, I sought for an answer I wasn't sure of myself. "I guess . . . I guess because she's my friend. Because I haven't given every waking moment to searching for her. Because I was at the mall today with Barbara instead of out hunting for clues." After a moment, during which Kyle patiently waited, I added, "I was with my mother when she died, you know. I was asleep, and when I woke up, she was gone. If I'd been awake, if I'd been there, maybe I could have gone for help or something. Maybe I could have saved her."

Kyle stood up and came around to the front of the desk, where he propped himself on the edge. "You were four years old, Persia. What could you have done? Hell . . . I remember in school. From the very beginning, you took everything so seriously. You assumed responsibility for so many of the underdogs. Nobody picked on Robbie Larson again after you beat the crap out of Pickett and Joe Snider. Your reputation as the class avenger still goes untarnished, according to Principal Whittaker."

I laughed then. Principal Whittaker hadn't known what to do with me. He sent me home so many times with notes encouraging Auntie to rein me in. But Principal Whittaker had been an underdog himself when he was young—I was sure of it. He'd been short and thin, with round glasses that made him look like an owl. Every time I ended up in his office, he started out with a lecture and ended up unable to continue, just telling me to be careful and think before I acted.

"Lisa's my friend, Kyle. What am I supposed to do? Just go on, as if she's still here? She's missing, and I think there's a chance she's still alive. I'm going to talk to Annabel's husband tonight. They went home early the night of the Gala, and she says there's a chance he might have seen something out of their living room window, which looks out over Lookout Pier."

With luck, Lloyd would be a snoop who couldn't keep away from the window. Of course, that was pushing the limits of good fortune, but one could always hope for minor miracles.

Kyle raised his eyebrows. "Good. We've talked to a number of residents up on the cliff but haven't had a chance to talk to Annabel yet."

"Have you subpoenaed Lisa's cell phone records yet? Or the house phone, for that matter? She might have received a call from somebody that would give us a clue. Maybe a call that Amy doesn't know about." I was struggling to come up with new ideas; anything that might help.

Kyle beamed. "At least I'm ahead of you on that one. The phone company should be faxing them over today." His smile died off then, and he closed the door before continuing. "Amy's mad at me. She blames me for the fact that we haven't found Lisa yet. I know she does."

I struggled to find something to say that would help. "Kyle, she's scared for her sister. You're an authority figure who just happens to be her boyfriend. She looks up to you to help her, both as a citizen and as a girlfriend. You're caught in a rough place, that's for sure."

"I never expected to fall for Amy. In fact, she didn't seem my type at all," he continued, and I heard the sense of wonder in his voice. The same sense that I felt about Killian. "But working on the antigun campaign for the school together . . . something just clicked."

"Kyle, I can tell you right now that Amy's the *perfect* woman for you. You two fit together like a hand and glove. I'd hate to see this thing with Lisa come between you two, but that means we have to find out what happened to her! Will you let me know if there's anything unusual about the phone records?" I stood up, stretched gently. "Ouch," I said.

"You be careful with that arm. I don't want Miss Florence on my neck about you hurting yourself," Kyle said, glaring.

"The longer I go without moving it, the less mobility I'll have. I don't care what the doctor said. I know muscles, and they need to be moved." I winced as the pain blended with the delicious ache of movement.

"Don't come crying to me if you make it worse," he muttered. "And yes, damn it, I'll call you when I get the records. Maybe between you, Amy, and me, we can figure out just who called her and why."

As I turned to leave, he stopped me with a gentle hand on my shoulder. "Persia, did you mean what you said? About Amy being perfect for me?"

I gave him a slow smile. "I sure did. Let's find Lisa so you and Amy can get on with your lives together, because I'm expecting to hear wedding bells before next year is out."

He snorted. "Me? Get married again? I don't think that's in my future."

As I put my hand on the doorknob, I said, "Don't be too sure, Kyle. You never know what's going to happen. And you're not a man who's happy as a bachelor. Amy would make a wonderful wife. And she'd be lucky to have you." Before he could respond, I slipped out the door and headed to my car.

By the time I got home it was almost two thirty, and the trees were up, the lights were strung, the swags were swagging their way around the room, and Auntie was making fudge. As I licked the fudge pan, she emptied the bags, clucking over my choices.

"Good job, Persia, these are lovely lights."

I'd chosen faceted twinkle lights that reminded me of stained glass panels—in a passing way. They were prettier than the plain ones, and slightly bigger. I'd finally chosen an ivory and gold theme for the tree in my study and had splurged on dozens of sun and star ornaments, as well as corded and fabric decorations to match. With multicolored lights, it would be stunning. Auntie held up one of the beaded ornaments that had a six-inch tassel hanging from it and nodded her approval.

"You have such good taste, Imp. All right, I'm going to call Trevor in and have him carry your decorations up to your study. Then we'll start on the living room tree. I figure by the end of this weekend, we'll have everything decorated."

"Okay, but I'm running over to Annabel's tonight for a little while." I told her how I'd managed to wangle myself an invitation over to the Masons'.

Auntie beamed. "You're a woman of many talents, Imp. Now, come along and help me with the tree. I'll make us some popcorn, and we can eat fudge and decorate while watching the *Forensics Files*."

I grinned, following her into the kitchen. Leave it to Auntie. Only she could mix watching a show about murder and mayhem while decorating for the season of peace and joy and see no contradiction in it at all.

☙

To use the word *house* for Annabel Mason's home was a misnomer. Annabel and Lloyd lived in a mansion. At least three stories high, the manor sprawled out across a well-kept parcel of lawn that must have been two acres if it was an inch. Not a lot of land unless you considered that it was smack in the middle of the rich and powerful suburbs cloistered on the hillside overlooking the inlet. Property was at a premium, so usually the lots were tiny, the houses large, and the taxes excruciating.

But Annabel didn't seem worried about taxes. Her home was smack in the middle of the wide swath of grass and manicured trees, buffering it from the neighbors. The house itself was one of those *Street of Dreams* houses, following no particular style yet ending up unique enough to be artistic but practical.

I parked the car in the semicircular driveway and slipped out into the chill weather, which was still trying to make up its mind whether or not to let loose with the white stuff. I pulled my jacket tighter. Though night was well on its way, the dusk couldn't drown out the silvery white of the sky that appeared when snowstorms were imminent.

As I strode up the flagstone path that led to the front of the house, I took note of the landscaping. Some estates felt soulless in their precision, but the flower beds and shrubs that bordered Annabel's walkway were all just a touch off; someone had guesstimated here and there, rather than using a ruler to plant the flowers and plants in exact intervals. That told me that Annabel wasn't as demanding as one might expect.

I stopped and leaned down to examine one of the rose-bushes. Of course, the roses were long gone, but even in the dim light I could tell it was an heirloom rose, not a hybrid, and that clued me in to yet another facet of Mrs. Mason, whom I was beginning to respect more and more. Annabel had a respect for the past, and she chose authenticity over perfection.

The front of the house was bereft of a porch, and my guess had been wrong. No Grecian pillars, no portico. Just two stone steps leading up to an entry presided over by a set of handcrafted double doors. Both doors were ornamented with stained glass windows shaped like roses the size of portholes.

I rang the bell, hoping that Lloyd was home. There were several cars in the driveway, but with money like Annabel's, there were bound to always be several cars in the driveway. One car in particular looked familiar, but I wasn't sure where I'd seen it, or even if I had.

After a moment, the door opened, and Lloyd stood there, looking puzzled by my appearance. I recognized him from the Gala but doubted if he'd remember me. "I'm Persia Vanderbilt, from Venus Envy? I talked to Annabel this morning. She said you might be able to answer a couple of questions for me and suggested I drop by tonight to talk to you."

He frowned, tipping his head to the side. I suppose he would have been considered handsome, in a tennis-pro way. All tan and white teeth, and something about him whispered "superficial" to me. I wondered what a woman like Annabel saw in him.

"Come in, then," he said, still frowning. "What's this about?" He led me into a living room that could have contained the entire bottom floor of Moss Rose Cottage. It was exquisitely decorated, but here and there I saw hints that somebody actually lived here, that it wasn't just one of those fancy homes mimicking a fine arts gallery. A lace shawl draped over the back of a wing chair, looking old but beloved. A stack of books sitting next to an end table, some with bookmarks holding the place where the reader had left off. A scattering of sheet music on top of the baby grand that was spotlighted beneath a scintillating chandelier of teardrop crystals.

He motioned for me to sit down, and I cautiously sat on the edge of the pale beige sofa until I noticed a faint stain on one of the cushions. I pushed myself back and relaxed.

"So, what's so important that you're dragging yourself over here on a holiday weekend?" Lloyd asked. He poured himself a Scotch and held up another glass. "Would you like a drink?"

"No thank you," I said. "I'm driving." Something about the setup of the bar bothered me, but I couldn't pinpoint just what. Distracted, I said, "When I met Annabel in the bank today, she mentioned to me that you both came home early the night of the Gala. I was wondering if you'd noticed anything unusual. Maybe if you looked out your living room window down toward Lookout Pier?"

Lloyd stared at me for a moment. "Why do you need to know?"

I shrugged. "A friend of mine disappeared from there the night of the dance. You might have read about her in the paper—Lisa Tremont? She works for us at Venus Envy, and we're terribly worried about her."

"Oh," he said, pulling a pipe out of his pocket. "Do you mind?"

I shook my head. It was his home, he could smoke it up if he wanted to, although I cringed when I thought of what the smell would do to the furniture and fine draperies. "No, please, go ahead."

Lloyd lit his pipe, puffing gently until smoke began to curl up from the bowl. He set his Scotch on a coaster on the end table, let out a long, satisfied sigh, and settled back in his chair, resting his feet on an ottoman. "So, your friend has gone missing? Are you sure she just didn't take off somewhere on vacation or with a boyfriend?"

I couldn't pinpoint why, but I didn't like Lloyd Mason too much. There was something too slick about him. I had the feeling Annabel had made a mistake in her choice of husband, unless he was hiding some exquisite quality that I couldn't see.

"No, we found her car down in the parking lot by Lookout Pier, and she hasn't contacted anyone since Saturday. There's something wrong. The police think she might have drowned, but I know her too well to believe that." I shifted in my seat and looked around. "You have a lovely home here."

He practically beamed. "Thank you, I like it, too. Annabel's handiwork, all of it. She's a talented woman, and I'm a lucky man." He cleared his throat. "I'm sorry to disappoint you, but I didn't bother looking outside once we got home. Annabel's nurse helped her up to bed. I'm a night owl and spent the rest of my evening reading in the study. Why are you so sure Lisa didn't drown?"

I almost didn't hear him; I'd glanced at the bar again and realized just what was bothering me. There were two wineglasses on the counter—used. Two, not one. Annabel was out of town, and I had my doubts that she'd ever left a dirty dish out after she'd finished using it.

"Uh . . ." I brought my attention back to him. "Lisa was terrified of water, and I was helping her overcome that phobia. She would never have willingly taken a walk on the pier—alone or with anybody else. There's no way she would have gone near the water. So she parked in that lot to meet someone. Either that or somebody drove her car there and left it, in which case her disappearance takes on a more sinister tone. Chief Laughlin is planning on talking to everybody over here during the next few days."

Lloyd nodded. "I see your point. And you say she's a reliable girl? That she doesn't just run off a lot on her own?"

"Lisa Tremont takes her work—and her family—very seriously," I said. "She'd never leave her sister hanging like this. No, you can be sure, something's preventing her from calling Amy." After a pause, I decided to go for it. "May I ask you about Candy Harrison? She's your wife's nurse."

Looking taken aback, Lloyd cocked his head to one side. "Well, that's a strange change of subject. She's been an exemplary employee, that I can tell you. What do you want to know, and why?"

"Oh, nothing, I suppose. She was working for Lisa's

father before she took on the job with your wife. He died of cancer. I thought maybe she might know something that would help. I spoke to her, but I have the feeling she didn't trust me. I can understand—who am I, that she would confide in me? If she says anything that might give us some indication of where Lisa disappeared to, you would contact the police, wouldn't you?"

He frowned. "Are you accusing Candy of anything?"

Now it was my turn to be taken aback. I hadn't said anything of the sort. I shook my head. "No, of course not. I simply have the feeling that she and Lisa might have had words, and that Lisa might have said something during that argument. The two girls didn't like each other very much, and I'm not altogether sure of the reason."

Standing up, Lloyd finished his drink and set his pipe in an ashtray after tamping it out. "Of course. I'll talk to Ms. Harrison next time I see her. I certainly hope you hear from Lisa soon. You must be frantic, and her sister, too. Allow me to show you out?" He motioned toward the door, and I walked past him. As I did so, I managed to catch my heel on the Persian rug and started to trip. Lloyd caught my elbow as I steadied myself.

As I stood close enough to touch him, my nose twitched. Something—a familiar scent. I frowned, searching my memories for what it was. A rare fragrance, one I seldom smelled. And then I knew. I knew who the other wineglass was for, and I knew what residue perfume was clinging to Lloyd.

Trying to not miss a beat, I gathered my purse and keys. "I appreciate you taking time out of your evening to see me. Thank you. If you think of anything else, you'll let me know?"

He opened the door and with a crocodile smile, waved at me as I dashed down the walkway toward my car. The snow had started, and I could tell we were in for a good night's worth of weather. It was starting to stick to the grass, though the road was bare and wet. But with the temperature dropping, we'd have a mess by morning.

"I'll let you know if I think of anything," Lloyd called after me. "Nice talking with you, and good luck!"

I reached the protection of my car and slid into the front seat. My windshield was almost covered with the white stuff, and the flakes were growing thicker and bigger. I fumbled in my glove compartment and found the camera I kept in the car just in case of an accident. Our insurance agent had recommended doing so, and it seemed like a good idea. Only this roll of pictures would be welcome, rather than dreaded. From where I was parked, I could just see beyond the house to the snow coming down over the inlet. The sight was breathtaking.

Before I headed down to Lookout Pier to take pictures from the shoreline, I glanced at the house. Lloyd had closed the door and was nowhere to be seen. I put the flash on the camera and slid out of the car, hurrying over to the car that had looked familiar. I knew who the car belonged to now, and I quickly took two pictures, one of the profile of the red two-seater BMW, and one of the license plate.

Then I slipped back to the car and eased out of the driveway, hoping that Lloyd and Candy hadn't seen what I'd done.

⋆❧

Once down at Lookout Pier, I snapped a few pictures of the snow as it slowly drifted down to kiss the inlet and melt into the dark and choppy waters while I thought things through.

So Lloyd and Candy were having an affair. That explained the perfume and clothing she'd been wearing the other day when we met. Lloyd was probably buying her gifts, and that would also explain his overdrawn account that Annabel was so upset over at the bank. Chances were that Candy never wore the fragrance—or the fancy clothes—around Annabel, though. Annabel was a smart cookie and would notice the changes, although I also had a sinking feeling that she was deliberately overlooking the signs of a cheating husband.

Sometimes it was easier to pretend something didn't exist until somebody shoved it in your face and rubbed your nose in it. Like Elliot embezzling money. I'd believed him when he told me he had a trust fund from his grandmother. It was easier to accept his word and not question it than to actually risk finding out he was getting his fortune the old-fashioned way—by stealing.

The two wineglasses on the bar told me that Candy must have been hiding in the house, listening to what I was saying. Of course she and Lloyd would take advantage of Annabel's absence. Feeling sorry for the older woman—she was too good a woman to deserve a louse like Lloyd—I walked out on the pier, cautious of my footing. While the railing was plenty sturdy, accidents could—and did—happen. The waves were cresting less than two feet below the pier as the snow silently melted into the darkened currents.

Lloyd and Candy's affair was none of my business, and yet I felt oddly guilty, as if I'd peeked in a room I knew that I shouldn't have. Should I tell Annabel? Did she even want to know? And how did it relate to Lisa's disappearance, if at all?

I was beginning to wish that I'd left the questioning to Kyle. I didn't want to know about cheating hearts and fading matrons who were being taken advantage of. Trapped by uncertainty, I decided to tell Auntie. If anybody could help me sort out my ambiguous feelings, she could. The truth was that, having met and talked to Annabel, I liked her. And I didn't want to see her get hurt. Squaring my shoulders, I turned and headed back to my car.

One last stop before going home. I checked my notebook for her address, then drove over to Candy Harrison's apartment, wondering if Lisa's suspicions were correct. The idea that Candy had been having an affair with Mr.

Tremont seemed much more likely now that I'd realized she and Lloyd were getting it on together, and the thought that Mr. Tremont might have squandered his money on the nurse made me vaguely nauseated. Gifts from boyfriends and lovers were one thing, but Candy struck me as a cunning little whore. She used people and had probably left a trail of heartache in her wake.

Candy lived six blocks from Annabel's, but the neighborhood was a world apart from the affluential suburb in which the Masons lived. The Villa del Mar Apartments were comprised of a series of two-story buildings, each of which contained sixteen units. Looking weathered and ratty in the dim evening light, they weren't exactly slumlord material, but it didn't take a genius to figure out that Candy wasn't rolling in Annabel's money yet. Either that, or she wanted to keep a low profile.

I looked for apartment C-5. After gathering a flashlight, my camera, and putting on a pair of gloves, I quietly dashed up the stairs. The lights were off on the upper floor, including the porch light, which told me that both Candy and her neighbor were out for the evening. I knew where she was, but I could only hope her neighbor didn't come home until I was done poking around.

Taking a deep breath, I pulled out my library card and jimmied the lock. Thank God I'd learned how to pick locks while infiltrating Bebe's factory. I wasn't all that skilled, but knew enough to jar a cheap lock like this one.

A click told me I'd met with success. I slipped inside and turned on my flashlight, determined to ferret out whatever secrets Candy might be hiding.

Chapter Fifteen

After latching the door behind me, I looked around the apartment. Small and cramped, it was a one-bedroom barely larger than a studio. The living room was filled with bags and boxes, and in the beam from my flashlight I counted a dozen bags from Northrup Department Store, three from Briarlane's Jewelers, and a garment bag from Sarina's. Somebody had been on an expensive shopping spree.

No family pictures decorated the walls or tables, and the furniture was thrift-store variety. Takeout boxes sat on the counter in the small kitchenette, some of them crusted over. Taking a chance, I turned on the light over the range and blinked as the dim bulb cast a soft glow around the tiny room.

Dishes filled the sink, and a sour odor lingered, as if milk had been spilled and then gone bad. Wrinkling my nose, I made my way into the bedroom. The bed was covered with a leopard print duvet. I turned on the light on the end table and hurriedly began to search the room. Clothes littered the floor, some obviously dirty; others looked like she'd tried them on then cast them off for another outfit. Ms. Harrison would not receive the award for House-keeper of the Year.

And then I noticed a handbag on her dresser. Marc Jacobs. Black, with a gold chain handle. My stomach lurched. It looked exactly like the one I'd given Lisa a couple of weeks ago. I gingerly picked it up by the chain and opened it. Nothing. Empty. But as I looked closer, I noticed an ink stain on the inner lining. The ink stain my fountain pen had made before I realized that the lid had come off. Shit—this was Lisa's purse! Which meant that Candy *had to know* what happened to her.

My heart racing, I set the handbag back where I'd found it and looked through the rest of the contents scattered on the dresser. Jewelry—some costume, some real. A topaz cocktail ring that had to cost a pretty penny. A string of pearls. A picture of Candy and Lloyd—

What? I picked up the photo. It was from a Polaroid, and looked like it had been taken through a window. I tried to pinpoint the location but couldn't place it. Candy and Lloyd were naked, on a bed, engaged in some hot and heavy dalliance that left me both blushing and thinking that I now knew what had attracted Annabel to him in the first place.

They didn't seem to notice the photographer, so I had my doubts that they'd taken this picture in order to remember their day together. I glanced at the back. The writing was familiar. In Lisa's handwriting, it said, "Candy and Lloyd, November 13th."

So Lisa had caught them together. Could this all be a case of blackmail gone awry? As I was mulling over how to piece together this tidbit with Lisa's disappearance, I noticed a savings deposit book sitting on the dresser. I opened it and gasped. Candy had a balance of $275,352. How the hell did a private nurse come by that much money, and what was she doing living in a dump if she was so well-off? Unless nobody knew she had it, and she wanted to keep it that way.

Had she been collecting it all from Lloyd? That seemed like far too great an amount for Annabel not to notice. As I scanned the list of deposits and dates, it became apparent where she'd gotten most of the cash. Candy had made a regular deposit every two weeks for over a year. The deposits stopped right around the time Mr. Tremont had died. Candy had been either extorting, embezzling, or cajoling money out of Lisa and Amy's father for a long time. Long enough to build up a nice savings account.

After a period of about five months without any regular deposits, they started again. In smaller amounts, yes, but once every two weeks for the past seven months, she'd gone back to making regular deposits. I had a feeling Lloyd was responsible for the renewed activity on her account. Was that why his account was overdrawn? Or had he figured out a way to filter it out from Annabel's accounts without her knowing?

Lost in thought, I sat on the edge of Candy's bed. Had Lisa came across some sort of evidence linking Candy to the loss of her father's money? And had she threatened to expose her? Was she blackmailing Candy for the return of her father's money by using the affair with Lloyd as leverage? And what was Lloyd's part in all this, other than willing paramour? Did he know about Candy's father? Did he realize he was being used? Was Lisa blackmailing both Candy and Lloyd?

No matter which way I looked at it, the situation provided some pretty powerful incentives for Candy to get Lisa out of the way. But what exactly had happened?

The thought that Candy and Lloyd might have killed Lisa raced through my mind, making me queasy. It wasn't out of the realm of possibility. But would a thief and an adulterer stoop to murder? *Could* they? Lloyd stood to lose a lot if Annabel found out he'd been cheating on her.

Winthrop had said Lloyd had agreed to an extensive prenuptial agreement. Just what did that entail?

Wondering if I'd left anything else uncovered, I scoured the room, quickly peeking through drawers, but there was nothing more that I could see. I longed to take the handbag with me for proof, but that would tip Candy off, and I wasn't sure just what Kyle could do based on my observations. Technically, I was breaking and entering, and Candy could have me arrested for that.

I used my camera to take pictures of the handbag, the photograph, and the open savings account book, then made sure everything was put back the way I'd found it, although with the mess rampant throughout the apartment, I doubted if Candy would ever know the difference. After I was finished, I let myself out, locking the door behind me. Nobody bothered me on the way back to my car, and I began to think that I might have a future with the CIA after all.

*

I reached home to find Auntie and Kane sitting by the fire with hot chocolate and cinnamon buns. Auntie motioned me over.

"We were waiting for you. We're about to watch *It's a Wonderful Life* and wanted to know if you'd join us." She held up a DVD, and I smiled. Sometimes it felt damned good to have family.

"I'd love to, but I have to make a call to Kyle first. I found out something that might lead us to Lisa."

Of course, Auntie had to hear about it, and Kane, too, so I told them what I'd been up to. Auntie only blinked when I mentioned breaking into Candy's apartment, but Kane raised his eyebrows and looked at me questioningly.

"So, do you make it a practice to go around picking locks?" he asked. "I don't think Kyle will be able to use your testimony to get a warrant."

"Maybe not, but there has to be some way we can use

what I found out." I punched in Kyle's number and waited until he came on the line. Before he had a chance to speak, I spilled out everything I'd found. "And I have pictures— they aren't digital, but I can get them developed at the one-hour shop tonight, if you want. The Delacorte Plaza's open till midnight for holiday shopping."

"Damn it," he said. "If you'd been invited into her house and saw everything, I could make use of it. But I can't possibly get a warrant based on an illegal search, re- gardless of *who* did the searching. It would never hold up in court. Is there any way you can get back in there legally? Get her to invite you over?" He sounded as frus- trated as I felt.

"I doubt it," I said. "If she and Lloyd are responsible for Lisa's disappearance, then what the hell are we going to do? You're right about one thing, though. If you arrest them, they may never tell us where she is. If she's still alive now, she might not be by the time we finished with them."

"I don't know if I can get the bank to turn over her records without solid evidence. Shit." Kyle let out a long sigh. "Let me ask around and see what I can find out. Meanwhile, see if you can find out anything more about Candy and Lloyd. Then we'll put our heads together, and maybe we'll have enough to piece together this puzzle."

I hung up and looked at Auntie. "Tell me everything you know about Lloyd and Annabel Mason, Auntie. Everything."

Auntie blinked. "Hold on, child. Let me call Winthrop. He would know more than me."

Within fifteen minutes, Winthrop, Auntie, Kane, and I were gathered around the dining room table. Winthrop looked none too pleased at being called out so late, but we assured him that this was on the clock, and he lightened up.

"You want to know more about Annabel and Lloyd Mason? There are things I can tell you that are public knowledge. You know that Annabel has a heart condition.

She's always had it, but so far has managed to avoid major illness, but she has to be careful, or she could easily go into heart failure." He looked at his hands, and I could tell the subject wasn't comfortable for him. "Annabel is a lovely woman; I just wish she realized how lovely. She settled for Lloyd Mason because she was afraid of losing her looks, losing her youth."

"And Lloyd Mason is using her for her money. What about the prenup? How tight is it?"

"I can't give you the details, but what I can tell you is that if Annabel dies before they hit their fifteenth anniversary, he's out with a minimal inheritance. If they divorce before their fifteenth anniversary, he's out with the clothes on his back and a sparse settlement. He has a lot to lose if she dies or if this affair comes to light. Quite frankly, I plan on setting a PI on Lloyd as of Monday. Annabel needs to know about this, but I want proof first."

Winthrop's voice was so harsh that I stared at him. What I saw in his eyes told me that he was in love with Annabel. Had they ever dated? Had she rejected him? Or had he just never had the chance to tell her how he felt?

"How long have they been married?" I asked.

"Nine years. Annabel was fifty-seven when they married; Lloyd was forty-three. Hence, the prenuptial agreement. If he's having an affair now, my guess is that he's had several over the years, but this time, he met his match in Miss Candy Harrison. He's a stupid man to risk that much money, but then again, as I told you before, Lloyd was never a very good lawyer, and he only passed the bar by the skin of his teeth. If I remember right, it took him five tries."

Auntie refilled our teacups. She handed around a plate of tomato and cream cheese sandwiches, and Winthrop gave her a grin. "You know the way to my heart, Florence."

"She knows the way to mine, too," Kane spoke up. He touched his nose and winked. "Just make sure you don't lure her away with those highfalutin ways of yours. She's all mine."

Winthrop almost choked on his sandwich, laughing. "Kane, if I wanted to lure Florence away, I'd do it in a second without any regrets. But she seems happy with you, and so I will remain a gentleman."

Auntie gave both of them a gentle whop upside the head. "You two take the cake. While you're eating the sandwiches, I'll get some apple pie and ice cream for us." Kane moved to help her, while Winthrop and I stayed at the table.

"So, have you found out anything else about Candy since we last talked?"

"Actually, yes. I did a little digging into her background after our last discussion. It seems our nurse here worked at a geriatric home in Olympia for awhile. She was fired—I told you that much. Well, I had a friend of mine ask around, and it seems that a few of the residents who had lived there ended up including Candy in their wills."

"She seems to specialize in taking care of people with money, doesn't she?" I asked.

"Well, leaving a bequest to a caregiver isn't in itself uncommon, but one of the sons of an elderly gentleman who Candy looked after didn't like losing part of his inheritance, and he investigated her. Seems that she was accused of *fraternizing* with a few of the male residents. Nothing could be proven, and shortly after that, the nursing home let her go." Winthrop shook his head. "I don't know how she managed to con them out of the money, but then again, old geezers like to think they're still attractive to young women."

"She can't be stupid enough to think that Lloyd would leave Annabel for her. Surely he's told her about the prenup. Even if he didn't, that seems to be fairly common knowledge." I tried to look at the matter through the eyes of a manipulator. In six years Lloyd would potentially be a rich man. Would they chance throwing that away for sex now?

Winthrop seemed to follow my train of thought. "There's one loophole that gives them a way out. If Annabel's health deteriorates so that she has to be confined to a nursing home, Lloyd can go to court and get appointed power of attorney. He might not be able to get the bulk of her money, but even the interest off what she's worth would be a powerful temptation for someone looking for a free ride."

"And a nurse might know just how to speed along that deterioration in health. Oh hell, Winthrop, Candy could be giving her the wrong meds in order to make her sicker!"

"Precisely, which is why we're going to talk to Annabel about this. I won't have them hurting her." His voice boomed through the room as Auntie and Kane brought our dessert to the table.

"Is there anything we can do now?"

"Not tonight. We have to go about this carefully." Winthrop concurred with Kyle. "Just owning a Marc Jacobs bag doesn't mean that she stole it from Lisa, even though *you* know she did. Any number of handbags have ink stains in them, and it's your word against Candy's— and seeing how you were in her apartment illegally, how do you think that would sound to a judge? And the X-rated photograph could have been taken by anybody. If we tip our hands prematurely, and Lisa's still alive, we might put her life in jeopardy."

Auntie and I walked Winthrop and Kane out to their cars. The snow had piled a good two inches thick already. Trevor would be busy with the shovel tomorrow, that was for sure. We waved as they pulled out, then stood for a moment, watching the thick flakes silently drift to the ground.

"It's beautiful, isn't it, Imp?" Auntie asked.

I nodded. "Doesn't it seem like it muffles everything in

a cushion of silence? Time seems to stand still when it snows."

"Kane walked the dogs for us, so we don't have to do that tonight," Auntie said. "Come on, let's get inside." She linked her arm through mine. "We'll find out where Lisa is. It seems like you're getting closer. I know you're frustrated and worried, but that's the reality of most missing persons cases. Not all fireworks and sudden discoveries like you see on the cop shows."

"I know," I said, shutting the door behind us. "I just hate wondering if she's still alive, waiting for help that may never come. It feels like tomorrow we'll just go back to work at the shop and eventually everybody will talk about 'Lisa Tremont, the girl who disappeared' as if it's all faded and over. But it won't ever be over till we find her—especially not for her sister."

Before I went to bed, a wave of nostalgia hit me, and I climbed the stairs to the landing at the door of the attic, standing with my hand on the knob, flashing back to all the nights I'd spent up here as a child, searching for comfort. Searching for the truth of my own thoughts.

As I entered the room, I felt for the light switch. It was where it always had been, and when I flipped it, a pale but steady light flickered on from a pair of sconces mounted on the wall.

I glanced around. There was the rocking chair in which I'd spent many a night, talking to the Cap'n and to my mother's ghost, who I never caught a glimpse of but who I was positive could hear me. I'd come here to think, to journal, to muse, and sometimes to cry.

I found myself drawn over to a large black trunk painted with ivy vines and roses. This was my trunk. Auntie had commissioned it from a local artisan, and I'd left it here when I took off for Seattle, not wanting to sever all connections I had with Moss Rose Cottage. Kneeling by its side, I lifted the lid. I hadn't looked inside since I was sixteen.

As I sorted through the memorabilia, I shook my head, wondering at the circumambulatory route that had brought me home. Here was the doll I'd been carrying when I showed up on Auntie's doorstep, four years old and holding the hand of my father who didn't care if he ever saw me again. The doll was a belly dancing doll, and she was dark and mysterious. Next to the doll were the souvenirs I'd brought home from my travels with Auntie. A Bast statue from Egypt, a bottle of perfume—long faded and evaporated—from France, a woven shawl from Ireland, a tiny heart pendant that Eva had given to me on my eighth birthday. And next to my treasure trove were several faded journals. My diaries.

"What do you know?" I said softly. "Hey, Cap'n! Remember these? I used to come up here and write in them. I'd tell you everything that I was thinking, then write it down so I would remember later. So I wouldn't forget all my dreams and goals."

I picked up one and flipped through it. I'd written one when I was eight, another at nine, the next I hadn't started until I was eleven. Two more, from thirteen and fifteen. Journals of my childhood, charting the route that I'd taken to become the person I am. Diaries holding all the secrets of my life.

As I fingered the brocade cover, I thought, *That's what diaries are—our most secret lives.* What we couldn't tell our family and friends, we could tell a blank page. Our most heartfelt moments, our fears, our dreams, and our plans.

Wait a minute! *Our plans.* I dropped the volume on my lap and sat up. Lisa kept a diary. I'd seen her writing in a journal from time to time. Had Amy even thought to look in her room for it? Maybe it could tell us something about where Lisa had been planning to go. I jumped up, closing the lid to the trunk, and checked my watch. It was too late to call Amy or Kyle now, but first thing in the morning, I'd be on the phone.

Before heading back to my suite I stood for a moment at the little porthole window overlooking the inlet. The ocean mirrored that silver sheen that lit up the sky, reflecting it upward to form a haze so that I couldn't tell where the sky ended and the water began. The roof was covered with a thick layer of snow, and the trees were swaying gently in the breeze that stirred up the flakes, swirling them into flurries of dancing snowmen. I sighed, feeling a tad melancholy.

"Please let her be okay," I whispered under my breath. "Please let them have hearts. Please, don't let Lisa be dead."

As I headed for the door, there was a faint creak behind me, and I turned. The rocker was moving ever so slightly—just a little—as if someone was gently rocking back and forth, and I thought for a moment I could smell pipe smoke.

Smiling softly, I whispered, "Night, Cap'n. It's good to talk to you again," and then headed downstairs for bed.

❧

A loud crash brought me to waking consciousness, and another shot me to my feet. I flipped on my light and, dressed only in my nightshirt, went racing downstairs. Most likely one of the dogs had managed to get in the cupboards again. I skidded to a halt in the hallway, about to head into the kitchen when I heard another noise, this one from the living room. It sounded like whimpering and, worried that one of the dogs had been hurt, I hurried through the kitchen, into the living room. The sight before me stopped me cold in my tracks.

Elliot was there, silhouetted by the kitchen light as he stood near the Christmas tree. He was holding Pete by the collar with one hand, his gun aimed at the dog with the other. He looked drunk, and he looked mean. I gasped and started toward him, but he gave me an evil grin and put the muzzle of the gun closer to the struggling retriever's head.

"You want me to shoot him? You want to see me blow this dog's brains out right in front of you? How would you like that, Persia?" His voice dripped with sarcasm, his words slurred. Elliot was high as a kite.

"Let him go. Pete never did anything to hurt you, Elliot. Let him go, for God's sake." I took another step toward him.

"What will you give me to let him go?"

I blinked. "What do you want? Money?"

With a harsh snort—and then a moan as he winced beneath the bandage covering his nose—Elliot spat on the ground. "Money? You think I'm here for money? That's a good one. No, baby, I left my dignity under your thumb last time I was here. I left my balls under your heel. I'm here to get both of them back."

Oh God, this was going to be bad. There was no way it _couldn't_ be bad. I struggled to keep my voice even. "Let the dog go. This is between us. Don't take out your anger at me on Pete. Just let him go, please?"

"It's _please_ now, is it? Well, that's a start. Beg me to let him go. Beg me, and I'll do it. And make it good." Elliot twisted Pete's collar a little tighter and Petey whimpered again, looking at me with bewildered eyes. The dog had known a harsh life before Auntie rescued him, and I was furious at Elliot for using him as a pawn.

"You want me to beg for Pete's life? All right, I will. He doesn't deserve cruelty, so I'll get down on my knees and beg you to spare him." Hating every minute of it, I slowly lowered myself to my knees. "Elliot, please, let Petey go. I'm begging you—he's a good dog. If you're angry at me, be angry at _me_. Please don't hurt Pete."

Elliot seemed taken aback that I'd actually done it. His fingers slipped, and Pete pulled away from his grasp. Elliot swung around, gun aimed, but then shook his head and turned back to me as Pete ran over to me.

"Go lie down, Pete. Go lie down in your bed and stay there. Go on!" Bless his heart, Pete listened and headed out of the room. One crisis down, another to go. I slowly stood up, trying to appear as unthreatening as possible.

"Elliot, what do you want? I thought you had left the island."

"I tried, but damn it, you wouldn't let me. You're in my head, Persia. You mock me every minute of the day. You and your boyfriend and your rich aunt and your oh-so-prissy business. And I'm stuck in a dump, no prospects, nobody will hire me. Who wants an accountant who was arrested for embezzling and laundering money?"

Back to his whiny self, I noted. Albeit once again, he had a gun. I could tell that even Elliot didn't know what he wanted from me, which was quite possibly the worst position I could be in. Without a plan, he might become so desperate he'd shoot us both.

I had to do something and do it quick. He was too far gone for me to just walk up to him and take the gun away. Then, as my eyes focused on the Christmas tree, I had an idea. I might be able to startle him enough to give me the one wedge I needed.

"Elliot," I said, "you just have to move on. Get away from the island. Go back to Seattle and start over there." And then I clapped my hands. Twice. The Christmas tree lights sprang to life, as did the lights lining the swag on the mantelpiece. Bless Auntie and The Clapper!

Blinded by the sudden brilliance of twinkling faerie lights, Elliot jerked around to stare wildly at the tree. Unfortunately, his gun went off, and he shot our three-foot-high wooden nutcracker in the head, but that was the kind of casualty we could recover from. I raced forward, throwing myself at him and knocking him to the ground, my shoulder screaming bloody murder with every jolt. Elliot grunted and lost hold of the gun, which went skittering across the floor.

"Persia, what the fuck—"

"That's enough! Hold it right there." Kyle's voice boomed out of the kitchen, and I glanced over my shoulder to see him and one of his officers rush in, followed by Auntie, who had her cell phone in hand. "We have to stop meeting like this, Elliot. People are going to talk," he added, and I stared at him incredulously. Kyle had made a joke?

He helped me up while the other officer cuffed Elliot, none too gently.

"Oh Imp, I was so afraid that he'd hurt you before Kyle got here," Auntie said. She was shaking pretty bad, and I put my arms around her, holding her close. "I heard a crash and called the police before I even set foot on the stairs."

"You made the right decision, Miss Florence," Kyle said. He picked up the gun and shook his head. "Yep, this is Officer Reed's gun. Elliot, didn't anybody ever teach you to not to play with firearms? You sure as hell can't shoot straight."

"The nutcracker took one in the head," I said, caught by a sudden fit of nervous giggles. I was too tired and in too much pain to think straight, and now that Elliot was safely cuffed—and shackled at the ankles, thanks to Kyle's fore-sight—I broke into a gale of laughter that was followed by a just as unexpected shower of tears.

Auntie and Kyle stared at me, shaking their heads.

"Imp," Auntie said, "*you* almost took one in the head. And Pete. This is no laughing matter—"

"I think she's just wound up from the stress, Miss Florence." Kyle led me over to the rocking chair. "You might want to go back to the doctor and have your shoul-der checked again. But you did good, Persia. That was quick thinking. I don't know if Christmas lights have ever saved anybody's life before, but you certainly know how to use whatever's available."

I swallowed both laughter and tears and gave him a wry grin. "Well, I don't teach those self-defense courses for nothing, you know. This is what I tell my students every time: you look around for anything that can be used as a weapon. I'm just grateful that Auntie thought to put them on The Clapper in the first place."

Kyle and the other officer carted Elliot away. This time, I hoped it was for good. Not only would he face the original charges, but now he'd face escape and another attempted murder charge. Or at least assault with a deadly weapon.

Auntie picked up the remains of the nutcracker and looked at me, a twisted smile on her face. "This little guy gave his life for you. Kind of. Persia, what should we do with him? I've had him for forty years, and I hate to just toss him in the garbage."

I looked at the wooden toy and indeed, every Christmas when I was a child, I remembered him showing up near the tree. "Maybe burn him? Send him back to ashes? Or better yet, why don't we fix him up and coat him with polyurethane and set him out to watch over the Memory Garden?"

Auntie had fashioned a little spot away from the shop gardens that held the remains of three beloved cats that she'd rescued and given a home to until they'd succumbed to old age. The graveyard would be there for the rest of the Menagerie as their times came, and whatever animals came to fill the empty spaces in our tribe after that. Replete with lilies and white roses, with daisies and white pansies and primroses, and delicate maidenhair fern, and little stone statues of cats and dogs, it was a garden in white and green. A memorial.

Auntie gave me a soft smile. "That would be lovely," she said. "What a wonderful idea. He can be their guardian." She gently laid him on the coffee table and motioned for me to join her in the kitchen. "I think we need some hot chocolate, don't you, Imp?"

"I'll be there in a minute, Auntie. I just want to tidy up around here." When Elliot had crashed to the floor, he'd knocked several of the ornaments off the tree. I carefully picked up the crystal balls—miraculously they'd all survived—and hung them back on the branches. Thank heavens the cats left them alone, though I could see Delilah snoozing away under the tree, and Buttercup was hiding out on a pillow nearby. I finished tidying up and stared at the scene.

The cats, the tree sparkling with light, the bedecked mantel . . . it was all so beautiful and so homey. On impulse, I switched on the radio and turned it to 98.1 FM. The crystal tones of "Carol of the Bells" rang out, lovely and haunting, and I closed my eyes, willing myself to relax and breathe deeply.

Auntie swept open the curtains, and we stared at the yard. The snow was still falling, and there must have been a good five inches on the ground already. "Imp, what do you say to a walk through the gardens before we have a bite to eat? Snow this deep is a rare treat around here." Auntie looked at me expectantly, and suddenly, that seemed the perfect thing to do.

I nodded and accepted the pair of sweatpants she handed me from the dryer. As we suited up in coats and boots, we didn't speak. We didn't have to. Sometimes, silence was the best antidote to anxiety, and by the time we opened the door, dogs at our heels, and set off for the gardens, the muffled hush of the night had captured both of us in its spell.

Our grounds had transformed. Covered in crystals, the bushes and trees took on an otherworldly glow, and the crunch of snow under our feet flashed me back to the story of Heidi. I'd loved the book as a child, and often imagined myself wading home to an alpine cabin where Auntie would be waiting with toasted cheese on bread.

"I hope it lasts," I said, my voice sounding swathed in cotton as the flakes continued to fall thick and fast. "We should take pictures tomorrow."

"Good idea, Imp. Oh, look at Beauty!" The little cocker spaniel bounded around with frantic joy, barking at the flakes with the frenzy only another canine can understand. Petey walked more sedately by my side, and Beast went rolling around, snuffling under a log after something buried there.

I stopped, staring up as the flakes hit my face and stuck to my hair. "Thank you," I whispered. "Thank you for helping me save Petey and trip up Elliot." The universe might be listening or not, but I believed in showing gratitude for favors granted.

When morning came, I'd go over to Amy's, and we'd search for Lisa's diary. And if we could find it, perhaps we'd find the key to where she was.

"That's all I want for Christmas, Santa," I whispered into the night.

"What did you say, Imp? And let's turn back now. I could go for some hot chocolate, a grilled cheese sandwich, and a bowl of chicken soup."

"That sounds perfect to me," I said. "I was thinking about Lisa and whether or not we'll find her." With a shrug, I added, "I was just telling Santa that all I want for Christmas is for my friends and loved ones to be happy, healthy, and safe. Can't hurt, can it?"

"No, it can't hurt. If you can't ask Santa for a favor, who can you ask?" Auntie slid her arm through mine. "Imp, being with family and friends . . . having health, safety, and well-being . . . they're the only things that really matter in the end. No matter who you were or what you accomplished, at the last gasp it comes down to this: Were you a good person? Did you leave this world a little better than it was when you came into it? And did you act with love?"

We whistled for the dogs and headed back to the house. In the distance, the waves crashed against the shore, and once again, the image of Lisa's face popped into my mind. I hoped that, wherever she was, she was safe and warm.

Chapter Sixteen

Morning saw me up and surprised to find my arm feeling a bit better. After the skirmish with Elliot, I was sure I'd done more damage, but it seemed to have had the opposite effect. I cautiously went through a short stretching routine and then hopped on my stationary bike for fifteen minutes before showering and getting dressed.

One look out the window told me the world was still swaddled in white, so I put on a pair of dark-washed jeans and a soft burgundy turtleneck. I slid my feet into a pair of candy cane–decorated socks and then a pair of stacked-heel boots. The bottoms were skid-proof so I wouldn't go sliding all over the place. I brushed my hair and decided to let it hang loose, holding it back with a velvet headband.

As I hurried downstairs, the sound of the TV told me Auntie was up. She was drinking a cup of tea and eating fresh-baked muffins while watching *Northwest Cable News.*

"Good morning," she said, motioning to the second cup

and saucer waiting. "I made tea and cranberry muffins for breakfast. There's also some smoked salmon. I'm heading out to the shop in a few minutes," she said. "You go ahead and go over to Amy's. I hope you find what you're looking for."

"So do I," I said, dropping into a chair. Nibbling on one of the muffins, I poured my tea and added lemon. "So what's on the news?"

"More of the same old, same old. They had a piece on Elliot. He's safely locked up, by the way. Kyle made sure to call me. I don't know why I watch," Auntie said. "The world seems to have gone crazy. Two homeless men were found dead—frozen—in Seattle. There was a seven-car pileup on I-5 that left three dead, and police logged eighty-three minor accidents on the freeway overnight because of the unexpected snowstorm. And at the Delacorte Plaza, one of the mall Santas got plastered, dropped his pants, and peed all over one of the elves. The little girl who was next in line started screaming, and her father got so angry he gave Santa a black eye. The holidays can be ugly, Imp." But even as she ticked off the incidents, I could see the twinkle in her eyes.

"Bad news or not, you love it, don't you? You just love this time of year," I said, sipping my Irish breakfast tea.

Auntie chuckled. "Guilty as charged. I know that it's a rough time for a lot of people, and I do what I can to help, but that can't negate the joy this time of year brings to me. We'll be together for Christmas, and you know how much that means to me."

At that thought, I shook off the gloom. "I know; I feel the same way, too."

"Speaking of family, I got a call from Mother today." Auntie raised her eyebrows, and I snorted. Grandma Dakota was as prim as Auntie was flamboyant. It was hard to believe they were related.

Grandma and I had a tenuous relationship; she hadn't approved of my mother's choice to follow my father to

Iran when he relocated there for the company he worked for. Especially since they weren't married. My mother never ended up with a proposal, and when she died, my father was only too glad for the opportunity to drop me off with Auntie.

"What did Grandma want?" I sliced off a piece of smoked salmon and gave a little smile of satisfaction when the taste of hickory hit my tongue.

"She wanted to let me know she's sent off our presents and to keep a lookout for them. Of course, she had to point out that it would be nice to have both of us there for the holiday, seeing that she's *not getting any younger and probably only has a few years left*." Auntie could do a perfect imitation of Grandma, and it never failed to make me laugh.

"Grandma may be eighty-three, but you wait and see, she'll outlive us all." I shook my head. My mother had been born thirteen years after Auntie, but Grandma Dakota never blinked an eye. She took it in stride and charged ahead. Grandpa William was just along for the ride—he'd been a lawyer, but even though he was terribly successful, he hadn't let it go to his head. Auntie told me that if he'd had his way, they would have taken me in, but Grandma was so put out about my mother dying overseas that Gramps quietly stepped aside and gave Aunt Florence his blessing.

"Well, I'm certainly not traveling to Virginia for the holidays. I love Mother, but I have no desire to sit there and have her try to mold me over in her image. Not at my age," Auntie said.

I had a frightening flash of Grandma forcing Auntie into a Chanel pantsuit and Mrs. Cleaver pearls. Nope, not a good scenario nor one likely to happen. Snickering, I picked up the phone.

"I'd better call Amy. She should be up by now."

Sure enough, she was, and when I told her what I was thinking, she was only too happy to invite me over. I gathered my purse and keys and shrugged into a warm suede jacket. As I stepped out onto the porch, the frosty air pierced my lungs like a row of needle-sharp daggers. The steps were iced over, and I cautiously navigated my way down them only to meet Trevor, who was climbing out of his truck, sandbag in hand.

"I thought I'd come in early," he said, "and deice Miss Florence's steps. I figured things would be pretty frozen over here."

I gave him a quick hug. "Thanks, Trev. You're worth your weight in gold. What does Auntie have on the list for you today?"

He snorted. "Apparently, this year we're lighting up the holly grove. She wants everything decked out in twinkles, so I'm off to A Christmas Carol today for more lights and other assorted goodies."

The holly grove was Auntie's name for a clearing around a giant holly tree on the outskirts of our land. Trev and Sarah had worked their butts off through September to clear out the brambles, plant wildflowers, and build a rock garden. The ring of cedars surrounding the lea gave the whole area a grovelike feel, and Auntie was intent on creating a magical place that could be used for Venus Envy–sponsored events during the summer.

"Well, that'll be pretty," I said. "How are the roads, by the way? Do I need snow tires or anything like that?"

Trev glanced back at his truck. "Wouldn't hurt. This winter's supposed to be a lot wetter and colder than usual, which means we could see several snowstorms. And watch out for black ice—the roads are pretty slick this morning. Don't take Randall Avenue. A tree blew down across the road and took the power lines with it. Electricity is out for blocks around, and it's a real mess."

I waved and got in my car. Trevor put down his sandbags and hurried over, motioning for me to stay inside while he deiced the windshield. As I was warming the engine, my phone rang, and I flipped it open. Killian! I quickly punched the Talk button and answered.

"Persia, I wanted to catch you before I get on the plane. I'm at the airport, and my flight's been delayed for an hour. Did I call at a bad time?"

I smiled softly. "There's never a bad time for you to call. Are you ready for your meeting?"

"Ready as I'll ever be," he said. "I've got all the graphs, charts, spreadsheets, and marketing analyses that you could ever hope to see. Once we finalize the deal, then I'll be able to start hunting for rental space. Possibly as early as December. I'm thinking of buying Bebe's old building." He gave a nasty snicker, and I cracked up. "Just think, Bebe Wilcox can rot in that jail cell of hers knowing that my new company took over her space."

"Just make sure you get Bran Stanton to cleanse the place for you." I stopped suddenly. Considering that Bran and I'd had a lovely fling for a few months, I wasn't sure that was the best idea after all. But Killian just grunted.

"Hell, I'd do it—extra insurance is always welcome. But didn't his sister say he's off on some reality show?"

"Come to think of it, yeah. *Castaway: Amazon Adventure*. And it wouldn't surprise me to see him win, either. Of course, if he wins a million dollars, he's going to be insufferable. He was talking about going to Everest earlier this year." As much as I loved being with Killian, I would have given just about anything to go on an expedition up Everest. It would be brutal, but I was up to the training.

"And you want to go," Killian said, laughing. "Don't deny it. Well, if you do, I won't stand in your way, but Stanton better not be your bed warmer if you go with him. Have you found out anything about Lisa yet?"

"No," I said. "But I'm warming up the car as we speak to go check on a lead. We're making headway."

"Okay, babe. I'll let you go, then. But Persia, be careful. And remember—you're all mine." Killian's voice slid over me like liquid fire.

"Trust me, I won't forget," I said. "Hurry back. And be safe. And good luck to you." I hung up and pulled out of the driveway. Killian and I bantered the words "Love you" around like a badminton birdie, but we hadn't landed them seriously yet. I didn't know if we would—or when we would—but the feeling was there. And that was enough.

~

Amy was waiting for me, her expression hopeful. My breath puffed out in little clouds of white as I hurried to the door and pulled off my gloves and jacket. Amy pressed a cup of hot chocolate in my hands. "I can't believe the snow—and the weatherman says we might have more this afternoon."

"Yeah, and for once it's not melting off right away." I sipped at the chocolate, grateful for the warmth. "So, what do you think? Any idea where Lisa might have hidden her diary?"

With a shrug, Amy led me back to Lisa's room. "Probably in here. Let's see what we can find. Feel free to look through everything," she said, starting at the desk. While she searched among Lisa's papers, I began hunting through Lisa's dresser, looking for anything that might be a journal. The drawers revealed an interesting array of lingerie, condoms, a few personal toys that I discreetly avoided mentioning, and a baggie that contained a few grams of marijuana. I handed it to Amy.

"You might want to get rid of this. I don't have any problem with it, but if the police ever come in to check the room, you don't want things getting ugly."

Amy sighed. "Yeah. Lisa's a party girl, but she's usually careful. I'll just dispose of this and be right back." She headed into the bathroom, and I turned my attention to Lisa's bed. I stripped the sheets and comforter and began searching between the mattress and box spring. A moment later, I hit pay dirt. At the foot of the bed I found a thin volume. It was lovely—as beautiful as my own journals—and the cover was a soft navy velvet. It was tied shut with a pale blue ribbon, and I sat down on the bed, holding the book in my lap. Amy joined me.

"Have you ever seen this before?" I asked.

She shook her head. "I don't think so. I've seen her write in another journal, but this is different. Maybe she keeps two? Some people do, one for very private thoughts."

I silently untied the bow and set the ribbon aside. I could tell that Lisa had used this journal with care. I wagered a guess that we wouldn't find any haphazard notes or scribbled-out pages.

As I flipped through the diary, I saw that I was right. Lisa had printed everything in neat block lettering. Tidy entries that looked like they'd taken some thought. No doubt her venting was left for the other journal. This book contained memories and poems and important notes.

"Why don't you keep searching for her other journal? We might need both," I said as I skimmed entries. Better I read these than Amy. They were sisters. Anything in here would roll off my back, but if there was something about Amy, it might hurt her feelings.

Toward the end, I came across an entry that mentioned Candy. Dated on the Saturday of the Gala, it was neatly printed like the others, but the pen pressure had been heavy, and I could almost feel the anger seething from the pages.

Our father's estate has been demolished by Candy Harrison. She sucked him dry and left us holding the empty purse strings. She's a manipulator, and though I can't prove she did it, I know she's got our missing money. And now we're going to get it back. All that snooping around and following her paid off. Yesterday

she made an appointment and begged me not to say a
word about her and Lloyd, but it's too late.

   I'm meeting them this afternoon down on Lookout
Pier in the parking lot. And if they don't show, they
know I'll just take my pictures to Annabel. If Candy
won't pay us back what she stole, then I'll do the next
best thing—see her reputation destroyed. It's the least
she deserves.

Two photographs were carefully taped by their corners
to the next page. They were Polaroids, and they showed
Lloyd and Candy doing the horizontal bump and grind.
Just like the one I'd found in Candy's apartment.

I jumped up and called to Amy, who was sorting
through the closet. "I found what we need to have Kyle
search Candy's apartment! Look at this."

As Amy read the entry and looked at the pictures, her
eyes grew wide, and she let out a little gasp. "Oh no!
Candy really took our money? Lisa hinted at it, but I
thought she was being paranoid."

I frowned. "I don't know if we can ever prove that
Candy stole the money, but yes, her bankbook did show a
lot of large deposits during the time she was caring for
your father. Call Kyle and ask him to come over, would
you?"

While we waited for him to get there, we sat at the
kitchen table, hot chocolate in hand. I wandered over to
the window, gazing out at the tidy lawn. Candy and Lloyd
were responsible for Lisa's disappearance. I knew it. But
what if they'd already killed her to keep her quiet? Could
they go so far? *Would* they?

A nagging suspicion pounded at the corners of my
thoughts, one I didn't want to explore. What if Candy and
Lloyd had dragged her out to Lookout Pier and pushed her
off the edge? She could be under the water there. Just because one body had surfaced didn't mean that Lisa wasn't

down there, too. Maybe Kyle was right, but in a way he never expected to be.

I suddenly wondered where Lloyd had been during the afternoon of the Gala. Whatever had happened to Lisa took place during the afternoon, because Lloyd was at the dance with Annabel, and Lisa was missing by then.

All of these thoughts racing through my head, I turned back to the table, only to find Amy silently weeping as she stared at a picture of her sister. She looked up at me, her composure crumbling before my eyes. I hurried over to her, and she rested her head against my side as I slid my arm around her shoulder.

She didn't speak, and I didn't ask her to. There was nothing to say. We both knew that there was a chance that Lisa had met with a violent end. It was one thing to think she might be in an accident somewhere; quite another to realize she was blackmailing a potential embezzler who wouldn't want the truth to come out.

The doorbell rang, and Amy hastily dabbed at her eyes. "I'll get it," I said, leaving her to compose herself. Kyle was standing there, looking grim. "Weather's socking in. It's going to be a long night and probably a lot of accidents. What have you got?"

I nodded him into the kitchen, where we showed him the diary and pictures. "Now can you search Candy's apartment? Now can you talk to Lloyd?"

"Yep," he said, closing the diary and slipping it into a bag. "We'll need this, but we should be able to get a search warrant. Once I find the other photo in Candy's apartment, we can arrest her and Lloyd on suspicion of playing a part in Lisa's disappearance. That alone might scare them into confessing. If Lisa's alive, we can play up the fact that they won't get nearly as bad a sentence if they tell us where she is."

We headed out, Kyle in his prowl car, Amy riding with me. Kyle stopped at the courthouse and within minutes returned, waving a search warrant. "I called ahead," he said, leaning against my door. "Let's go over to Candy's. I assume you want to come along?"

I nodded. "We won't interfere, though. I promise."

"Uh-huh. Right. I know what your promises are worth. Just don't do anything without my permission so we don't botch up the admissibility of any evidence we recover." He jogged back to his car, and we followed him over to Candy's apartment building.

The Villa del Mar looked as run-down as ever. Kyle took the lead, and we headed up the stairs, stopping at Candy's door. He knocked three times, and when nobody answered, he sent me to find the superintendent, who brought the master key. The super let us in, standing beside the door rubbing her arms against the cold as we entered the apartment.

The place looked just about the same as it had when I'd been there before. I pointed to the handbag, and Kyle bagged it. He sifted through her things, turning her desk inside out, checking every drawer. On her dresser, he found her bankbook and bagged that for evidence, too. And then, the picture.

As he gingerly picked it up, gloves on, he said, "This is our link. This gives me probable cause to believe that Candy played a part in Lisa's disappearance." He looked through a few more things, but nothing seemed out of the ordinary. Returning to the super, he asked, "Do you know when Miss Harrison will be home?"

The super shook her head. "Nah, that girl is a wild one. I don't like her much, but she pays her rent on time and doesn't play her music too loud. She done something wrong?"

"Maybe. If she returns, please call the station and tell us where and when you saw her. Someone's life may depend on it." Kyle handed her a card with the station's number on it, and we took off back down the stairs.

"What next?" I asked.

"I'll get one of the boys over here to keep a watch in

case she returns, and put out an APB on her. Hold on," he said, running back up to exchange notes with the super again. When he returned, he held up a piece of paper. "Her license plate and make and model of car. Makes it easier for the APB to work," he added, a short grin tweaking the corner of his lips.

"Where do we go from here?" Amy asked, her eyes flickering. I could hear the faint glimmer of hope in her voice, but it waged war with fear, and I knew she was fighting a battle against expecting too much.

Kyle glanced down at her protectively. I could tell he wanted to gather her in his arms, to whisper that it would be okay. He settled for lifting her chin and giving her a soft smile. "We go to Annabel's and have a little chat with Lloyd. Candy might be there, too, for all we know."

The streets were getting slicker. Not only had the snow remained on the roads, except along the main thoroughfares, but the temperature was still below freezing, and now tiny flakes began to skitter through the air, whirling as the breeze whipped them into a frenzied dance. We avoided the downtown area where shoppers would be clogging the streets, but in doing so, found ourselves on a back road that had patches of black ice and frozen slush.

Cautiously navigating around several downed tree limbs, I pulled into Annabel's driveway behind Kyle and let out a long sigh. While I knew how to drive on snow, it had been awhile. I turned to Amy. "Here we are. Keep your spirits up, hon. Lloyd doesn't strike me as a killer. And I doubt if Candy has the brains for it."

She gave me a weak smile and followed me up the path as we joined Kyle at the door. He rang the bell, and to my surprise, Annabel answered. She frowned at his uniform, then saw me and, looking confused, said, "Is something wrong? Did something happen to Lloyd?"

Kyle winced. "Is your husband home, ma'am? I need to talk to him."

Annabel shook her head. "No, he went out to our beach

house on the other side of the island. He's going to make sure it's battened up tight because of the storm. He won't be home until evening. What is it? Persia, tell me—I know something's wrong."

By the edge in her voice I realized that she did, indeed, know something was up. She probably suspected Lloyd was doing something on the sly because of his overdrawn account. I would, if I were in her shoes.

I looked at Kyle, who gave me a nod. "Annabel, may we talk to you for a moment?" She let us in and led us to the living room, where we sat on the edge of the sofa. She lowered herself into an armchair.

"Now, what's this all about? I haven't reached my age without learning a few things, and believe me, it's never a good sign when a police officer shows up at the door asking to talk to your husband. What's going on?" She nervously twisted a handkerchief in her hands.

I wondered just how the shock might affect her and hesitantly said, "This is going to come as a bit of a surprise, Annabel, but we suspect that your husband may know something about Lisa Tremont's disappearance."

Annabel closed her eyes for a moment and then slowly opened them. "Tell me everything," she said. And we did.

While Kyle and Amy were laying out the facts, I slipped out to the foyer and called Auntie. "Can you come over to Annabel's? I know you want to be at the shop, but she needs you." Quickly, I laid out what had happened, and Auntie said she'd be right over.

As I returned to the living room, Annabel was in the process of giving Kyle permission to search Lloyd's office. We all trooped in, though I held back for a moment.

"Annabel, I called my aunt. I thought you might like some company . . . someone who . . ." I left off, feeling uncertain. How do you tell someone you're afraid they might keel over with a heart attack so you're calling in the cavalry? But she saw through me, and even though her eyes were filled with betrayal, her gratitude was evident.

"I'm a tough old bird, my dear. Tougher than a lot of people think. But you're a sweetheart for thinking of my health, and I'll welcome Miss Florence's company. She's a good woman, and I see she raised you to be just like her. Now come, let's see what Chief Laughlin finds in my two-timing husband's desk."

Kyle was sifting through Lloyd's desk. One drawer—the bottom left—was locked. "Do you by chance have a key to this drawer, Mrs. Mason?" he asked.

She shook her head. "Lloyd has it. I give you my permission to break it open."

Kyle stared at the desk, which was obviously an antique. "Are you sure you want me to do that? I could ruin the wood—"

"My dear Chief Laughlin, I said you have my permission. Since I bought that desk for Lloyd as a wedding present, it's up to me whether or not you may bust it to smithereens. Please, be my guest." Her voice hardened, and I thought, *She's enjoying this.* "I'll get you a crowbar if you like."

"No, no—I don't think that will be necessary," Kyle said. He braced himself and yanked on the drawer. The second time, it came shooting off on the runners as the wood splintered and the lock broke. Kyle fell backwards, the drawer and its contents landing on the floor in front of him.

"Shit, that was close," he muttered, staring at his crotch. I stifled a snort.

"Should have used the crowbar," Annabel said, raising her eyebrows. I quickly stepped over to Kyle and offered him my hand, but he waved me off.

"Hello, what's this?" he said, lifting a wallet out of the drawer. The plastic ID window held a driver's license. The face staring out at us was Lisa's.

"Lisa!" Amy gasped. "He knows where she is!"

"So it isn't just Candy," Kyle said. He looked up at Annabel. "You said he might be out at your beach house?"

She nodded, pale. "Yes. Oh my God, if he hurt that girl, I'll never forgive myself." She started to shiver, and I led her to a chair.

"What's your doctor's name? Let me call him," I said. The doorbell rang, and I motioned for Kyle to go answer. He came back, leading Auntie. By the time they entered the office, I could tell she'd been given a bullet list of what we'd found out.

"Auntie, call Annabel's doctor. This is quite a shock for her," I said as I stood up. "We'd better get out to that beach house. Annabel, can you give us the address?"

Looking grim and shaken, she whispered, "48023 Terrace Lane Drive. It's on the other side of the island, about a twenty-minute drive from here. On the waterfront near Silver Sky Cove."

Silver Sky Cove? Something rang a bell, and then I remembered Bran's words. *"All I can see is silver . . . something about silver,"* he'd said. "That's it! Lisa's there. I know it," I said and motioned for Amy and Kyle to follow me to the door. I turned back to Auntie. "I've got my cell. I'll call you as soon as we know anything."

Auntie blinked, and I could see her eyes glistening. "Be careful, Imp. I don't want to see you hurt."

I paused to run back and grab her around the waist, hugging her tightly. "Oh Auntie, I'll be careful. Kyle will be there, so don't worry. Please, just take care of Annabel. She needs support right now."

"Go on, Persia. Go and bring that girl back." Auntie turned back to Annabel, and I heard her ask something about doctors. As we left the house, I hoped that the strain wouldn't do Annabel in. She didn't deserve any of this.

Amy and I dashed to my car while Kyle hopped in his cruiser. "Let's go find Lisa and bring her home," I said. I only hoped we wouldn't be bringing her home in a body bag.

Chapter Seventeen

Neither Amy nor I spoke much on the drive. The road passed under our wheels, a ribbon of concrete and ice. I concentrated on my driving; the windshield wipers were working at top speed. Ahead of us, Kyle was speeding silently, and I thought how grim police cruisers looked when they were on a mission. It was almost as if you could tell they were racing the clock—the car moving quickly, no sirens, no lights flashing, but only a fierce determination to get to their destination in time to prevent tragedy.

Several roads led to the other side of the island, but we were taking the most direct one, Route 79. Once an old logging road that cut directly through the center of the island, it had been turned into a smooth, two-lane highway twenty years back, shortly after Auntie bought Moss Rose Cottage. Lined on both sides with wooded ravines and rural suburbs, Route 79 was most frequently used by visitors coming in off the bridge that led to the peninsula, the only way off Port Samanish Island other than the ferry. If

Elliot had been smart, he would have sped along this route as soon as he escaped and escaped over the bridge before they put up roadblocks. Lucky for me, he hadn't been that bright.

The snow was sticking—at least six inches on the ground. The storm must be a gift from La Niña, which made winters in the Pacific Northwest a lot wetter and colder. The road was patchy with compact slush and ice, and up ahead, Kyle swerved into the other lane, then back into ours. A branch, big enough to raise havoc to a sedan like mine, lay in the road. I steered to the left, then back into our lane.

Beside me, Amy sat silent, clenching and unclenching her hands. After another moment she said, "Do you think she's alive? I want you to be honest. I don't want to get my hopes up and then have them crash to the ground."

I blinked, not certain what to say. "I don't know," I finally answered. "In my heart, I think she has to be. But my head . . . I just don't know, Amy. My intuition tells me Lloyd isn't a killer. As far as Candy . . . she's so young. And yet, earlier this year I helped catch two killers who were young women barely into their early twenties. You can never really tell what goes on in somebody's heart. I don't know if you can ever really know someone—not down to their core."

"Then how do you do it? How do you make friends, get married, have kids, if you can't trust?" There was a catch in her voice, and I knew she was struggling. Her sister might be dead, and if so, how could she face the people who murdered her?

"Those are questions I ask myself every day," I said. "And yet . . . you just go on. You love, you hope, you trust as much as you can trust. I suppose it comes down to having faith. Faith that perhaps luck will be good to you, faith in the knowledge that there are good people in this world, that not everybody is out to get you. I don't think I'm the right person to ask about this, Amy. I'm still learning these lessons myself."

Out of the corner of my eye, I could see her bite her lip. She stared out the side window for awhile, then asked, "Do you love Killian?"

The question took me by surprise. It wasn't what I expected. I thought for a moment. "I don't know, to be honest. I love being around him. I love the time I spend with him. I enjoy his company and have no real desire to date anybody else. But love . . . that's such an intangible feeling. I suppose I do, in a way, and I think that feeling might grow, given time. I'm skittish about commitment, Amy. I'm not wired for the picket fence and the two-point-five kids."

She seemed to be mulling over my answer for a moment, before saying, "What about Kyle? Do you like him?"

Suddenly, I knew where this was going. I flashed her a quick smile. "Kyle is a good man, Amy. He's courteous, intelligent, and I'm glad he's my friend. I like to think that he feels the same."

Another mile passed as she settled back in her seat, looking a little less tense. Ahead of us, Kyle turned to the right onto Terrace Lane Drive. I flipped on my blinkers and followed suit. To the left, through a thin band of fir and maple, we could see the shoreline. I was thinking that we had to be nearing the beach house when Kyle suddenly made a swing across the road into a driveway that sloped down past the thicket of trees. I saw the number 48023 on the mailbox and turned left, skidding slightly on a patch of ice.

Edging forward cautiously, I followed Kyle down the drive and into an open space in front of a lovely little beach house. The parking area was flat, bordering the lawn in front of the cottage. There were two cars in sight: one a Lexus that I didn't recognize, the other a red two-seater BMW. Candy's BMW. I coasted to a stop behind Kyle, and Amy and I slowly stepped out of the car.

The bungalow was one story, probably a two-bedroom, and looked like one of those charming English cottages with ivy growing up the sides of the stone walls and onto the roof. A terrace off of what was probably the dining room was enclosed by a short stone wall—only a foot or so high and flanked with what looked to be roses. All-weather patio furniture sat on the lanai, covered in snow. French doors led into the house, their curtains drawn. No signs of activity . . . I wondered if they knew we were here.

As I gazed at the house, Amy gasped and pointed to one of the windows on the far right. "That window. Don't you recognize it?"

I looked at it carefully. A window box that had held flowers only a few months ago, a mullioned window covered with what looked like white lace drapery . . . It looked familiar, and I tried to place it. And then I snapped my fingers and turned to her.

"The pictures," I whispered. "The pictures Lisa took of Lloyd and Candy—ten to one they were taken through that window. Then, that should be a bedroom."

Kyle hurried over to us, and we told him about recognizing the window. He pulled out the pictures and looked at them, then at the house. "You're right," he said, frowning. "Okay, I'm going in, I want you two to stay here." He headed for the door, gun at the ready.

Amy's gaze was glued on his back, but I had an odd feeling and turned around, slowing walking over to Candy's car. I could still smell her perfume in the chill of the day. It lingered like a fine wine on the palate, and I closed my eyes, sensing the trail of scent that she'd left behind. It didn't lead to the house, though, but toward a small path off to the right. Without a second thought, I began to follow the trail.

The path led through a patch of Scotch broom that had

grown to a towering height. Around here, Scotch broom grew with a vengeance, choking out the other plants and killing off endemic vegetation. This patch looked like it hadn't been cleared all year. As I pushed through the foliage, I noticed that the snow along the path had been disturbed; here and there I could see individual footprints, but it looked like something had been dragged along the trail. Something . . . *or someone*.

Oh hell. I began to run.

I kept my arms in front of me to ward off the prickly broom overshadowing the path, blinking as snowflakes spiraled out of the sky to land on my eyelashes and face. As I neared the end of the trail—it couldn't have been more than two hundred yards—my toe caught on a branch hidden under the snow, and I went flying face-first to the ground. A broken branch off of one of the broom plants scratched my cheek when I hit the snow.

I picked myself up and crept forward, peering out of the thicket. There, on the shoreline, Candy and Lloyd stood, arguing by the look of things. On the ground next to them I could see Lisa. She was slumped forward, her eyes closed. Candy pointed to the inlet, and I could see that there were a couple of garden bricks—the kind with holes in them—tied to Lisa's feet. My stomach lurched. Was she already dead?

"We have to do this," Candy was yelling.

"I don't know if I can," Lloyd countered. "Baby doll, this is *murder*. We aren't talking kidnapping here, but cold-blooded murder. I used to be a lawyer. How can you expect me to do this?" Lloyd's voice rose in answer to Candy's. He looked scared out of his mind, and I began to understand the dynamics of their affair. Candy was the mastermind. And a bully at that.

"Can you think of a better way? We can't let her go. There's no way to let her go and be safe. We have no choice; we *have* to get rid of her. Now help me get her into the damned water. Jesus, you sound like an *old man*."

Candy reached down to pick up one of Lisa's arms, and Lloyd reluctantly reached for the other.

I lunged out from the path and raced toward them without a word. They heard me as I was almost upon them, and Lloyd spun around, his eyes wide, just in time to say hello to my boot as I nailed him with a kick to the stomach.

"Persia!" Candy screamed, then whimpered as I moved toward her. She turned and started to run down the shoreline. Lloyd was doubled over, and I gave him a shove for good measure, which knocked him down, and took off after Candy. I was stronger, taller, and faster than she was and managed to tackle her with little problem, slamming her to the ground. I jerked her head back, holding fast to her hair.

"You'd better pray that Lisa's still alive, or I'll make sure you regret every single day you have left to live," I said.

"She's alive, she's alive!" Candy let out a yelp as I twisted a handful of her hair in my hand and gave it another good yank.

"You'd better hope she is," I said. Jumping up, I dragged her to her feet. She resisted, and I lost my temper and backhanded her. "Try that again, and I'll knock you silly, you little bitch."

She cowered then, losing what fight was in her, and I jerked her along behind me as I strode over to Lisa. It was apparent that neither Lloyd nor Candy was conversant in self-defense, nor were they carrying guns.

Lloyd started to get up. I gave him a long look. "Move a muscle, lover boy, and you get it right in the balls," I warned him. "Kyle Laughlin is on his way down here right now. You don't want him thinking that you're resisting arrest, now do you? I don't have a gun, but he does, *if you get my drift.*"

Pale, Lloyd shrank back to the ground, staring at the sand. I shoved Candy down next to him and knelt beside

Lisa. At that moment, Kyle and Amy came racing out from the trail.

Kyle didn't say a word, just took out his handcuffs and motioned for Lloyd to stand. "Is Lisa alive?" he asked me, his voice gruff.

I felt for Lisa's pulse. There it was, thready and weak, but definitely strong enough to keep her going. "Yeah, she is. Phone for an ambulance though. I think she's been drugged."

Kyle pulled out his phone and dialed, calling for backup and for an ambulance. He turned to Amy. "In the squad car, you'll find extra handcuffs. Run up there and get me a pair, would you?"

She glanced at Lisa, visibly torn. I motioned for her to take my place. "Lisa's going to be okay, honey. Here, you stay with her, and I'll go get them." I jogged back to the driveway, where I poked around in the front seat of Kyle's cruiser and found an extra pair of cuffs. By the time I returned to the beach, Kyle was reading Candy and Lloyd their rights.

I told him about the conversation I'd overheard. "So they were going to kill her by pushing her into the water. Essentially, they were going to drown her."

Lisa murmured something and blinked, opening her eyes a crack. When she saw Amy's face, the relief that flooded her face made me want to cry. She tried to talk, but Amy shushed her, kissing her gently on the forehead. Just then, we heard the sound of sirens. Help had arrived.

Turning to Candy, I said, "What did you give her? We're going to search the house, so we'll find out anyway. Make it easier on yourself by cooperating. Tell us what shit it was that you used to drug her."

Candy frowned, then muttered, "Succinylcholine chloride. She'll be okay, I didn't give her enough to kill her. Though maybe I should have—it would have saved us a whole lot of trouble."

Lloyd stared at Candy, the light in his eyes going out. I had the feeling he was starting to realize just how much he had lost. "It was all her," he told Kyle frantically. "I didn't want to hurt Lisa. It was all Candy's idea."

Shouts erupted from the Scotch broom as three officers and a paramedic team came into sight. I gently drew Amy back so they'd have enough room to work on Lisa, and told them what she'd been drugged with.

"Shit, that's a strong muscle relaxant. It's lucky she's still breathing," one of the medics said. The other one nodded. "Her blood pressure's too low and her pulse is weak, but we should be able to pull her through without a problem." They strapped her on a stretcher and put her on oxygen and then, with Amy following, started the journey back to the house.

Kyle and I looked at each other, then at Candy and Lloyd. "Let's go back to the station. You can call your lawyers, though I suggest you think really hard on the trip back. Since Lisa's still alive, you can save yourself a lot of pain and heartache by cooperating."

Candy snorted, but Lloyd's gaze flickered to me, then back to Kyle. "I'll tell you what you want to know," he said. "I used to be a lawyer; I used to be respected in this town."

Kyle gave him a hard stare. "Times change, and so do people. But if you're willing to cooperate, the judge might take that under consideration." He motioned to his officers, and they led Candy and Lloyd away. A third officer began gathering evidence, including the bricks that had been tied to Lisa's feet.

"My God, they were just going to push her into the inlet, weighed down by stones? What kind of person does that?" He looked shaken.

"The kind of person," I said slowly, "who's only out for number one. I don't think you'll have a problem getting the story out of Lloyd. He seems willing to talk. I have the feeling Candy managed to manipulate him all the way down the line."

"That doesn't exonerate him," Kyle said. "People make choices. He could have said no to an affair, he could have accepted responsibility for his actions when that affair was uncovered."

I nodded. "I know, and I'm not making any excuses for him. He's weak, Kyle. He's weak-willed and wanting other people to hand him the world on a silver platter. People who aren't willing to put in the work to make their life meaningful are prime targets for the bullies. And Candy's a bully."

I walked down to the water's edge, shaking off the flakes that spiraled into my hair. The world lay hushed and silent.

"I think Amy's in love with you," I said.

Kyle joined me, staring out at the water. "What makes you say that?"

"Call it women's intuition. Don't let her get away, Kyle. She's good for you. Don't be afraid to take a chance. And make certain she knows she can trust you. Keep her faith, Kyle. She's looking for an honest man." I turned to him, tossing my hair back, smiling. "You saved her sister—"

"*You* saved her sister," he said, holding up his hand. "Even if she thanks me, it was you. So, you think I should give love another chance? It was so hard when Katy died, Persia. I never thought I'd be able to even think about loving someone again . . . but . . ."

"But Amy makes you laugh, and smile, and you want to curl your arm around her and protect her from the evils of the world." I put my hand on his arm as he blushed. "And that, my dear, is what you call love."

Kyle motioned toward the path. "We'd better get going. So, how are you and Killian doing?" he asked as we headed back toward the path. "Any wedding bells in your future?" And for once, I heard nothing but a friendly interest in his voice.

I snorted. "We're good, Kyle. We're good. And that's all that matters."

He held out his arm, and I took it and, heads bent against the chill, we hurried back to the beach house as the snow fell in a soft shroud around us.

Chapter Eighteen

A week later on Saturday morning—almost two weeks after Lisa had disappeared—we were into December, and the holiday spirit filled the air everywhere on the island. The storm had stayed over Gull Harbor for several days, dumping a surprise foot of snow on us, and the weather was still icy cold. The streets were clear, thanks to the city crews, but lawns and trees and houses bore the unmistakable kiss of Old Man Winter.

I woke up to another chill morning and stuck my head out the window, gasping as the shock of cold air reverberated through my lungs. As I gazed into the overcast sky that still glittered with the possibility of snow, I saw a red-tailed hawk circle, and then it flew west. Feeling blessed—hawks were one of my favorite birds—I yanked my head back in and slammed the window, shivering.

We'd been so busy at Venus Envy that we had barely had time to think, but we were taking the day off and again leaving the shop in the capable hands of Tawny and Betsy Sue. Killian had gotten back in town last night, though I hadn't seen him yet, and Auntie was hosting a brunch to celebrate his success. He'd landed his funding and next week would start proceedings to buy the building Bebe Wilcox had owned. Turnabout was the best revenge.

We were also celebrating Lisa's return to work; she'd be starting again Monday. She'd spent several days in the hospital recovering from the drug, from being tied up, and from malnutrition. Candy and Lloyd hadn't thought to feed her more than once during the time she'd been kidnapped, although she'd had access to water, so she wasn't terribly dehydrated. Her wrists were covered with sores from the ropes, and she'd developed a rash on her body from wearing the same clothes day after day.

As for Lloyd and Candy, they were facing kidnapping and attempted murder charges. They wouldn't be seeing the light of day for a long time, and neither one was likely to ever set a free foot in Gull Harbor again after the trial. And since Elliot had violated his parole, he'd been carted away to prison to serve the rest of his term for embezzlement. He'd be heading to trial for the new charges within a few months. Either way, he wasn't breathing the air of freedom for twenty years at the very least.

I spent a good half hour on a light workout—my shoulder was indeed better, and the bruising was almost gone—and by the time I finished, I was beginning to feel like my old self. I showered and sifted through my closet, looking for something festive to wear.

Sliding on a black silk skirt, I added a royal purple and hunter striped V-neck sweater with sparkling gold trim, and black Chanel pumps. I brushed my hair back, holding it with jeweled barrettes, and quickly applied my makeup and slid gold hoops into my ears. Satisfied that I looked as good as I felt, I headed downstairs.

Kane was in the kitchen, helping Auntie. Barb and Dorian had already arrived, pastries aplenty in hand. They looked radiant, and I pulled her into the kitchen with me after kissing Dorian on the cheek.

"You look good. What's shaking?"

She beamed. "Dorian's taking me to Fiji next month—just the two of us, for a second honeymoon! That's his Christmas present to me this year."

I gave her a hug, thinking that the big lug had finally come to his senses. "Good for you. It sounds divine. I wish I could go!"

"Well you can't, at least not with us," she said, grinning. "Meanwhile, where's that man of yours?"

I snickered. "He'll be here. I can't wait until he gets his shop going again, though I think he's going to be surprised when he finds out Betsy Sue has asked if she can stay with us. She has a knack for retail, and she loves making friends. It won't be for long, anyway. She's due in a couple of months, and since Julius will be working again for Killian, she'll be able to take some time off for maternity leave."

"Are Lisa and Amy coming to brunch?" Barb asked, tossing her coppery bob back. I gasped as I saw the twinkle of amethyst in her ears.

"New earrings, my dear? And yes, they should be here any minute."

She beamed again. "Another present. Dorian apologized for putting me through what he did when Mama Konstantinos was here. He's promised that on the next trip to Greece, we'll stay at a hotel, and I won't have to put up with her bitching at me. He'll stand up for me from now on."

"Well, it's about time," I said. The sound of chimes echoed through from the living room. "Come on, there's the doorbell."

Auntie had already gotten the door by the time we got there, and Amy, Lisa, and Kyle stood there. Lisa still looked a little unsteady, but she sported a dazzling smile, while Amy and Kyle kept gazing at each other in a way that told me Kyle had grabbed the brass ring and discovered it was actually gold.

We gathered near the tree, and Auntie plugged in the

Christmas lights while Kane opened the curtains so that we could see the snow-covered yard. Auntie's idea of hooking the lights up to The Clapper might have saved me, but like I had predicted, it proved to be a strobe light nightmare every time one of us clapped at the dogs or cats to make them behave. The Clapper was now safely back in the kitchen drawer.

"So tell me," Barb said to Lisa as we settled in the living room. "How did they kidnap you? If it's not too traumatic."

Lisa rolled her eyes. "I was so stupid. I never expected Candy to fight back, or I wouldn't have agreed to meet them in private. I guess I was greedy," she said in a quiet little voice. "I knew she'd stolen Dad's money, and I figured she'd do anything to avoid having her affair with Lloyd exposed because it might lead to other secrets being uncovered."

"Did they kidnap you at Lookout Pier?" Barb asked.

She nodded. "Yeah. Candy was armed with a syringe of that damned drug. Lloyd was talking to me—distracting me, now I know—when Candy stuck the needle through the leg of my jeans. She injected me before I knew what was happening, and the stuff works quickly. It leaves you feeling paralyzed. You can still think, you just can't react. Terrifying stuff."

"What were they going to do with you?" Dorian asked, his eyes wide.

"I think Candy planned to kill me all along, but she had to convince Lloyd to go through with it. At first, I heard her tell him that they'd just keep me there. That they'd figure out what to do with me and let me go when they were safe. He's so stupid, he bought it," she said, shaking her head.

"Lloyd told us pretty much the same thing," Kyle said. "He said he never would have agreed to kidnap you if he thought that Candy meant to kill you. I tend to believe him. He was a lousy lawyer because he never could think on his feet in court."

"Too stupid to live," I said. Everybody looked at me. "He's one of those people you look at and think, *Jeez, you're just too stupid to live.*"

Lisa snorted. "That's the truth. He came out to the beach house and talked to me a couple of times. I tried to convince him to let me go, but he kept saying that Candy would fix it all—that she'd think of something, and everything would be okay."

"Well, it's not going to be okay for the two of them, that's for sure," Kyle said dryly.

"Is there any chance you can get your money back from her?" Kane asked.

Lisa shook her head. "No, there's no clear-cut way to prove that she actually stole it. We're still fighting to save the house."

The doorbell rang again, and I answered. Annabel Mason stood there, and I could see Daphne wading through the snow from her car. I hugged Annabel and welcomed her in. Within moments, Daphne was helping Auntie and Barb fill the table with food and mimosas. While Dorian and Kane debated the merits of real versus artificial trees, Amy and Kyle snuggled in front of the fire. Annabel sat beside Lisa, holding the girl's hand.

"Again, I am so sorry for the trouble Lloyd caused," she was saying.

Lisa shook her head. "You didn't know; it wasn't your fault. I should have tried some other way to get my father's money back. It was a stupid mistake. I'm sorry about your husband and Candy, though. You don't deserve that kind of treatment."

Annabel smiled gently. "Well, you two didn't deserve to have your inheritance stolen from under your noses. Which is why I'm giving you an early Christmas present." She opened her purse and pulled out a letter, handing it to

Lisa. "I only hope that this makes up for your pain and trouble, my dear."

Lisa slowly opened the letter and gasped, then showed it to Amy. Amy paled. "We can't possibly let you do this—" she started to say, but Annabel held up her hand.

"Of course you can. If I can't do good in this world with my money, then I'm not the person I hope to be. You girls have had to cope with too much over the past few years. Let me help you. Please."

Annabel's voice was wistful, and I saw Amy look at her with understanding. Sometimes people needed to be needed. Amy put her arm around Lisa and hugged her, then gave the older woman a broad smile. "Thank you. You're most kind, and we're honored to accept your help."

Lisa stood up. "May I escort you to the table? It looks like brunch is ready." As she led Annabel into the dining room, I turned to Amy with a questioning look. She silently showed me the letter. Annabel had paid off every one of their father's creditors, and the house was free and clear, no longer in danger of being taken away to satisfy debts.

"Congratulations," I said. And then, because I was feeling mischievous, I grinned. "And congratulations on your engagement, too. Don't think I don't see that hunk of ice sitting on your finger there!"

Amy and Kyle blushed.

"We know it's awfully quick, but sometimes, you just know you're doing the right thing," Amy said. "We won't be getting married until June, though."

"We're going to make the official announcement during brunch," Kyle whispered. And then he startled me by asking, "Persia, would you be my Best Woman?"

I snorted. "As long as you don't put me in a tux, sure." I glanced at Amy. "And Lisa will be maid of honor, of course?"

"Of course," she said, giggling. "Do you think we'd

better get to the table? It looks like Miss Florence is almost ready."

I motioned for them to go ahead. "I'll be there in a second," I said. As they bustled away, I turned back to the window. Delilah was sitting on the ledge, watching the lace-covered world outside. The snow was as white as her coat, and we stared at the front yard as I stroked her throat. She began to purr, her body vibrating as I leaned down to plant a kiss on the elderly cat's head. As I straightened up, Killian's car pulled into the yard.

I yelled out, "Killian's here, don't start without us!" and raced out the door and down the steps, ignoring the cold blast as the arctic chill slammed into me.

Laughing, Killian held out his arms and caught me up in a flurry of kisses. "I missed you, babe," he said, holding me so tight I almost couldn't breathe.

I buried my face in his neck and sighed contentedly. "I'm glad you're home. It's been a hard two weeks, but everything's going to be okay now that you're back."

"I have an early birthday present for you," he said. "I know it's a month away, but I want to tell you now so you can make arrangements for it."

I looked up at him, my heart skipping a beat. *Please don't let it be a ring, please don't make me decide now.* "What is it?" I asked slowly.

Killian pulled a bottle out of his pocket and pressed it into my hand. "Smell that and tell me what it is."

Puzzled, I twisted the cap off and sniffed. The fragrance of tropical nights and molten earth rose to intoxicate my senses. "Oh, that's lovely! Let me see . . . jasmine and white ginger, ylang-ylang, and . . . hibiscus?"

"And a few more. That's a bottle of Tropical Fire, a little combo I had specially blended just for you. And it's a hint as to what your birthday present is." He grinned, then slowly handed me an envelope. I opened it. Inside were two tickets to Hawai'i. I beamed at him.

"A trip? For us?"

"Not just us. Miss Florence and Kane are going, too. Kane and I rigged this up before I left. We're taking the two of you to the Big Island next month. No arguments. We're going to spend two luxurious weeks lolling about the beaches and go visit Kilauea and the observatories on Mauna Kea. Kane said he thinks Miss Florence is ready to go back now."

I flew into his arms again. "You know exactly the right thing to say and the right gifts to give," I murmured.

He pushed me back and stared into my eyes as the snow began to fall again. "Persia, I know you aren't ready to hear what I want to say, so let me say this instead: There's nobody else but you. *Nobody*. Do you understand?"

As the flakes grew fat and thick, I glanced back at the house. The lights were glimmering against the winter landscape, and for a moment I felt like I'd been swept into a Currier & Ives print. Beauty and Beast and Petey had gathered around the screen door, staring out, and Delilah was sitting in the window now, her gaze captivated by the snowflakes.

I turned back to Killian and searched his face. What if things fell apart? What if I couldn't say the words, *ever*?

As I gazed into his eyes, I realized that Killian understood and was giving me exactly what I needed. I had my space, and yet we were together. A couple in a way that I'd never been with anyone. I reached up to gently rest my lips against his and realized that I didn't need to say a word. He heard me loud and clear.

~~~

From the pages of Persia's Journal

Yuletide Pomanders

~~~

It's that time again—time to create Yuletide pomanders for friends and family. We sell them at the shop, too, but mostly, I like to give these as gifts because they're so labor-intensive. But I'm giving the directions to our customers, because these are fun to make for the whole family. Sit down in front of a good movie and enjoy whipping up a few for your own home and as gifts to good friends.

Other ways to make the holidays less stressful and more fun:

- Hold a Christmas or Yuletide dessert party. Have everyone bring a different dessert that originates in a different country (and provide some cheese and crackers and fruits for those who can't eat sugar), light a fire in the fireplace, put on good music, and nosh as you relax and enjoy the company of friends. One person might bring an English trifle. Another might bring baklava. Other dessert ideas: tiramisu, mochi, Linzer torte, flan, granita, pepperkaker . . . all sorts of goodies that will give your gathering a worldwide flavor.

- Get together with your grown siblings and agree that instead of scrambling to buy gifts that you don't even know will be appreciated, that each family will donate to a charity of their choice.

- Spend time at a homeless shelter, serving meals to those less fortunate. This is a good lesson for children, to show them just how much they have to be thankful for.

- Splurge and hire a housekeeper to come in for a couple of hours before decorating for the holidays. A little luxury can save a lot of time and stress.

- Place bowls of lightly scented potpourri around the house to add a holiday scent all season long.

- Find fun-shaped candles (like snowmen or trees) and cut the wicks down to the very edge so they can't be burned. When stored properly, these can become decorations that will last for years.

- If the old traditions don't mean anything, develop new ones that do.

- Go out to watch the moon on a cold and frost-filled night. There's a certain look to it that is so haunting, so beautiful, that it will make you forget the stress of the day.

- Don't forget—there are *many* winter holiday traditions celebrated, all around the same time. Using the phrase *Happy Holidays* is a wonderful and thoughtful way to incorporate them all and not make anybody feel excluded or left out.

To make your pomander you will need:

One large orange for each pomander
A lot of whole cloves
¼ cup each dried and ground: cinnamon, cloves, ginger,
*   nutmeg*
A length of red ribbon
A yard of red netting

Over a tray so the juice won't stain your clothes, push the cloves (long end first) into the orange. Fill in the entire surface, placing cloves as close together as possible while focusing on joy and love filling your home. Mix the ground spices in a shallow tray. Roll the orange in them until covered. Set in dry place that isn't too warm or too cold. Once a day, roll the orange(s) around in the spices. Within three weeks, they should be dry. Gently tap off the excess spices, wrap each orange in netting, and tie the ends together with ribbon (like you would a sachet). Hang from the ceiling in your kitchen, family room, living room, or dining room.